sign language

sign language

a novel

AMY ACKLEY

VIKING
An Imprint of Penguin Group (USA) Inc.

VIKING
Published by Penguin Group
Penguin Group (USA) Inc., 345 Hudson Street, New York, New York 10014, U.S.A.
Penguin Group (Canada), 90 Eglinton Avenue East, Suite 700,
Toronto, Ontario, Canada M4P 2Y3 (a division of Pearson Penguin Canada Inc.)
Penguin Books Ltd, 80 Strand, London WC2R 0RL, England
Penguin Ireland, 25 St Stephen's Green, Dublin 2, Ireland (a division of Penguin Books Ltd)
Penguin Group (Australia), 250 Camberwell Road, Camberwell, Victoria 3124,
Australia (a division of Pearson Australia Group Pty Ltd)
Penguin Books India Pvt Ltd, 11 Community Centre, Panchsheel Park,
New Delhi – 110 017, India
Penguin Group (NZ), 67 Apollo Drive, Rosedale, Auckland 0632,
New Zealand (a division of Pearson New Zealand Ltd.)
Penguin Books (South Africa) (Pty) Ltd, 24 Sturdee Avenue, Rosebank,
Johannesburg 2196, South Africa

Penguin Books Ltd, Registered Offices: 80 Strand, London WC2R 0RL, England

First published in 2011 by Viking, a member of Penguin Group (USA) Inc.

10 9 8 7 6 5 4 3 2 1

Copyright © Amy Ackley, 2011
All rights reserved

LIBRARY OF CONGRESS CATALOGING IN PUBLICATION DATA
Ackley, Amy.
Sign language : a novel / Amy Ackley.
p. cm.
Summary: Teenaged Abby must deal with her feelings about her father's cancer and its
aftermath while simultaneously navigating the difficult problems of growing up.
ISBN 978-0-670-01318-0
[1. Grief—Fiction. 2. Death—Fiction. 3. Fathers—Fiction. 4. Family life—Michigan—
Fiction. 5. Interpersonal relations—Fiction. 6. Middle schools—Fiction. 7. High schools—
Fiction. 8. Schools—Fiction.] I. Title.
PZ7.A1829Si 2011 [Fic]—dc22 2011003001

Printed in U.S.A.   Set in ITC Esprit Std   Book design by Kate Renner

For my dad, Norm Ballou

"Suffering has been stronger than all other teaching, and has taught me to understand what your heart used to be. I have been bent and broken, but—I hope—into a better shape."

—Charles Dickens, *Great Expectations*

PART ONE

Before and During

One

June

The first thing Abby remembered about It was the scar.

Mr. North had had a kidney removed; that much Abby knew. Abby's mom and dad had broken the news about the operation right before they dropped Abby and her older brother, Josh, off at their aunt Fran's to stay for a few days. Dad had found blood in his urine, Mom had said, so he was going to have a kidney removed. She would stay with Dad at the hospital. To Abby, that sounded preferable to Aunt Fran's.

It wasn't fair. Mom's claws came out when she spent more than five minutes with her husband's sister, and yet she expected Abby to grin and bear Aunt Fran's barbs for days on end. "Don't you two have any manners?" Aunt Fran would say, or, to Abby, "You were a homely baby, but I guess you turned out all right." And then there was the killer, knowing that Mom's feelings for Aunt Fran were mutual: "You're just like your mother." They tolerated each other because they both adored Dad.

"I don't get why we can't stay with a neighbor," Abby had whined on the way to Aunt Fran's.

"Because Aunt Fran is family," Dad replied. Mom made a choking sound, and Dad grinned at Abby in the rearview mirror. "Just think of all the members of our family as the different ingredients of one great big, delicious cookie. Aunt Fran is the salt. Too much of her can raise your blood pressure, but the cookie wouldn't be the same without her."

Abby had rolled her eyes and pinched her nose, but she couldn't help but laugh. Dad was in his usual good spirits, so she figured she didn't need to give the operation much thought. When her older half sister, Deanna, Mom's daughter from her short-lived first marriage, had had an operation to remove her tonsils, it hadn't seemed too bad. Deanna's throat had been sore, sure, and she couldn't talk for a couple of days (which was heavenly for Abby), but what Abby remembered most was that Deanna got all the ice cream and Popsicles she'd wanted for a week. Abby had wondered where she could sign up.

So now it was Dad's turn. Mom was tense about the whole thing, but that was her modus operandi. The previous summer a mother rabbit had nested in a hole beneath the Norths' backyard shed. She'd had her babies there—Abby had peeked in at them once when the mama had gone out—and other than those few essential grocery trips, that mother rabbit spent her days darting in and out of the hole, ears perked, alert for any danger that might lurk about. Abby's mom was just like that—always looking out for the big, bad wolf.

Not Dad. He was cheerful as ever as he gave Abby a quick hug and an "Adios," and she'd shot him back a "Good luck." Away her parents had gone to Beaumont Hospital, just outside Detroit, leaving Abby with only one concern: how to make herself scarce for the next seventy-two hours. The only thing she could do to completely avoid Aunt Fran's glares of annoyance and disapproval would be to stop breathing entirely.

The next afternoon Mom called with good news: Dad's operation had gone well. Then came the bad news: he needed to stay in the hospital to recover longer than they'd expected. Thus a few days turned into a long, torturous week, but somehow Abby and Josh made it out alive. When Dad was finally discharged and Aunt Fran got the call that she could release her charges from custody, it didn't take Abby and Josh more than a few minutes to get their bags out of the house and into the driveway.

They'd never unpacked.

Abby bounced and fidgeted in the backseat of the minivan all the way home. The thirty-minute drive took a lifetime. When Aunt Fran pulled into the cracked asphalt driveway of the Norths' brown tri-level on Summit Drive, Abby clicked the button to release her seat belt and let it snap loudly as it recoiled. She slid open the car door before Aunt Fran had even put the gearshift in park. "Hang on a minute," Aunt Fran hollered as she heaved herself out of the front seat. "Come back here and get your bag."

Shifting from foot to foot, Abby waited as Aunt Fran fumbled with her mess of car keys to pop the hatch. Josh, fourteen and full of himself, stood beside Abby, nonchalant as usual, as if he couldn't have cared less about seeing Mom and Dad. That probably wasn't much of a stretch. Spending quality time with his family wasn't exactly high up on Josh's to-do list.

Aunt Fran snuck inside as Josh and Abby hoisted their duffel bags onto their shoulders. Abby stuck out her tongue at the back of Aunt Fran's head.

"Hey!" The voice was as familiar and warm as curling up in her own bed at night. Abby turned and found her best friend since forever across the street at the Shotwells' house, wielding a power washer spray nozzle. Spence Harrison, willing to do just about any job to earn a few bucks.

"Hey yourself!" Abby called back.

Spence meandered toward the road so he could talk to Abby a little more easily.

"I saw your mom's car in the garage, so I figured you'd be home soon." Spence wiped sweat from his brow with his wrist, leaving a smear of dirt across his forehead and making the front of his ash-blond hair stand at attention. "How's your dad doing?"

Abby shrugged. "I guess he's fine, but I haven't seen him yet. Just got home. Duh."

Spence laughed. "Duh."

Abby's shoulder hurt from the weight of her duffel bag. She shifted it to the other side. "I'm going in," she said.

Spence nodded. "How 'bout going for a swim after I finish up over here?"

"Maybe in a little bit." Abby had already turned and was heading toward the house. "Later."

"Later," Spence echoed. As Abby stepped inside, she heard the rumble of the power washer starting up.

Josh was waiting in the living room. Abby chucked her bag near the front door and followed him upstairs. Aunt Fran was already in the master bedroom, where Dad was sitting upright on the bed, propped up with pillows. Mom stood beside the bed, hovering over him. Dad wasn't eating ice cream or nursing Popsicles. He looked tired and a bit down—his face was longer, somehow—though he was able to manufacture a smile when he saw Josh and Abby standing in the doorway. Aunt Fran quickly shooed them away.

Josh flew to the phone in the kitchen like Aunt Fran to a bingo hall, presumably to make plans for a quick getaway. Abby, on the other hand, was so happy to be home that she didn't think she'd ever leave again. Not only because Aunt Fran was mean—Abby just didn't like being away from her parents for long. When she was apart from them—which, aside from during school and work hours, was next to never—she felt like a shoe without laces.

She was twelve going on thirteen; she knew she was too old to be so attached. Josh called her a homebody; Mom said she was more set in her ways than a little old lady. Dad had tried to break her out of her shell. When she'd been nervous about going off to fifth-grade camp, starting her first day of middle school, or moving up to the twelve-and-over age division in softball, Dad had pulled her aside and said: "The Earth never stops spinning, Abby, no matter how fast you run in the opposite direction." As was the case with most Dad-isms, she hadn't a clue what he was talking about.

Abby wandered downstairs and flipped on the TV, stretching out on the carpet in front of the cheap wooden television stand. You could see the TV better from the couch, but Abby knew from experience that on a hot day—and it had to be ninety-five degrees today—the corduroy made your legs and back sweat. The Norths' couch, one of her mother's prized garage-sale finds, had zigzags and striped blocks of pattern that made you dizzy if you stared too long. It was a burnt orange shade that Mom called "rust." Abby could never figure out what had possessed Mom to buy an orange corduroy couch. Aside from that couch and Mom's watercolor paintings that decorated the off-white walls, the house was absent of color. The kitchen linoleum was brown—a faux-brick design—and the carpeting a brown calico. The furniture throughout the house was dark, and the bedroom quilts were brown and cream. The tri-level's exterior was—yep—dark brown. Every once in a while Mom got nutty and purchased something beige, like Dad's living room recliner, but other than that she stuck with brown. Mom's orange couch stuck out like a peacock in a turkey pen.

Turned out the carpet was as hot to sit on as the couch, so Abby stood loitering near the bottom of the stairs waiting for Aunt Fran to leave. Abby was dying to run down to the Point to cool off in White Lake, but she wasn't about to go without getting a good dose of Mom and Dad first.

Eventually Aunt Fran waddled down the stairs. She huffed as she passed Abby, clearly disgusted that Abby'd been eavesdropping. She hadn't been, really—they'd been talking too quietly upstairs to hear—but she blushed anyway.

"Where's your brother?" Aunt Fran asked as she wedged her plump, bunioned feet into her Stride Rites.

"He's gone already," Abby replied. "I think."

Aunt Fran shook her head. "Okay," she said after a moment, hugging Abby with as little of her body as possible. "I've had enough of you."

She always said that.

"Bye," Abby said, starting to pull away, though Aunt Fran had already beat her to it.

"You be good for your mom and dad. The last thing they need right now is a bunch of crap from you kids."

When the screen door banged shut behind her, Abby bounded up the stairs two steps at a time. Approaching Mom and Dad's open bedroom door, she saw Mom sitting on the bed beside Dad with her head on his shoulder. They weren't talking or sleeping, so Abby invited herself in.

"Dad needs to rest," Mom said softly.

"Naw," Dad said, dismissing Mom with a wave of his hand. "She can come in."

Mom shot Abby a disapproving frown, but Abby leapt for the bed anyway, plopping tummy-down on the mattress and resting her chin on Dad's knees.

"Be careful," Mom scolded.

"Oh, Helen," Dad said, tousling Abby's already messy strawberry-blonde hair, "she's not hurting me."

"How ya feeling?" Abby asked.

"I'm fine, honey. Did you have a good time at Aunt Fran's?"

Abby gave Dad a "don't ask" look. He didn't. Neither parent spoke a word. "So the doctor got the kidney out okay?" she finally said.

"Yep," Dad said, reaching down beside the bed. "I've got it here in a big jar. They preserved it in pickle juice. Wanna see it?"

Abby nodded excitedly. She'd dissected a frog and a worm, and even a cow's eyeball, at school, but she'd never seen a human body part. Now *that* would be something for her science fair project.

"He's kidding," Mom said with a grin, playfully patting Dad on the arm.

"Oh." Bummer.

Dad leaned his head back on his pillow, looking up at the ceiling. The view from Abby's angle was of Dad's salt-and-pepper-bearded chin, his skinny lips, his mustache, and then straight up into his nose.

"You know," Abby said, "your nostrils are shaped like kidney beans. Do your kidneys look like kidney beans?"

Dad laughed aloud then winced, gently laying a hand over his abdomen.

"Does it hurt?"

"A bit," Dad half whispered, pain leaking out through the cracks in his voice.

"So did you see it when they took it out? Did it look like a kidney bean?"

"No." He chuckled. "I didn't see it. But maybe it did."

"A kidney bean with a Siamese baseball," Mom added. Abby cocked her head inquisitively. "There was something growing on his kidney. Dad's doctor said it was the size of a baseball. That's why the kidney had to come out."

"Hmm." Gross. Abby pictured this mushy organ sprouting stuff like an old potato. Man, she wished he'd brought it home. "Can I see where they took it out?"

Dad lifted the bottom of his short-sleeved sweatshirt to reveal his swollen abdomen with fresh stitches running up the middle, practically from his chest to the button of his tan cotton pants.

"Geez," Abby said. "You *look* like a baseball."

Mom and Dad roared. Dad held his stomach and kind of cough-laughed and Mom snorted. She did that when she found something really funny.

And Abby was on a roll.

"Maybe," she continued, "it's like a zipper, so the doctors can unzip you in case they have to take anything else out."

Ba-da-bum-ching!

This joke, however, was a flop. Dad smiled and Mom tried, but instead her lips straightened into a line. Her face held the expression she normally reserved for Jehovah's Witnesses and Aunt Fran. Abby wondered what she'd said wrong.

"He's got another kidney," Mom said, "but they can't take that one out. Everyone needs at least one kidney. We're hoping the remaining one will be okay."

"Hoping?"

"Yeah. But if it isn't, it's possible that someone could donate a kidney to Dad. In fact, Mr. Beasley said that if Dad needed it he'd give Dad one of his kidneys."

Abby wrinkled her nose. Mr. Beasley lived next door. He was a quiet, nice man and Abby was sure that he had very nice kidneys, too, but the thought of Dad having one of Mr. Beasley's body parts inside him was downright creepy.

"Doctors do it all the time," Dad said. "Don't worry."

Abby hadn't been worried.

Dad yawned and Mom told Abby to skidoo so that he could sleep a while. Abby patted his knee and left the room. Mom came out behind her and followed her down the stairs.

"That was nice," Mom whispered, gently patting Abby's back. "He really needed that. Thank you."

Thanks for what?

Abby darted into her bedroom and snatched her faded yellow one-piece bathing suit from its usual spot on the closet doorknob. She could hear the hum of motorboats on the lake, the noisy turf wars of geese and the faraway shrieks of "Marco!" and "Polo!" Her grin started somewhere in the bottom of her stomach and spread outward, tingling her fingers and toes and spreading wide across her face. There was no place on earth that she would rather be than on her tiny little peninsula in Highland, Michigan. Out of the six square miles that comprised Highland, probably five were water. The land kind of floated in between. Highland was Abby's own private island. It was home.

Abby suited up, threw her long hair into a ponytail, grabbed a towel, and galloped downstairs and out the front door.

"I'm going!" Abby yelled to Spence. He turned, and she couldn't help but laugh. His hair was soaked flat to his head, his wet clothes clinging to his skinny frame like they'd been glued on.

"You're supposed to spray the water on the *house*!" She laughed. Spence stuck out his tongue and turned back to his work. As he did, Abby noticed that Spence's back seemed to have gotten wider, a little more muscular, while she was gone. When he looked over his shoulder again, Abby gave him a quick wave and started toward the Point. She didn't want him to get the idea that she was looking at him *that* way. Then things would just get weird.

Eight houses dotted the neighborhood peninsula, four on either side of the road, which was really a dirt path just wide enough for one car at a time. The road led gradually uphill; the last houses were at the crest, and then it sloped steeply downward to the Point.

When Abby passed by the house next door, Mrs. Stover, who had to be eighty if she was a day, glanced up from her flower bed long enough to wave and shake her head. For years, Mrs. Stover had scolded Abby for walking barefoot down the gravel road. She'd finally given up because the soles of Abby's feet had become thick with calluses before she'd even reached kindergarten.

"Abby North!" Mrs. Stover hollered. "Where are your flip-flops?" Well, she'd *almost* given up.

Abby lowered her chin to hide a smile.

"One day you'll wish you'd listened to me," Mrs. Stover shouted too loud. She always talked too loud. "When you can only dream of having pretty feet. How's your dad feeling?"

"Good," Abby replied. "He's tired, but he'll be okay."

"That's right, honey. He'll be just fine. Don't you worry."

Abby wasn't worried.

She *was* worried, however, when Mrs. Stover struggled to her feet and stretched the kinks out of her back. She was a sweet old lady, but if she made it to the road before Abby got out of there, Abby could be stuck talking to her for hours.

She waved and continued quickly down the road, eyeing the rocks underfoot to avoid the sharpest.

As she descended the railroad-ties-turned-steps that led to the water she spotted Fred, the Fischers' old basset hound lounging underneath the only shade tree.

"Hey, Fred." The dog wagged his tail in greeting but didn't move. It was Fred's shade tree; he rarely left it during daylight hours and would wander home at dusk only to return to his beloved tree the next morning, come rain, snow, or blistering sunshine. At the base of the trunk a Fred-size patch of grass had been worn away to expose bare earth, marking Fred's territory.

Abby understood completely.

Spence made his usual descent, hollering like a warrior as he ran full out down the hill. He still wore all of his clothes. He didn't let up as he approached the lake, but simply splashed and thrashed through the shallow water until it was deep enough for him to roll in. He did an impressive handstand before popping up and shaking the water out of his hair like a dog.

"High-class," Abby said, sticking her feet into the water to let them get used to the cold. Spence splashed her, the shock of the cold water making her catch her breath. Abby growled. Sometimes Spence was like the brother she wished Josh could be, but sometimes he was just like Josh.

Grabbing a clump of duckweed bobbing near the shore, Abby threw it at Spence's head, but missed. He splashed her again. Abby took a fistful of weeds and charged toward Spence, but he swam away quickly, and before she realized it she was chest-deep in the water. So much for easing in.

"Refreshing, huh?" Spence teased.

Abby dove in and swam underwater. She grabbed his legs and pulled, wrestling him under. When they both emerged together, Spence was blowing water and snot from his nose.

"Refreshing, huh?" Abby snickered.

She read Spence's smile like a book.

Yeah, I missed you, too. Jerkwad.

TWO

July

On the Fourth of July, Abby sat on a blanket on the Point's grassy plateau, listening to the Frank Sinatra tunes the Fischers pumped out their screened windows and mindlessly dipping her hand into a bag of Cheetos as she watched the annual boat parade. Mom and Dad sat in folding chairs beside her, and they were surrounded by their extended family—the neighbors.

Abby's parents had moved to Highland when Mom was pregnant with Josh, but most of the neighbors had grown up in the homes they owned. There was no uniformity in the style or colors—the Beasleys' house was a yellow tri-level, the Norths' brown; the Stovers lived in a green Cape Cod, the Fischers a chocolate box; the Danielses owned a red colonial, the Mulligans a white bungalow; the Shotwells had a tan ranch, the Longmans a small gray cottage that had been added on to in so many directions that it looked abstract. Most of the kids from Abby's school lived in the newer cookie-cutter neighborhoods across town; Abby preferred her LEGO village on the lake.

As they all watched the line of speedboats and pontoons, decked out in red, white, and blue, motor slowly past, Josh was busy conducting a mini-fireworks display near the water, quickly setting up the next as the last sputtered out, lighting them with the long butane lighter Dad normally used for the grill. Josh was in his glory.

In years past he had been the assistant while Dad lit the fireworks. Josh, a closet pyromaniac, had been denied the use of lighters or matches ever since he caught the side of the garage on fire when he was seven. But he was fourteen now, Dad had said as he ceremoniously passed the lighter to Josh that evening, old enough to act responsibly. Mom had looked on uneasily but did not object, though during the whole little show she yelled: "Put it closer to the lake!" and "Stand back! Stand back!"

Mom had hollered the same commands to Dad. Like Dad, Josh pretended not to hear but did as she said anyway.

As the sky drew a black curtain, Josh ran out of the small stuff, and the chattering crowd began to quiet, awaiting the start of the big display put on by the White Lake Homeowners Association. Abby had seen TV footage of the International

Freedom Festival, where millions of dollars' worth of fire-works were shot off from a barge floating upon the Detroit River, and while the White Lake fireworks weren't as long (ten minutes, tops), they were every bit as good. In Abby's eyes, anyway.

At ten p.m. on the nose, the first bursts of light illumi-nated the sky and the crowd went wild, gasping and clapping and cheering. You could hear the applause clear around the lake, where people from other lakefront homes were perched on their back porches or docks or at neighborhood beaches. The lake was a stadium.

Dad started at the applause and rubbed his eyes drowsily. He'd tried to stay awake as best he could. Over the explosions and the oohing and aahing, Abby heard Mom ask if he wanted to go home. Abby expected him to decline—Dad never left a good party early—but was surprised when he said yes.

Mom and Dad rose to their feet, and as Mom packed up their folding chairs, Dad leaned down to kiss Abby on the forehead. She wrinkled her nose and wiped the kiss off with the back of her hand in mock disgust. She'd been spurning Dad's kisses for years, but that hadn't kept him from sneak-ing them anyway. It was a game they played.

Mom instructed Abby to come right home after the finale. Abby nodded and watched her parents walk slowly up the hill toward home. Though the Point was jam-packed with people, Abby felt oddly alone with Mom and Dad gone, sitting on her ratty old blanket with only her bag of Cheetos to keep her company.

Until Spence came along.

Spence didn't actually live in Abby's neighborhood; he lived across the small bay, his house about a five-minute walk around the water's edge. He'd started out doing chores in his own neighborhood, but when business dried up there Abby had helped him secure a couple of odd jobs with the Beasleys and the Stovers. At first they'd hired him because he was "cute as a button," according to Mrs. Stover, but they had continued to call on him for help because he was "so darned conscientious," said Mr. Beasley. He'd since become the golden boy to Abby's neighbors—the kid who was never too busy to help mow a lawn or paint a fence or wash a car—and they'd adopted him as one of their own.

So of course Spence was at the Point for the fireworks, having his cheeks pinched by Mrs. Stover and getting a lesson in conservative politics from Mr. Shotwell, until he saw Abby sitting alone. He immediately excused himself and butted in beside Abby on her blanket, helping himself to her Cheetos.

"Where'd your mom and dad go?" Spence crunched in her ear.

She shrugged. "Home."

When the next firework went off, two miniature versions of it exploded in Spence's eyes.

"Wanna do something after the fireworks?" Spence asked. "Maybe take the boat out?" It never failed to annoy Abby that Spence had no curfew. His parents were divorced—and had been long before Spence had offered Abby the bus seat beside him on their first day of kindergarten. While Josh had sat in the back laughing at Abby for smuggling her beloved Winnie-the-Pooh to school in her new pink backpack, Spence had told her lame knock-knock jokes all the way there so she wouldn't cry.

Spence and Abby had been two halves of a whole ever since—and Spence had gradually became an afterthought to his mother as she spent most of her time looking for Husband Number Two. Lots of prospects had moved in and out of their house, but she still hadn't found The One and spent her Friday and Saturday nights out on the town, desperately trying.

"Can't," Abby said, almost feeling guilty that she had a mom who cared where she was and what she was up to. "You can come over if you want."

"North!"

Abby spun around. She knew that voice. She dreamed that voice, night after night.

Josh, who had been sitting with his neighborhood buddy

Billy Mohr on the wooden steps that led down to the water, stood and waved at the newcomer.

Logan Pierce.

Dear God. Abby quickly licked the Cheeto goo from her fingers and wiped her face with her blanket.

"What's he doing here?" Spence asked.

"Hey, Logan," Abby said, but her voice was drowned out by a loud *boom*. Abby put a hand to her chest to make sure that no one had heard her heart beating so loudly.

And then the fireworks started going off like popping corn. The grand finale.

The sky lit up with exploding fire in shades of periwinkle and pink and jade and gold. That's what Abby could see out of the corner of her eye, anyway. She was too busy studying the way the fireworks illuminated Logan's face, making his presence even more surreal.

Logan was Josh's best-looking friend, and the most popular boy in middle school. That he was standing little more than ten feet away from Abby was like having a celebrity step right out of the movie screen. Logan had been over to the house to see Josh a couple of times, and Abby had been starstruck every time.

Logan had even stayed overnight once, sleeping on the foldout couch downstairs beside Josh while Abby lay awake upstairs nearly hyperventilating all night. Logan's mom had picked him up early the next morning, scolding him for losing the T-shirt he'd worn the day before. No one knew that the shirt was under Abby's pillow, and there it stayed hidden until Abby went to bed at night and pulled it out and slept with it under her cheek, inhaling Logan's scent.

Logan Pierce was Abby's obsession: the ultimate unattainable guy. If she hadn't lived in the same house as Josh, Logan wouldn't have known she existed. Logan dated popular girls, Mock Election winners for "Greatest Hair" or "Prettiest Smile." Abby ached to be part of that group, though she was more the type to be shoved off to the end of the bottom row in the Mock Election yearbook photo—the winners of the "Most Likely to Succeed" category—if anyone even remembered her name. It didn't much matter that Abby had earned a 4.0 since the beginning of her middle school career or that she had been the district spelling bee champ every year since the third grade. She was invisible.

The crowd cheered, and large puffs of white smoke crept across the black sky. The chatter started immediately thereafter, everyone commenting on how much better this year's display was than last as they packed up their belongings and started toward home. Josh disappeared into the darkness around the Fischers' backyard with Logan and Billy, leaving Abby to haul all the snacks and blankets home. Spence scooped up the stuff before Abby could and led the way up the hill toward the Norths' house.

Spence was yakking about something, but she had no idea what. She was nearly going out of her mind, imagining that Logan Pierce might be at her house at that very moment. Maybe he'd see her and smile. Perhaps he'd even invite her to hang out with them. Abby put a little more distance between Spence and herself. She didn't want Logan to get the wrong idea.

Abby was nearly breathless with anticipation when she got home. The television was on in the living room and Channel 4 was broadcasting the tail end of the Freedom Fest. Mom was in the kitchen loading the dishwasher. There was no sign of Josh. Or Logan.

Abby plopped down on the couch. Spence took the other end. Dad was asleep upstairs already.

"Where's Josh?" Abby asked loud enough for Mom to hear her in the kitchen, but quietly enough not to risk waking Dad.

"He's staying the night at Billy's," Mom replied.

"And you let him?"

"Sure. Why not?"

Abby looked at Spence and shook her head in disbelief at her poor, gullible mother. Josh would have her head if Abby told their mother about the secret stash of fireworks in the bushes. Abby knew that Josh and Billy, and probably Logan, would sneak out in the middle of the night and set them off in Wardlow Field.

Abby sighed and stared glumly at the television. After the fireworks ended, Channel 4 broke to a commercial, and by then she had bored Spence enough for him to say his farewells and head for home. She stretched out on the couch. Mom was bustling about, picking up a stray sock here, an empty soda-pop can there—she despised waking up to a messy house—but Abby wasn't about to make Mom's obsessive-compulsiveness her problem and let her heavy eyelids close. If she couldn't see Logan in person, she'd find him in her dreams.

Just as she started to drift off to sleep, however, a loud thumping jarred her awake. When she opened her eyes Mom was already halfway up the stairs. Abby jumped to her feet and followed.

"Sam!" Mom shouted from the door to the master bedroom. "What are you doing?"

It took Abby's eyes a few moments to adjust to the darkness, but when they did she saw Dad standing beside the bed. He was facing the wall, pounding it with one fist, his other hand frantically searching for . . . something.

"Dad?"

Mom touched Dad's shoulder gently, but when he didn't stop flailing she shook it with force.

"Sam! Wake up!"

Dad spun around with his hands raised in surrender. His eyes, wild with fear, darted from Mom to Abby and back again.

"Where's Josh?" Dad yelled, his voice breaking.

"He's at Billy's," Mom said. "What—"

"We have to get out of here!" Dad took Mom by the arm and tried to lead her away. When Mom didn't budge he stopped, grimaced, and held his side.

"The house is on fire, Helen! One of the fireworks . . . it caught the roof . . . the room . . ."

Dad surveyed the bedroom. No flames. No smoke. He rubbed his face and shook his head.

"I'm sorry," he said, his voice back to normal. "I guess it was just a dream. But it seemed so real. The bedroom was on fire and the door handle wouldn't turn. . . . I couldn't open the door to get out. I banged on the door but no one answered me; I didn't know if you all were okay. I was trapped."

Dad ran his fingers through his hair. "You must think I've lost my marbles."

Mom hugged him and rubbed his back. "You're just over-tired. Go back to bed."

He looked at Abby and smiled a sad smile. "I'm so sorry, honey," he said. "I didn't mean to scare you."

"It's okay, Dad," Abby assured him. But she had been scared. Dad wasn't prone to nightmares. Maybe his dream about the fire was some kind of premonition about Josh and the fireworks. Maybe Josh was out in the woods as they spoke, trapped in an inferno, screaming for help.

Abby followed Mom downstairs and spilled her guts about Josh. A quick call to Billy's mom put Abby at ease, and Mrs. Mohr placed Josh and Billy and Logan on all-night surveillance, foiling their plans. Abby instantly wished she'd left Josh to deal with his own consequences. Now he was going to kill her, leaving her destined to go to her grave before Logan Pierce even knew she was alive.

BY THE END OF THE MONTH, DAD HAD RECOVERED FROM his surgery, and already the scar on his abdomen was beginning to fade from bright purple to violet. After the Fourth he'd started going to the hospital every couple of weeks for "treatments" that left him feeling nauseated and puny for a few days, but in between he seemed okay. Then his treatment schedule increased to a couple of hours a day. Mom would come home early from work to drive him to the hospital, where they'd spend an hour or so before coming home. Dad sometimes threw up afterward. Mom said that was normal.

Mom and Dad never discussed the details of the treatments, and Abby didn't ask. When Abby had come down with strep throat the previous winter she'd had to take some pretty nasty-tasting medicine that had made her want to puke. She decided Dad's treatments were like that.

She pretended Dad's treatments were like that.

Other than that, the summer was the same as always. Since all of the other kids in the neighborhood were boys, Josh had plenty of buddies to chum around with and Abby was left chasing them around. Since he'd turned fourteen, Abby had become a royal thorn in Josh's side. Besides, he still hated her for spoiling his Fourth of July.

A few girls from school lived in Seven Harbors, a neighborhood on the other end of White Lake, but Dad wouldn't let her walk that far by herself. She had Spence, of course, but summer was his busiest odd-job season. He came to visit during every break and after finishing up for the day, but he had other friends from his neighborhood to hang out with. He always invited Abby along to go Jet Skiing with Griffin or fishing with Kevin, but she had learned that not all guys were as accepting as Spence. It had been fine when they were little kids, but now the guys tended to clam up when she was around. Abby felt like she was stifling their conversations and endangering their manliness.

Abby went to her weekly softball practices for the summer Hi-White league, and her parents came to the Saturday morning games. She loved softball and had played since third grade, but she'd never been much good at it. She was a decent hitter and had an arm strong and accurate enough to throw from her usual position at third to first, but her head had never quite gotten into the game. When the ball came her way, she panicked. Fifty percent of the time she could catch or otherwise stop it—but she'd get befuddled about what to do next. And fifty percent of the time her teammates wanted to strangle her.

Abby wasn't a fast runner, either. What would be a triple for most batters might be a single for her, if the ball didn't make it there first, which in most cases it did.

Her lack of speed was a handicap in the outfield, too. "Put a hustle on it!" her coach, Skip, would yell, and she would put her heart and soul into trying to make her legs move faster. But they wouldn't. She felt like the Roadrunner in Looney Tunes, the way his legs spin so fast they're a blur before he speeds off. Only Abby never sped off.

That summer, determined to help her rise above her current level of mediocrity, Dad played coach. He made her run sprints in the backyard. Batting practice was too dangerous—they'd learned that after a putting a few too many dents in the Stovers' shed and almost having to replace their kitchen window—so they'd just toss the ball around, Dad squinting and pursing his lips when he wound up to throw. Abby was afraid to hurt him, so they played catch, which wouldn't do her much good, but she didn't say so.

Afterward the two of them would sit on the back porch, absorbed in their own books. They were together; they were worlds apart. Before his operation, Dad had toyed with a cigar while he read. And while he mowed the lawn. And while sitting at the Point watching Abby and Josh swim. He didn't smoke anymore. Abby missed the sweet aroma of his Crooks.

Dad never got through more than a few pages before nodding off, which was fine when he was in the living room recliner, but when he fell asleep on the back porch in the rusty metal rocking chair Abby had to stand guard. Though Dad had lost some weight, he was still a good 185 pounds and could tip that chair over with the slightest movement. Abby was glad when Mom replaced it with a long lounge chair. Dad couldn't get in and out of it easily—he had a pain in his side that wouldn't go away—but at least it wouldn't dump him. Abby was still distracted from her books, though; the moment Dad fell asleep he sent out gnat-and-mosquito radar. Abby had to keep one eye on Dad, waving the bugs away.

One muggy afternoon Dad had dozed off in his turquoise lounge chair while reading O. Henry, and a pesky bee was hell-bent on sinking its stinger into his flesh. So Abby stood over him, swatting the bee away until it came after her. Abby hollered when it stung her hand; Dad didn't even wake up. Inside, she mixed up baking soda and water and applied it to extract the stinger. After she got it out, she went back outside to fish for sympathy.

Dad was still asleep. Now he'd rolled onto his side and was dangerously close to falling facedown onto the patio.

Abby tried to figure out the best way to ease Dad onto his back, fearing that if she tried to pull him backward he might startle and accidentally hit her. Once, when Abby was little, she'd snuck up on Dad when he was working downstairs, and when she had shouted, "Boo!" he'd flailed an arm on instinct. Though he'd missed, he was so upset that he could have hurt her he nearly cried.

She decided to try to move him from the front. She could hold his arm down and gently push him backward; that way he would see her if he awoke and perhaps not be so alarmed.

As Abby faced Dad, her eyes were drawn to his lower abdomen where bare skin was exposed underneath his creeping shirt. There she saw a patch of red, blotchy skin with a small blue X in the middle. The thought that an advanced form of clever bees had marked their target almost made Abby laugh. It did look like her dad had been stung, but not just once; the mottled patch of skin was at least the size of a tennis ball, and there appeared to be several spots where the bees had injected stingers. And what the heck was that blue X all about?

Abby didn't know what to do. Dad's wound looked tender and Abby didn't want to hurt him, but he was right on the edge of that flimsy lounge chair.

Holding Dad's right arm firmly at his side and grabbing him by his right shoulder, she pushed gently and his body slumped backward. He twitched as he woke, shooting upright and nearly banging his head against hers.

"What are you doing?" Dad sputtered.

"You were about to roll off the chair," Abby replied.

"Oh," Dad said, wiping sweat from his brow. "Thanks."

"Does your stomach hurt?" Abby asked. "It's all swollen and nasty looking down by that blue X. What's that there for?"

Dad smiled. "The doctor put it there so they'd know which area to treat. At the hospital they use something like a laser to treat my . . . problem. It makes my skin look that way. It's called radiation."

"Does it hurt?"

"No. It's a little sore, but not bad at all."

"Oh."

"Don't worry about it, honey. I'm fine."

Abby wasn't worried.

THREE

Abby turned thirteen just before the start of the new school year. Finally she was a teenager, and finally she was starting to look like one. The baby fat she had worn far past toddlerhood had melted away. There was no longer a trace of what Dad called Abby's "hearty German build," and she was ready to sport her longer, leaner (though still a little too boyish) physique for her final year at White Lake Middle School. And her first year there without Josh.

Abby envied Josh. Not only did he get to leave middle school, he was taking Logan Pierce with him. She found solace in the new morning routine. Josh had to get up an hour earlier than she did, and this made bathroom shifts much easier. Mom woke up and showered first, then Dad. Then Mom got Josh out of bed, and while he showered she tried to wake Abby, knowing full well that she never succeeded in one try.

After Mom resorted to threats, Abby would finally roll out of bed and watch out her bedroom window as Dad started up his gold Chevy Impala, drove it around the semicircle driveway, and disappeared down the gravel road to the high school where he taught. Abby had watched Dad leave every morning for as long as she could remember, and it still made her feel a little sad that everyone had to go their separate ways.

Abby took a little extra time in the bathroom nowadays, applying a little mascara and lip gloss and messing around with her unruly hair until Mom had a conniption about Abby missing the bus and making her late for work.

Mom was actually an artist, and had sold some of her watercolors—but for a living she designed brochures for a marketing company, and seemed to think that if she was not at her desk by 8:00 each morning all business operations would come to a screeching halt. She would contend that Abby was welcome to get her fanny out of bed earlier to beautify; Abby would argue that their one full bathroom was too crowded in the morning; Mom would tell Abby to put on her makeup in the half bathroom downstairs; Abby would complain about the lack of counter space in the half bathroom and whine about their lousy house with only one full bathroom. What were they, Amish?

In the end Mom would get mad enough that Abby knew to shut her trap and haul her butt to the bus stop before missing her ride.

Yet despite the beauty arguments, her brother's contempt for everything familial, and Dad's sick stomach and exhaustion, things were fine. Life was good.

For a while.

Dad's internal motor started to sputter. He'd always had an affection for the occasional late afternoon nap, but this was different. He usually got home soon after Josh got off the bus, and almost always before Abby did, and in years past they'd sit at the kitchen table after school and eat snacks Mom forbade when she was home. Then Josh and Abby did their homework or goofed off while Dad corrected English papers and prepared lesson plans until Mom got home and fixed dinner.

That fall, however, Dad slept. A lot. If his Impala was in the driveway when Abby got off the bus, nine times out of ten he'd be upstairs snoozing when Abby walked through the front door. Dad was still going in for treatments occasionally, and while in the beginning they had wiped him out for only a few days, now he seemed eternally tired. Abby just figured— well, she didn't know what to figure. She didn't feel the need to figure anything. Napping didn't seem all that alarming.

Abby took full advantage of the Dadless time by

hanging out with Spence or, more and more often, with Leise Spangler, a new girl at school who lived across town. Leise had taken the empty seat next to Abby at lunch on the first day. Even boys who had never before seemed remotely interested in girls craned their necks to stare at blonde, blue-eyed, beautiful Leise. Her flawless complexion and enviable figure and plate of salad, no dressing, made Abby suddenly, acutely aware that her hot dog and Doritos contained very little actual food. So she'd pushed aside her tray and listened to Leise's stories about her old school in Akron, Ohio.

She'd hung on Leise's every word and studied every gesture—the way she flipped her hair when she laughed and fiddled with her earrings when she was listening intently and pouted her glossed lips when she was thinking— deciding that if she were ever to become popular she needed to shuck her nerdy, tomboy ways and become less like Spence and more like Leise.

Leise was a real girl. She wore makeup and jewelry and knew how to use a straightening iron. She and her mom used a spare bedroom as a closet for their designer clothes. Leise always looked pretty, even after running a mile during gym class, and was kind enough not to point out how frumpy Abby looked, even though 99.9 percent of the time Abby wore baggy jeans and her brother's T-shirts. That's what made Leise different from the other popular girls at Abby's school. She was nice.

They established an after-school routine that consisted of eating Reese's Peanut Butter Cups on Leise's living room floor while watching soap operas. Abby hated soap operas, and Leise was constantly shushing when she talked. At four they'd read their horoscopes from the newspaper, help each other with homework, and gossip about people at school, and Mom would pick Abby up around five.

Dad would be awake when they got home, and after dinner he and Mom would head out onto the back porch to talk. They used to go for long walks together, or take a leisurely paddleboat ride, but now Dad was too tired to walk very far, and it was too cold for the lake, so they held their heart-to-hearts at the picnic table on the back porch.

Josh hardly acknowledged her existence, so Abby would retreat to her bedroom, pull her seventh-grade yearbook out from under her bed, and open it up to page sixty-seven. The yearbook opened to page sixty-seven on its own, actually, from hours of staring at the photo near the top of the page—the boy with the shaggy blond hair and the cocky grin. Abby studied his face, the slight downward slant of his eyes, the dimple in his right cheek, the faded scar above his lip, and imagined that Logan Pierce was smiling not for a camera but for her. It would take a miracle, and for that Abby turned to God.

He spoke to her. Not directly, mind you. Abby didn't hear God's voice; He communicated with her in writing, on a three-dimensional pyramid afloat in deep blue liquid inside a black orb, answering only closed-ended questions.

God spoke to Abby through her Magic 8 Ball.

It went something like this:

Abby: Will Logan Pierce ever like me?

God: CANNOT PREDICT NOW

Abby: Will *any* boy ever like me?

God: AS I SEE IT YES

Abby: *Does* a boy like me?

God: BETTER NOT TELL YOU NOW

Hmm.

Abby: If you *could* tell me, would it be Logan Pierce?

God: DON'T COUNT ON IT

Abby: Okay, that's not a no. And even if he doesn't like me now, he still could at some point, right?

God: WITHOUT A DOUBT

Abby wouldn't push her luck any further; the signs were pointed in the right direction. She had one simple goal. She'd study hard as Leise's apprentice, and her hard work would pay off when Logan looked at her one day in disbelief, amazed that he'd passed her by so many times without seeing her. He'd realize that Abby was meant for him and that she would make his life complete. And then everything would be perfect.

SOMETIME IN EARLY WINTER MOM STOPPED SMILING. ABBY couldn't pinpoint exactly when it happened, and her mother wouldn't let on as to why. Perhaps she was going through "The Change" that some of the neighborhood men joked about. All Abby knew was that Mom looked frazzled and edgy all the time and had started treating Dad like he was a newborn.

"Don't do that," she'd tell Josh and Abby as they tried to wrestle each other to the floor in an attempt to determine once and for all who was the ruler of the remote control. "You could bump into Dad."

"You're sniffling. Are you getting a cold? Stay away from Dad if you're getting sick."

"No more friends here after school. I don't want you waking Dad. He needs his rest."

Dad himself would dismiss Mom's anxious babble. "I'm fine."

"No, you're not, Sam."

"I'm fine."

In January Dad retired; he was too worn out to keep trolling the halls at work and keep up with grading papers at night. Abby could tell Dad was bummed out about it. He'd been teaching high school for over thirty years, after all. Abby, on the other hand, was elated. She loved the idea of having him around all the time.

After retiring Dad slept even more; otherwise, he was generally just sitting around. He'd read the newspaper, *Time* magazine, books—anything he could get his hands on. Mom couldn't keep enough reading material around, so she went out and bought loads of old movies she knew he loved: *The Thin Man*, every Abbott & Costello flick she could find. Abby found *The Thin Man* excruciatingly boring and thought that Abbott and Costello were obnoxious, but she watched anyway. He'd sit in his recliner with Abby on the sofa beside him, reciting along with him lines he'd repeated for years:

"Ni-aaa-gara Falls. Slowly I turned. Step-by-step. Inch-by-inch."

"What's on second. Who's on first?"

Abby would have her homework scattered out across her lap during the movies, and every now and then she'd feel eyes upon her. She'd look up to find Dad studying her.

"What?" Abby would ask.

"Nothing," he'd reply. "What are you working on?"

Abby would tell him and go back to it. A few minutes later she'd feel him staring again.

"What?"

"Nothing," he'd say with a wistful smile.

Sometimes, she would challenge him to a game of Scrabble—though when competing against Dad, Abby was the one who was challenged. Dad was Scrabble king.

One Saturday in mid-February Abby convinced Dad to put off his afternoon nap long enough to play a quick game. She pulled a couple of tray tables over to the side of his recliner and put them together, creating a spot just large enough to hold the game board. Abby sat on her knees across from Dad, holding the box out to him so that he could choose his pieces, then she picked her own. Choosing her pieces was easy; Abby had figured out long ago that the wood on some of the higher-point pieces like *J* and *X* was slightly darker than the wood on most of the others. Dad knew that, too, but he avoided choosing those pieces, allowing Abby the handicap.

Dad and Abby placed their letters on the wooden stands, and Abby started first with all she had: *run*. A big, bad three points.

As usual, Abby's creativity increased as the game went on, but so did Dad's. After half an hour their word maze had stretched to cover the upper right quadrant of the board, with Dad's score ridiculously high. She didn't know why she even bothered keeping score. Even though they always vowed they would only play until one of them—meaning Dad—earned one hundred points, they never stopped playing. Neither of them could give up at only a hundred.

Then, grinning in amusement, Dad scored big with *Belize*, landing his ten-point *Z* on a triple-word-score square.

"Dad," Abby said, "that's not how you spell *belies*."

"Not *belies*," Dad chuckled. "*Belize* . . . Buh-*leeze*."

Abby crossed her arms across her chest, eyeing Dad suspiciously. "*Belize*? That's not a word."

"What exactly is it they're teaching you in school?"

"Social skills."

Dad chuckled and crossed his arms over his chest in response. "Go look it up."

Abby rolled her eyes and sighed as she rose to her feet and headed for the stairs. Their Scrabble games always led to Abby going online, looking up words to prove her dad wrong, though he was never wrong. With Dad you could never be sure, though, that he wasn't pulling your leg, and Abby was determined to at least once call his bluff.

Abby hopped up the stairs two at a time and went into her parents' bedroom. She fired up the computer at the corner desk and typed in *Belize* on Dictionary.com. Okay, so it was a word. A country, actually, in Central America. Foiled again. Now Abby would have to go back downstairs and listen to Dad gloat about his infinite wisdom and share all the facts and figures he knew about Belize.

Hang on a minute. Names of countries aren't allowed in the official rules of Scrabble! Dad himself had established that after she'd tried to lay down *Fiji*. She danced down the stairs, leaping over the last two and racing into the living room.

"Gotcha this time!" Dad didn't flinch. He was fast asleep in his recliner, wooden Scrabble letter holder still balanced delicately upon his lap. Abby left it there. She'd announce that she'd one-upped him and they'd resume their game when he woke.

She heard the ancient washing machine start up and went downstairs to check in with her mother. Mom was queen of the laundry room, surrounded by several meticulously separated piles of clothes: whites, brights, darks, lights, and towels. It was one duty Mom would never delegate to anyone. She had a deep-seated fear of her white underwear and socks being permanently altered to light blue or pink.

"Mom," Abby said, hoisting herself onto the top of the dryer, "have you ever heard of Belize?"

"Of course," Mom replied as she dabbed stain remover onto the collar of one of Josh's white T-shirts. "It's a country."

"Where?" Abby asked, playing dumb.

"South America, I think. Someplace near the equator. People go there on vacation. Why do you ask?"

"No reason." Were Central America and South America considered the same thing?

"Are you planning a trip or something?" Mom chuckled.

"No. A vacation would be sweet, though. Where are we going for spring break?" The Norths always went somewhere during spring break, even if only down to the Great Wolf Lodge in Sandusky.

Mom sighed, grabbing another shirt from the pile and doctoring it.

"We won't be going anywhere this year."

"Why not?"

"Well, now that Dad's not working, money's a little tight and, besides, Dad couldn't make the trip."

"We could go somewhere relaxing. He could still sleep."

Mom refused to look at Abby.

"Dad really can't go anywhere. I'd be afraid that something might happen while we were away. His doctors are here."

Abby decided not to press the issue. She didn't want Mom to feel guilty about not having enough money to go anywhere. Abby knew Dad would want to go, even if he wasn't feeling too good. He loved vacations.

"Well, maybe when Dad's feeling better, then."

Mom froze, Josh's shirt still in her hand. She stared out the small window in front of her.

"I don't think Dad's going to get better."

"What?"

"He's not going to get better."

Dad had said he was going to be fine! Mom could be a real killjoy, a pessimist: always worrying, always waiting for the sky to fall. She never saw the silver lining, ever. True, she was sometimes pleasantly surprised when things turned out better than she'd expected, but her endless suspicion of doom and gloom just plain ticked Abby off. Dad's sickness wasn't something to jinx.

From the laundry room window, Abby saw Spence down at the lake, clearing the ice with a shovel. She hopped off the dryer and left the laundry room without saying another word.

Abby grabbed her coat off the coat hook near the back door, jammed on her boots, and headed outside. She immediately wished she'd taken the time to get her gloves and hat, but her desire to get as far away from her mother as possible overrode her longing for comfort and warmth. So she pulled the hood of her ski jacket over her head—which did nothing but create a hollow cave for the bitter cold wind to seek refuge—tucked her hands inside her sleeves, and took off down the hill. She was running too fast to notice when her right boot got stuck in the snow. Since she wasn't wearing socks, it didn't take her long to figure it out. Growling in frustration, she shook out her snow-filled boot, slid it back on, and resumed her progress down the hill, more slowly this time.

Abby was shivering all over by the time she reached the edge of the lake. Spence was too busy shooting pucks into the hockey net he'd set up at the far end of the rink to notice her standing there. He had the pucks lined up in a row, and he smacked them in one by one until they were gone. He was getting really good. And he looked so different—so tall and rugged—in his hockey skates. Had he looked like that last year?

Spence skated toward the net to retrieve his pucks, and Abby joined him out on the ice.

"Hey," he said when he saw her. Abby's teeth were chattering too violently to allow her to answer. She jogged in place to try to warm up.

"Wanna take a shot?" Spence asked, offering her his stick. Abby shook her head. Spence nodded toward a thermos behind him. "Hot chocolate?"

Abby flew to the thermos, uncapped it, and took a swig, burning her tongue and throat. She didn't care. At least she could talk now. She held the thermos cupped in both hands for heat.

Spence shot a few pucks. Abby whistled.

"Lookin' good, Harrison."

Spence took a backward glance at his rear end. "You think? Really? I've been doing *Buns of Steel* with my mom."

Abby laughed. "Shut up. I didn't mean your butt."

Spence took another shot. "Oh, you must be admiring my stick."

Abby shook her head. "That's it. I'm outta here."

"You are not." Spence skated over and took the thermos from Abby's hand. He sipped gingerly.

Abby took the stick and slipped and slid toward the center of the ice. She took a shot at one of the pucks. It skidded across the ice, way left of goal, and came to an abrupt halt in a snowbank.

"Oops." She giggled.

"You'd better work on that," Spence hollered. He set the thermos on the ice and skated toward Abby. "Here, let me show you."

"No thanks," Abby said, backing away.

"No, seriously, you just—"

"I don't care if I'm any good," Abby said. "It's just a game."

Spence looked at her, aghast. "I'll pretend I didn't hear that." He shot another puck, landing it smack-dab in the middle of the goal. He looked at Abby smugly. "Now *that's* how it's done."

"Bravo." Abby slid her boots back and forth on the ice. "Do you have a big game coming up or something?"

"They're all big," Spence corrected. "But over the next few weeks the high school coaches are coming in to watch, so I'd better be at the top of my game."

"You're trying out for the high school team?"

Spence laughed. "What do you mean? Of course I am!"

Abby's heart skipped a beat. "Oh my gosh, you know who's on the high school team?"

Spence knit his brow. "Who?"

Abby's body was finally warm. In fact, she felt sweaty underneath her coat. "Logan Pierce!"

Spence nodded and looked away. He took a forceful shot, slapping the ice hard with his stick and sending it flying way past the goal.

"So that's how it's done?" Abby teased.

Spence didn't answer her. He went on shooting his pucks, retrieving them and lining them up to shoot again, ignoring Abby completely.

"What's your problem?" Abby asked after a while.

"No problem," Spence mumbled, continuing on as if Abby were invisible. Huffing, Abby stomped away. She'd go home and see if her father was awake yet so they could continue their game. Dad was the only person in Abby's life who made any sense anymore.

FOUR

March

One morning mid-March Abby woke up with a stomachache. It wasn't like the stomach flu, but more of a heavy, cramping feeling.

Mom banged on the door and told Abby to hurry up and get into the shower. Abby opened the door and complained about not feeling well, asking if she could stay home from school.

Mom gave her usual response: "You'll feel better after you take a shower."

Abby always wondered why the drugstore had an entire aisle with shelves stocked with expensive over-the-counter medications if every ailment was curable with hot water and steam.

Abby showered and pulled on a pair of jeans. Trying to zip and button the fly about killed her. It felt like there was a water balloon about to burst in her lower abdomen. She changed into white sweatpants and a maize-and-blue University of Michigan sweatshirt that Josh said looked like pajamas. She needed to be comfortable and didn't care what she looked like.

Then she trudged down the stairs, sat hopelessly on the bottom step, and watched Mom as she scurried around the kitchen making coffee, toasting bagels, and pouring orange juice. Abby told her she still felt awful.

"Do you feel like you're going to throw up?" Mom asked.

"No, not really," Abby replied, wanting to kick herself for not fibbing and saying that she might.

"Do you have to go to the bathroom?"

Abby shook her head, knowing what Mom was going to say next.

"It's probably just gas. You'll be fine. Now hurry up before you miss the bus."

Abby knew she and her brother were to blame for Mom's lack of empathy that morning. It was Monday, after all. Abby and Josh always feigned illness on Monday morning, though they usually got a jump start Sunday night. Mom called it "Sunday-nightis."

After putting on her coat and boots, Abby shuffled to the bus stop near the mailboxes at the end of the road. She moaned and groaned with every turn the bus made, but by the time the bus reached Spence's stop the crampy feeling had subsided a little. Maybe Mom was right.

Spence slid into the seat beside Abby and surveyed her comfort clothes and the hair she'd pulled back into a bird's-nest ponytail.

"You all right?" he asked.

"I'll live," Abby replied, but by the time the bus pulled into the middle school parking lot she wasn't so sure. Her stomach-ache had come back full force. Abby pitifully shuffled to her locker, shoved her coat and boots into the long bottom portion, and extracted her English book from the top. She wanted nothing more than to hide inside and take a nap.

Somehow Abby made it to her first class and slumped down into her assigned seat next to Leise.

"You look like crap," Leise said just before the bell rang.

"I think I'm sick or something."

"Oh," Leise said, moving away.

Mrs. Lawson, the English teacher, immediately assigned the students to groups of five according to who sat by whom and told everyone to review each other's homework. The assignment had been to write a haiku with the first line beginning: "If I were a bird . . ."

Abby had stood up to move her desk when Mark Sanderson,

who had a big mouth both literally and figuratively, started to cackle behind her.

Abby spun around to find Mark pointing at her and howling.

Leise gasped.

"Abby," Leise said, panicky, "go to the bathroom. I'll tell Mrs. Lawson where you are."

Abby opened her mouth to ask why.

"Just go!" Leise hissed.

So Abby went. She could hear Mark Sanderson chortling as she sped down the hallway toward the bathrooms. Thankfully the girls' room was empty. Abby looked at her reflection in the mirror, but nothing appeared out of the ordinary.

Until she turned around.

Oh, God.

She rushed for the stall furthest from the door.

Blood was everywhere. On her underpants, her white sweats, her inner thighs.

Oh, God.

This was how It started with Dad; he'd found blood in his urine. He'd gone to see a doctor and the doctor discovered the growth on his kidney. A tumor, Mom had called it.

Abby tried to breathe calmly but couldn't. Her breaths

came fast and shallow, and she feared she might hyper-ventilate.

Oh, God.

Dad had been having a hard time breathing, too. The symptoms were identical.

"Abby?" came a girl's voice from outside the stall. It was Leise. "Do you have anything with you?"

Abby exhaled sharply and shook her head, feeling stupid for overreacting. The difference between Abby and Dad?

Dad wasn't a girl.

"These machines are always empty," Leise said, but Abby wasn't listening, not really.

Abby cleaned herself up the best she could and opened the stall door. Leise stood just outside, smiling weakly, holding up a purple sweatshirt.

"I had this in my locker," Leise said. "You can wrap it around your waist to cover up your pants."

"Thanks." Abby accepted the sweatshirt and tied it around her waist. Not too tightly, though. Her bloated stomach was still tender. Leise smiled sympathetically as Abby washed her hands.

"Let's go call your mom," she said, taking Abby by the arm and leading her to the hallway. "I'll walk you to the office."

Abby plodded zombielike through the hallway. Leise still had Abby by the arm, like she was blind or something. A couple of kids stared, but they were sixth-graders, so who cared what they thought?

"She needs to call her mom," Leise announced as soon as they walked into the office.

The secretary, Mrs. Cartwright, nodded knowingly and escorted them to the nurse's station, the "sickroom." She handed Abby the phone receiver, dialed 9 to get an outside line, and whispered something to Mrs. Rasmussen, the school nurse.

Abby dialed Mom's work number but got her voice mail. She hung up.

"My mom's not there," Abby told Leise.

"How about your dad?" Leise asked.

Dad. Abby couldn't call Dad. Abby had to call Dad. There was no other choice.

Abby nervously dialed her home number. Dad answered on the fifth ring, sounding groggy.

Abby couldn't speak. She started to bawl like a little kid. It wasn't supposed to happen this way. Mrs. Rasmussen took the receiver from Abby's hand.

"Mr. North?" she said calmly. "This is Dana Rasmussen, the school nurse. . . . No, no, she's fine." Now the nurse was chuckling softly. That drove Abby nuts. "Happens to every girl at some point. . . . Yes, that's all it is. . . . She'll need you to bring her some pants; hers are soiled. Okay, Mr. North, see you then."

Mrs. Rasmussen hung up and beckoned for Abby to follow her to the bathroom attached to the sickroom. Opening up a cabinet above the sink she pulled out a small pink package and removed the plastic wrapping.

"Do you know how to use these?" she asked, handing Abby a maxi-pad.

"Yeah," Abby replied meekly. She now knew for sure that you cannot really die from embarrassment. She was still around.

Mrs. Rasmussen reached into the cabinet again and pulled out a pair of new white granny-style underwear.

"You'll need these, too," she said, handing both items to Abby. "I forgot to remind your father to bring some." She winked and whispered with a smile, "Dads don't think about that stuff."

After changing her underwear in the bathroom and affixing her new thingamajig, Abby sat on a towel on the bench in the sickroom until Dad showed up. Mrs. Cartwright had sent Leise back to class, so Abby was forced to sit and listen to Nurse Rasmussen ramble on about growing up and becoming a woman and the importance of good hygiene until Dad walked in twenty minutes later.

Dad stood at the door of the sickroom smiling uncomfortably and holding a pair of green jeans Aunt Fran had bought for Abby the previous Christmas.

"Dad!" Abby was horrified. "Why did you bring those?"

"What?"

"They're green! I must have ten pair of blue jeans in my drawer, but no, you have to bring green ones."

"What's wrong with green?"

"Do you see any green in my shirt? Those won't match!"

"How was I supposed to know?"

Abby groaned loudly, exasperated. "I wanna go home."

Dad sighed impatiently. "Just put the pants on. You're not going home."

Mrs. Rasmussen handed Abby a plastic bag for her soiled pants, and Abby stormed into the bathroom, fuming. The bell rang, signaling the end of class. First period was over. Mark Sanderson was likely running his mouth all over the hallway. Abby was ruined.

Why couldn't she go home? What was the big deal? It was one day of school, one crappy day. She was tired and crampy and wanted to go home and crawl into bed. Dad was tired and he got to stay home and sleep. It wasn't fair.

Now Abby had to wear those stupid green pants for the rest of the day, and anyone that didn't know about her problem via Mark Sanderson would know because of those ridiculous pants. She would never wear that shirt with those pants. Everyone would know something was up. They'd assume—

"Would you mind if I sat down?" Abby overheard Dad ask Nurse Rasmussen.

"No," she replied, "of course not." She paused. "Are you all right, Mr. North?"

"I'll be fine," Dad said, his standard answer. "I just, ah, get winded sometimes." Dad lowered his voice considerably, and Abby pressed her ear against the bathroom door, straining to hear him.

"I've got cancer," Dad explained. "I've been going through chemo and radiation, but it's spreading. It's in my lungs."

Though Abby wasn't naive enough not to know what It really was, no one had ever called It cancer before. And she hadn't known It was growing. Abby suddenly felt guilty for being snotty with Dad, yet angry with her parents for not telling her the truth. Why did they always keep Abby and Josh in the dark?

Because they knew they felt safe there.

Abby stopped eavesdropping, stuffed her demolished pants in the plastic bag, and walked out of the bathroom. Both Dad and Mrs. Rasmussen fabricated smiles.

"Could you take this home?" Abby asked Dad, handing him the bag. "You might as well throw those pants away, though. The stain will never come out."

Dad wrinkled his nose. This was not one of his most treasured father-daughter moments.

"I'll soak them in cold water when I get home," he said, accepting the bag without standing. "That's what Mom does, right?"

Abby nodded.

"Did you miss much of first per—your first class this morning?" Dad asked.

"Most of it."

"Well, you'd better get going, then. I'll be on my way out in just a minute." He started to lean in to give Abby a kiss but stopped himself. The game was only funny at home. Dad was a schoolteacher; he knew that parental displays of affection were only permitted until a kid reached third grade.

Thing was, this time she wouldn't have minded.

Abby turned back when she reached the door. "Thanks for bringing me some pants. Even these God-awful green ones."

"You're welcome," Dad said. "See you after school."

Abby walked through the door and bumped into Leise. Leise's eyes were as wide as silver dollars, her lips tight. How long had she been standing there? What had she heard?

When Abby brushed past her, Leise walked alongside her into the hallway.

"Why didn't you tell me about your dad?" Leise asked quietly as swarms of students buzzed around them.

Abby froze and looked Leise in the eye.

"Please," Abby begged. "Please don't tell anyone."

FIVE

March, Continued

Leise kept her mouth shut, Abby survived the "first period in first period" jokes from Mark Sanderson and his buddies, and she traveled safely back to Neverland where Dad wasn't sick, where her world centered around improving her social status, daydreaming about Logan Pierce, and obsessing about her nonexistent curves.

But a few days later, Abby arrived home from school and was greeted by a hideous noise. It went like this:

Suck-swoosh. Pause. *Suck-swoosh.* It sounded like Darth Vader had moved in.

Curious, Abby followed the sound into the living room where Dad sat in his recliner with a clear plastic tube running under his nostrils, over his ears, and down to a gawky metal contraption.

"Luke," Dad said in an ominous voice, "I am your fathah."

Great minds think alike.

"It's an oxygen machine," Mom explained from the top of the stairs. "To help Dad breathe."

Mom came downstairs and gave Dad a once-over to make sure all connections were in place and all systems were go.

"What are you doing home already?" Abby asked loudly, to be heard over Darth.

Mom sighed and balanced a full laundry basket on her hip. "I'm taking a leave of absence from work."

This was big. Come child care or car problems, fever or flood, Mom never missed work.

"For how long?"

A quick flash of anger darkened Mom's already brown eyes. Then she looked away, at something, or nothing, in the kitchen.

"For a while," she said, almost too quietly to hear, before escaping downstairs with her laundry.

Dad shifted in his chair uncomfortably.

"Are you okay?" Abby asked him.

"Oh, yeah, yeah," Dad said, reaching around the side of the chair and trying to lift Darth. He dropped the thing, yanking a tube out of his nose.

"Let me help you," Abby said, reaching down to pick it up as he repositioned the tubes.

"I'm okay, honey, really," Dad insisted, trying to get out of the chair. He stood, using the back of the chair for support, while he tried to catch his breath.

"What happened?" Mom was already there. Her hearing had become so fine-tuned she could probably hear the Fischers licking envelopes down the street.

"I have to use the bathroom," Dad said quietly.

Abby backed away, letting Mom take over and tote Darth as she walked behind Dad. He started to climb the stairs.

"Why don't you use the bathroom down here?" Mom asked.

"It's not big enough for both of us," he replied, taking two steps up and pausing for a breath. Taking two more. Pausing. Mom trailed behind him like a bridesmaid with a train.

Abby's sinuses stung and her eyes began to fog. She went over to the kitchen window to let the sun shine in and dry it all out.

The world outside had no idea anything was out of the ordinary. Spring had officially sprung. Though the air was still chilly, the sun was brighter than it had been in a long time, strong enough to warm Abby's face through the window glass. Far off in the distance she could hear the geese: "We're back! Time to put out the patio furniture!"

The trees were still naked, but the birds didn't seem to notice. They were chattering away and flitting from branch to branch on the backyard trees, gathering whatever they could fit in their beaks to build nests, like day-after-Thanksgiving shoppers at Macy's.

Abby thought back to that haiku she'd never written for Mrs. Lawson's class.

If I were a bird
I would carry Dad up high
To enjoy the air

Splat!

Abby jumped back from the window and watched the dirty scum of leftover snow trail down the glass. She looked out to see her brother standing on the back porch wearing a wicked grin.

Josh started for the back door of the garage with Spence trailing behind. No. Spence couldn't come in. One thing she loved about Spence was that he was friends with everyone. One thing she hated about him was that he was friends with Josh, too.

Abby leapt to the kitchen door to stop them before they came inside.

"What are you doing here?" Abby asked, blocking the door when Josh opened it.

"I live here," Josh said, shoving her aside.

"I don't mean you."

"Thanks for the warm welcome," Spence said, inviting himself into the kitchen.

"I can't do anything today," Abby said quickly. "I have homework."

Spence shrugged. "Josh and I are going to shoot some hoops."

"The basketball hoop is outside," Abby said, standing in front of them with her arms folded across her chest.

Josh rolled his eyes and tossed his hiking boots aside. "Move. I need my shoes."

Abby had no choice but to let Josh pass by. He stopped at the bottom of the stairs to make way for Dad as he gingerly descended the stairs with Mom close behind carting Darth. Dad stopped to take a breath after each step. Josh didn't seem surprised by Dad's new machinery. He must have seen it earlier when he came home from school.

Abby studied Spence's face closely. He tried hard to hide his shock, but it didn't work. His eyes were glassy, and he bit his lip. Abby closed her eyes and massaged the bridge of her nose. She was getting a headache. This wasn't right. Spence wasn't supposed to know about all this, and he certainly was not supposed to look so pathetic about it. The last thing Abby wanted was his pity. Pity was for lost causes.

Since the cat was already out of the bag, Abby let Spence

into the kitchen. They watched Dad settle into his living room chair and Mom struggle to get the apparatus repositioned.

And at once Abby saw her father through Spence's eyes. Dad's hair had grayed, though she couldn't remember when that had happened. It seemed to have faded overnight. And with the oxygen tubes hanging off of him this way and that, he suddenly looked really old. He was old, sure—he'd turned fifty-five in December—but suddenly Dad seemed ancient. Spent.

"Hi, Mr. North," Spence said cheerily, skillfully disguising his unease. "Anything I can do for you?"

"No," Dad said. "Thank you."

Josh came bounding down the stairs with his cross-trainers and sat down at the kitchen table to lace them up.

"Wanna come out with us?" Spence asked.

"It's, like, forty-five degrees out there," Abby replied.

"Heat wave, I know." Spence was trying hard to act normal. "Come on, don't be such a girl."

"I *am* a girl," Abby mumbled.

Spence shrugged. "Suit yourself." He turned toward Mom. "I'll come by tomorrow after school and help Josh and Abby rake the leaves out of the flower beds."

Josh's jaw fell to the floor.

Mom smiled. "Thank you. That would be nice."

When they were halfway out the door, Josh slugged Spence in the shoulder to thank him. Mom began digging pots and pans out of the kitchen cupboards to make dinner, and with the banging and clanging accompanying the bouncing of the basketball on the pavement outside and the noisy birds and geese and the *suck-swoosh* of Darth, Abby knew there was no way Dad could sleep.

Abby went into the living room. She was right. Dad wasn't even trying to get any shut-eye. Instead he held a pen in his right hand and a folded section of newspaper in his lap. His eyes were narrowed in concentration.

"Crossword?"

Dad nodded. He put his pen to the paper, but retracted it again. Abby circled his chair and peeked over his shoulder. All the squares were empty.

Crossing her arms across the back of the chair, Abby leaned down and rested her head on her forearms. One Across was a big, long word. That in and of itself would have made Abby move on to the next word to get more squares filled up in the long word so that she'd have some clues. Not Dad, though. Oh, no. He always had to start at the beginning and just plow on through.

When Abby read the clue for One Across her heart sank.

"The formation of a word by imitation of a sound," she read. Dad shook his head.

"Like boom, Dad, or bang."

Dad sighed in frustration. "It's on the tip of my tongue. . . ." He set his pen down on the paper. "Forget it."

"Onomatopoeia," Abby said quietly.

"What?"

"Onomatopoeia, that's the word."

"Right you are!" Dad picked up his pen and started to fill in the squares, but he spelled the word wrong. Abby gently corrected him, wanting to cry, wanting to cry foul. Dad was an English teacher. He knew this stuff. What was happening to his brain?

"It must be the medication," Dad said softly, reading Abby's mind.

"What medication?"

"For the pain. My doctor said the medicine might make it difficult to concentrate but, God, this is ridiculous." He turned in his chair to face Abby. "I'm not going to use it anymore."

Dad's cheeks were drawn and his eyes were saggy. He looked so tired.

"It's okay, Dad," Abby said, settling onto the armchair beside him. "We'll do this together."

So the two of them went to work on the crossword puzzle, Dad shaking his head every time Abby had to help him.

And the next night, Abby beat him at Scrabble.

That was when she stopped playing games with Dad altogether. It wasn't any fun anymore.

SIX

April

When Abby got off the bus one balmy April day, Mom's car was parked in the driveway with its trunk wide open. There was a suitcase inside. Mom was in the house, talking on the phone. As Abby kicked off her shoes near the front door she overheard something about a "last-ditch effort," and "lucky to have this chance."

Wandering through the living room and into the kitchen, Abby found Mom stuffing Dad's medicine bottles into a toiletry bag. Her hands were shaking.

"Oh, hey, Nancy," Mom said into the phone when she saw Abby. "I've got to run. Abby just got home. . . . Uh-huh. . . . No, not yet. . . . Okay, sure will. . . . Talk to you soon, Nancy."

The only Nancy whom Abby knew was Mrs. Beasley, the next-door neighbor. Abby had never heard Mom talk to Mrs.

Beasley on the phone; normally she just walked next door to visit.

"What's up?" Abby asked after Mom had hung up the phone.

"Honey, Dad and I have to go on a trip," Mom said, buzzing around the kitchen doing Lord-knows-what. "There's a team of doctors at the National Institutes of Health in Bethesda, cancer specialists, some of the best in the country, and it's near impossible to get in to see any of them but someone called from the hospital this afternoon and a doctor can see Dad tomorrow so we're flying out first thing in the morning and I've got to get everything ready tonight."

"Huh?" Abby's brain could process only three words: *doctor*, *flying*, *tomorrow*. "You're going where?"

"Bethesda. That's in Maryland."

"Oh. Can I come?"

Mom laughed nervously as she scurried back and forth through the kitchen, now doing absolutely nothing productive. "No. We're going to be there for a few days, at least. Maybe a week or more. Dad's going to see this doctor, then they've got to run some tests and they're going to try some experimental treatments on him."

More treatments.

"You can't miss that much school," Mom continued.

"Besides, it would be boring for you. You'd have to sit in the waiting room at the hospital."

Abby sat down at the table watching her mother pace. "So where are Josh and I going? Aunt Fran's?"

"No, she wouldn't be able to get you to school. Deanna's coming. Dad and I will head out early tomorrow morning, so I'll need you and Josh to get yourselves up and off to school. We'll leave the car at the airport and then Deanna will drive it home tomorrow night. Her flight comes in at seven thirty, so she should be here no later than nine thirty."

Deanna was twenty-two, nine years older than Abby, and a pain in the drain. She watched way too many soap operas, and she lived her life like one; there was always some crisis she invented to keep things exciting. The two of them had fought constantly, especially when they'd shared a bedroom. Abby had been delighted to see Deanna follow her boyfriend, Brad, out to Milwaukee, where he studied civil and environmental engineering at Marquette University. Deanna attended UW-Milwaukee, training as an interpreter, of all things (a career that required her to keep her mouth shut? Fat chance). Deanna had changed majors four times in her four years, so she'd most likely not graduate from college until Abby did.

Abby had barely been able to tolerate Deanna's holiday visits home, but now, to her surprise, she was excited.

Plus, Deanna coming meant they wouldn't be shipped off to Aunt Fran's.

"Mrs. Beasley will be around if you need anything," Mom said. Read: *You've got a watchdog.* "I've gotta go switch the laundry. Be right back."

Mom shot downstairs, but Abby didn't wait. Instead she went upstairs. She found Dad in the bedroom and, surprisingly, he wasn't sleeping. He was up and around, without his oxygen even, pulling clothes from his dresser drawer and stuffing them into an open suitcase while singing his favorite Beatles song, "Michelle." He appeared livelier than he had been in weeks—he didn't even seem out of breath.

"Hi, Dad," Abby said, leaning against the doorway.

Dad stopped singing and grinned. "Hope smiles from the threshold of the year to come whispering 'it will be happier.'" He raised an eyebrow. "Who wrote it?"

Abby rolled her eyes and sat down on the bed beside the suitcase. "I haven't the slightest idea. Shakespeare?"

"Tennyson." He wagged a finger at her. "I've got some work to do with you."

Without missing a beat he broke into song again, horribly off-key.

Abby laughed. "Don't quit your day job."

"Don't have one," Dad replied. He bent over to put a stack

of T-shirts in his suitcase and twisted toward Abby, startling her with a big, soggy smooch.

"Gross!" Abby said, wiping her wet cheek with the bottom hem of her shirt. But she was laughing. This trip was a good thing. It was a wonderful thing.

ABBY MADE IT TO THE BUS STOP EARLY THE NEXT MORNING. She knew Mrs. Beasley would be watching through her kitchen window, waiting to see her head out the front door, and there was no way she was going to screw this up. This was the first shot she and Josh had ever been given at proving that they could handle some responsibility. If they passed the test, chances were good that they'd be given even more freedom.

Instead of going to Leise's after school, Abby took the bus home. When she trekked up her street from the bus stop, Mrs. Beasley was in her garage vacuuming the car, no doubt keeping a lookout for Abby. Abby smiled and waved and continued next door, intending to start on her homework ASAP, in case Mrs. Beasley came around to check.

Abby could hear Josh and his friends before she'd even opened the front door. Leave it to Josh to be given an inch and take the whole mile. Didn't he know Mrs. Beasley was watching? Abby could feel the heat rising from her chest to her neck as she stormed through the front door.

Not even bothering to take off her muddy shoes, Abby stomped through the living room and down the stairs, fully prepared to let Josh have it.

But Abby didn't see her brother. Not at first, anyway. She was too stunned to see clearly; she was having hallucinations. It appeared as if Logan Pierce was in her house, kneeling on the floor beside Billy Mohr.

Logan caught Abby staring. She turned away, blushing.

"Hey, Abby," Billy mumbled.

"Hi," Abby squeaked. She couldn't have picked a worse day to throw her hair into a messy ponytail and wear Dad's old STUCKEY'S—EAT HERE AND GET GAS T-shirt. "Um, what are you guys doing?"

"What does it look like we're doing?" Josh barked, his thumbs tapping furiously upon the Xbox controller. As usual, the guys were playing Halo 3 on multiplayer mode, blowing the enemy away with a seemingly endless array of weapons.

"You wanna play?" Billy asked.

"No," Josh said before Abby could answer. "Can't you go find something to do? Oh, that's right, you can't. You don't have any friends."

"I have friends," Abby said, trying not to whine. She'd never hated her brother more than she did at that moment. Josh was the popular one, Abby the shy one. That was how it had always been, and probably always would be. But pointing this out was uncalled for.

"Then why don't you go bug one of them instead of us?" Josh said with a snicker.

On the verge of tears, Abby turned and schlepped up the stairs into the kitchen. As she rounded the corner to head up the next flight of stairs she heard Logan say, "Man, North, you're a real jerk to your sister."

"Oh," Josh said, "and you're real nice to yours."

"Yeah," Logan replied, "but my sister's not nearly as good-looking as yours is."

Abby's heart skipped a beat. She floated into her room, unsure of what to do with herself. She wanted Logan to think she was upstairs doing something cool, but she had no idea what cool people did in their rooms.

Maybe they listened to music. Yes, cool people always listened to music. But Abby had left her iPod in her school locker. All she had in her room was a clock radio that could only get one station without a bunch of static, and that station played "soft rock."

Cool people definitely didn't listen to Neil Diamond.

Leise was at cheerleading practice, so Abby couldn't go to her house. The lake had thawed and Abby could have taken a paddleboat across the bay to Spence's, but that didn't seem right, somehow. Josh would ask where she was going, and Logan might think she and Spence were an item and, besides, Abby didn't want to give Mrs. Beasley any reason to think she was up to no good.

So Abby did what she usually did when faced with such a dilemma: she turned to religion. She grabbed the Magic 8 Ball from the top of her dresser and flopped onto the bed.

Abby: Should I take the boat to Spence's?

God: MY REPLY IS NO

Abby: Should I stay home?

God: WITHOUT A DOUBT

Abby: Should I do my homework?

God: YES—DEFINITELY

Abby: Does Logan Pierce like me?

God: REPLY HAZY, TRY AGAIN

Abby bit her lip and listened to the boys downstairs, straining to hear Logan's voice. She heard him yell, "Oh, yeah!" at the television, and took this as a sign.

Abby: Am I really good-looking?

God: SIGNS POINT TO YES

Abby: Does Logan Pierce like me?

God: OUTLOOK GOOD

Thank you, God!

Abby left her room and went into the bathroom to fix herself up. If Logan thought she was cute before, well, wait until he saw the new-and-improved Abby.

A manicure was first on the agenda. Leise had her nails done by a "technician." Abby, on the other hand, had only just recently started clipping her nails before they looked haggard and filthy and Mom threatened not to allow her to leave the house until they were trimmed, so nail polish was a giant leap. Mom had four bottles in a Ziploc bag in the linen closet, and the names of the "colors" should have been "blah," "bland," "skin," and "slightly off-skin." Abby started with the toenails on her right foot and made such a mess of them she was thankful for the less-than-bold selection. She clearly needed some practice before moving on to pink or red.

Her wrists felt like they'd been scoured with sandpaper after rubbing against her prickly ankles during the toenail session. Mom had started allowing Abby to shave her legs over the summer, and though she'd gotten pretty good at it— sometimes not nicking the skin even once—it had been exciting only briefly. Now the thrill was gone, so Abby shaved only once every other week or so. Since it was still chilly outside, pants covered her legs and, besides, her leg hairs were blonde. You couldn't really tell her legs were hairy unless you touched them.

Though Abby knew Logan wouldn't be touching her legs, she shaved them anyway. Being in such a hurry to make her grand appearance before Logan left, she cut herself twice, once in the right ankle and once on her left knee. She cursed herself as she applied bandages: *This is taking up precious time! Who cares about the legs? The face! The hair!*

Abby plugged in the hand-me-down straightening iron she'd gotten from Leise and dug hair spray out of the cabinet under the sink. While the iron heated up, she took a stab at applying some makeup. All she owned was brown mascara and pink lip gloss, and she had become pretty adept at putting those on, but she wanted to look more sophisticated, so she broke into the linen closet where Mom kept her cosmetics. She pulled out the only blush and lipstick Mom hadn't packed and put some on. She wasn't impressed. The blush looked orangey, not the pretty pink shade that Leise wore, and the lipstick was nude—a condition, not a color—which was just about the same shade as Abby's lips but shinier.

Okay, forget the face. Next assignment: hair. Holding a handful of hair straight out with her left hand, Abby pressed the lever on the straightening iron with her right hand to open it up and then attempted to slide her hair neatly inside as Leise had taught her to do. She missed and burned her hand. Without Leise to help, it was awkward trying to do it while looking at the reverse image of herself in the mirror.

She tried again and fried her left ear. The clamp shut and she leaned forward to get the thing away from her head and then yanked it off, along with a clump of hair. What was left was a gigantic crease, surrounded by unruly waves. She couldn't quit. Her hair couldn't stay that way. Logan would take one look at her and crack up.

Abby gave it another go and this time succeeded in getting the iron clamped on without hurting herself. Starting at the top of her head, she slowly pulled the iron down toward the bottom fringe of hair. The hair was straighter—certainly not silky like the models in magazines, but it would do. She had just begun to repeat the process when she heard the boys downstairs preparing to leave.

Panicking, Abby wet her hair down again—wet was better than half-frizz and half-smooth—and let it be. She stepped out of the bathroom, hoping to catch Logan before he took off.

But the house was still. Abby tiptoed downstairs and found that the boys had left without a word while she was primping. All that work for nothing.

The quiet was unsettling. Abby had become accustomed to being quiet when Dad was resting, but even then there was always a hum from the washing machine, the drone of Darth, glasses clinking against forks and spoons as Mom did the dishes, the *tap-tap-tap* of Josh's fingers on the Xbox controller, and, of course, Dad's snoring.

This was a different quiet. It was silence. Abby didn't like it.

Abby turned on the TV for companionship, grabbed her

book bag, and sat on the living room floor, spreading her folders, books, and notepads across the coffee table. Josh could goof off all he wanted; Abby was going to do her homework, hoping to increase the odds of earning favorite-child status.

She thought she'd get algebra out of the way first, since she hated it most. Numbers were bad enough—but why did they have to be combined with letters? After she had worked a while, there was a knock on the door. Maybe it was Logan, who had ditched Billy and Josh to come and see Abby looking done up and gorgeous! She raced to the door, opened it, and found Mrs. Beasley smiling on the other side of the screen door, holding plates of food covered with plastic wrap.

"Hello, Abby! Dinnertime!" Mrs. Beasley said, strolling past Abby and into the kitchen. "Where's Josh?" she asked, setting the plates on the counter.

"A friend's house," Abby guessed.

"So you're here alone?" Mrs. Beasley asked, raising an eyebrow. "When's Deanna coming?"

"Not until later. Mom said around nine thirty."

"Why dontcha come have dinner with us? Mr. Beasley and I would love to have you."

"Thanks—that's really nice, but I have too much homework." It wasn't that Abby didn't want to have dinner with the Beasleys, but she needed to prove that she could take care of herself.

Assuring Mrs. Beasley that Josh would be home soon and that she would be all right, Abby thanked her for the food and led her to the door. Just as she opened it, though, Spence greeted them. He held up one of those disposable GladWare containers filled with macaroni and cheese.

"Spencer!" Mrs. Beasley exclaimed, ushering Spence in. The moment he smelled Mrs. Beasley's cooking, he hid the mac 'n' cheese behind his back.

"So glad you'll have company," Mrs. Beasley said, patting Spence on the shoulder and giving Abby a quick hug before walking out the door. "See you two later. Holler if you need anything."

"I didn't know he was coming," Abby said, but Mrs. Beasley didn't appear to have heard her. So much for her thinking Abby was on the straight and narrow. Here her parents hadn't even been gone a day and already Abby was having boys over.

Spence followed Abby into the kitchen, where she uncovered the plates of pot roast, carrots, and mashed potatoes Mrs. Beasley had left behind. Spence plunked his plastic container on the counter and laughed.

"Guess you won't be wanting this," he said, blushing. Abby reached up and grabbed an extra plate from the cupboard, then divided Mrs. Beasley's meal between the two of them. She made sure to add a heap of the macaroni and cheese to each plate as well. Spence looked at her gratefully.

"Shouldn't you save some for Josh?" he asked.

"Oh, yeah," Abby said. "Like he's so considerate of me." But she left some scraps for Josh anyway.

Spence and Abby sat down at the kitchen table to eat. Abby put the dishes in the dishwasher and wrote herself a note on the phone pad to return Mrs. Beasley's plates promptly the next day, thus impressing upon Mrs. Beasley just how grown up she was. Now, as much as she loathed the idea of being left home alone, she had to get rid of Spence.

Spence had already found a comfy spot on the couch and was reaching for the remote control.

"Spence," Abby said firmly, "you have to go."

Spence looked bewildered. "Why?"

"Because my parents aren't home and I don't want anyone to think . . . you know."

Spence laughed heartily. "Why would anyone think that?"

Abby shot him a look. What, was she so grotesque that anyone in his right mind would know better than to think Spence might look at her any other way than as just one of the guys? Logan Pierce thought she was good-looking, Abby reminded herself, and she had half a mind to inform Spence of this tidbit of information as well. But she didn't. What was the point? As if he would care.

Ignoring Abby, Spence turned on the television. Abby stepped in front of the TV and turned it off.

"Really, Spence. I think you'd better go."

Spence nodded and slapped his knees as he stood up. He took a step toward Abby.

"I'm sorry," he said. "I just didn't want you to be here alone."

"Josh should be here soon."

"Okay." Spence saw himself to the door. For some inexplicable reason, Abby felt like crying. As Spence reached for the doorknob, Abby reached for his arm.

"Thanks for coming over," she said.

"No problem," Spence muttered.

"And Spence?" Spence turned around to face her. His face was hopeful, expectant. "You don't, like, talk about this to anyone, do you?"

"Talk about what?"

"You know . . . my dad."

Spence's face softened. "No, Abby. I don't."

Abby breathed a sigh of relief. "Good. Thanks."

Spence and Abby looked at each other a little too long, so that Abby had to look away in discomfort. There was something unspoken hanging in the air, but Abby couldn't reach out and grab it.

"See ya," Spence said finally.

"See ya." Abby watched Spence release the kickstand on his bike and maneuver it down the driveway. She didn't take her eyes off of him until he was down the road and out of sight.

Swallowing the lump in her throat, Abby returned to her homework and waited for Josh.

And waited. The living room darkened with the sunset, and Abby turned on all the inside lights and the light over the garage so Josh could see when he came home.

An hour passed and Josh still wasn't home. Abby wasn't worried about him; she was furious. Furious that he was being so reckless and irresponsible, furious that he'd left her home alone for so long. Abby had never been home alone at night.

It was ten o'clock, and Mom and Dad hadn't called yet, either. What could be so important that they couldn't call?

At quarter past ten Josh opened the front door, scaring Abby out of her wits. He headed straight for the kitchen.

"Where were you?" Abby hollered from the living room.

Josh didn't answer. Abby was so mad that she thought her head might pop right off her neck.

"Where were you?" Abby demanded, barreling into the kitchen.

"What's it to you?" Josh was standing at the kitchen counter, digging into the plate of food. It was room temperature, but that didn't bother Josh. Josh ate anything.

"I deserve to know where you've been all night," Abby said, crossing her arms in front of her. She almost stomped her foot but then remembered that she was no longer three years old.

"All night?" Josh laughed. "It's ten o'clock."

"Quarter after!"

"Same diff."

"Mom never lets you stay out this late on a school night!"

Josh looked around in an exaggerated way. "Haven't you noticed? Mom's not here."

"I'm telling."

"Shut up," Josh said, brushing past Abby and barging up the stairs, slamming his bedroom door behind him.

"I'm telling!" Abby yelled up the stairs.

"Shut up!" Josh hollered back.

Josh didn't come out of his room, so Abby resumed her place on the couch, planning to stay there until Deanna arrived. She'd long since finished her homework, even the extra credit.

Some news program was on TV that Abby had zero interest in, so she passed the time by doodling on her notepad:

Logan Pierce

I hate Josh.

Mr. & Mrs. Logan Pierce

Spence. Abby quickly scribbled that out, not knowing why she'd written it in the first place.

Mrs. Abby Pierce

Josh sucks.

By eleven Deanna still wasn't there. Abby's eyes were stinging she was so tired, so she decided to call it a night. After putting on her version of pajamas—Dad's white under-shirt and a pair of his faded paisley boxers—Abby brushed her teeth and crawled into bed.

She rolled around in the quilt until it wrapped her up like a tortilla. She was nice and comfy, and tired as all get-out, but sleep wouldn't come. Abby found herself still waiting for Deanna. Her alarm clock read 11:58; Deanna was over two hours late.

Where could Deanna be? Did she miss her flight? Had her plane crashed? Did she wreck Dad's Impala on the way home?

If Deanna had missed her flight, she'd surely have called by now. If her plane had crashed it would have been breaking news, and Abby had had the television on.

Crashing Dad's car was still a possibility. An image of Deanna's body pinned inside the smashed Impala popped into her mind, and Abby did her best to force it out.

She'd probably met up with friends at the White Lake Inn. Yep, that's exactly what Deanna would do.

But where were Mom and Dad, and why hadn't they called? Abby couldn't say whether they normally called when they left Abby and Josh home alone, because they never left them home alone. What if their plane had crashed? *No, breaking news*, Abby reminded herself. What if something had gone terribly wrong at the hospital?

What if none of them, Deanna, Mom, or Dad, was coming home? What if Josh and Abby were sent to foster homes? Separate foster homes? What if the foster parents were child abusers? Pedophiles! Would Abby go to a different school?

Well, now that was a thought. Abby stuck with that, imagining how popular she'd be at a new school; the mysterious orphan. She created a bedtime story for herself inside her head, snuggled with Logan Pierce's T-shirt, and eventually fell asleep.

SEVEN

April, Continued

A mound in her parents' bed the following morning was Abby's first and only clue that Deanna had made it there. Trying to wake her, Abby bustled about noisily as she prepared to shower, slamming her dresser drawers and stomping down the hallway and banging around in the bathroom, but Deanna didn't stir. Abby guessed it was a good thing that she did not succeed in rousing her sister. Deanna made Abby's morning persona seem sunny.

When Abby looked at her reflection in the bathroom mirror she was greeted by a killer zit—a mammoth, near her right cheekbone. Should have taken her makeup off before bed, like Mom always did. The pimple was red and inflamed; even touching it lightly was painful. Abby wasted five minutes abusing it, though, squeezing and picking at it in the bathroom. After all that mutilation, it looked infinitely uglier than it had before.

After showering, Abby found a bottle of Mom's foundation and dabbed a glob of it on her swollen pimple. The makeup only made the zit look worse, but it would have to do.

After drying her hair and dressing, Abby peeked in at her still-slumbering sister. The quilt was pulled up to Deanna's neck, and though her sandy-blonde hair half covered her face, Abby could tell that Deanna hadn't changed a bit. She was still the pretty one.

Deanna had always liked to tell Abby that when genes were divvied out Abby had gotten the brains and Deanna the looks. Abby really wanted to wake Deanna up to see if she thought Abby had gotten any prettier, but she didn't. Deanna would see nothing but the monster zit.

She really didn't have anything to say to Deanna anyway. She was still mad at her for being late.

Mom and Dad hadn't called, either. Phooey to them, too.

And Josh was a jerk.

Abby hated everyone in her family that morning.

But by the time the last bell rang at the end of the school day, Abby's attitude toward her sister had sweetened. So she was late, big deal. It just went to show that Deanna thought Abby was old enough to handle things on her own. On the bus ride home Abby envisioned a weeklong slumber party of sorts: after Deanna helped Abby with her homework they would watch movies and eat popcorn and braid each other's hair and reminisce about old times and talk girl talk.

As soon as Abby arrived home from school and greeted her sister, though, she found out that the fantasy couldn't have been further from the reality. Deanna and Abby did talk girl talk, but Deanna-style, which meant that Deanna talked about Deanna while Abby listened, unable to get a word in edgewise. Deanna had nothing to say about Abby aside from a below-the-belt comment about her nasty zit, from which Abby had accidentally wiped off its foundation camouflage, and which was now the color of shame. After listening to Deanna gripe for an hour about Brad, about Milwaukee, about her job, about her car, and about her friends, Abby was ready to scratch her own eyeballs out. Or, better yet, Deanna's.

To make matters worse, every day that week Deanna invited a slew of her trashy old high school girlfriends over to sit at the picnic table on the back porch to drink beer and smoke cigarettes and complain about the lack of fairness in their lives. They made Abby feel homesick, even though she was home.

To be fair, Deanna did give domesticity the old college try. Each evening she would take a break from the grumbling long enough to pop a batch of frozen chicken into the oven or fix grilled cheese sandwiches. When "dinner" was ready she'd set a couple of plates on the counter beside the stove and return to her posse.

Long after dark the phone would ring and Abby would leap to answer it in hope of hearing Mom's or Dad's voice on the other end. They did call a couple of times, giving Abby a quick hello during the brief periods that there wasn't a doctor or nurse in the room, but usually Mom called while Abby was at school. It made Abby crazy. She was the one who came home, did her homework (extra credit included), and went to bed on time while Josh and Deanna partied. Didn't Mom know that Abby was the responsible one? Didn't she care?

Most often it would be Brad on the phone when Abby picked up. He would greet her buoyantly and ask about school and summer plans and whatnot. Her loneliness would slowly dissipate as they talked, and she started to look forward to their five-minute conversations. He seemed to be the only adult that cared anymore. She liked Brad, in a big-brother sort of way, and had no idea what he saw in her sister.

Then Brad would unenthusiastically ask to speak with Deanna, and Abby would holler out the kitchen window, "Deanna, phone's for you!" Deanna would come stumbling in and snatch the phone from Abby's hand, ripping into Brad immediately.

"Brad! Where have you been? I tried calling you three times!"

Deanna would listen with a scowl.

"You expect me to believe that?" More listening. Eyes narrowed, nostrils flared, mouth opens.

"Come on, Brad, I wasn't born yesterday! Tell me the truth!"

This would go on longer than Abby would have thought humanly possible for any guy to bear, until Deanna hung up on Brad and rushed outside to give her friends the play-by-play. They'd rile her up even more with their "compassion" and "support," and then Deanna would whip out her cell and dial Brad again. Yelling would ensue, followed by silence and tears. Amid the sobbing, Deanna's friends would become uncomfortable enough to announce their departure, and Deanna would wave them out while blubbering to Brad about how much she loved him.

All this drama was more than Abby could take. She went to bed earlier that week than she had since she was four. Abby prayed for Mom and Dad to come home early.

Her prayers were answered.

When Abby arrived home after school on Friday, she was surprised to find that the Impala was the only car in the driveway. Deanna's friends weren't there, and Josh was nowhere in sight, as usual.

Deanna jumped from the couch and put on a dopey-looking smile when Abby walked through the front door. Her eyes were red and puffy and her nose was running, so Abby assumed she'd had another squabble with Brad.

"Hiya, kiddo!" Deanna announced, her voice unsteady. "How was school?"

"Fine," Abby replied, eyeing her suspiciously. Something was up.

Abby tossed her book bag onto the floor beside the couch and wandered past her sister into the kitchen. Deanna had ignored Abby all week. Clearly she wanted to make up and make things look good before their parents came home.

"Are you hungry?" Deanna asked, following Abby. "I was thinking about ordering a pizza."

"I had pizza for lunch," Abby fibbed, getting a kick out of being difficult. She could see why Josh enjoyed it so much.

"Okay," Deanna said. "We've got some ground beef thawed in the fridge. I'll make tacos."

"I'm not hungry," Abby said flatly, grabbing a Coke from the fridge and popping the tab with a *snap-hiss*.

"Me neither. You want to play Monopoly or something?"

"I've got homework to do."

"It's Friday! Your homework can wait, can't it?" Some adult supervision Abby was getting. "Come on, we haven't played Monopoly in a million years."

"How about Scrabble?" Abby always kicked Deanna's butt in Scrabble. Abby kicked everyone's butt in Scrabble now.

"How about Monopoly?" Deanna held her ground.

Chicken.

"Fine," Abby sighed, as if doing her a giant favor. "One game. Houses, though. No hotels. That would take forever."

Deanna spread the game out on the living room floor and doled out the cash. Abby sat down across from Deanna, watching her carefully. It wasn't out of the goodness of her heart that Deanna always assumed the role of banker. She cheated. Abby had caught her twice pretending that two hundred dollar bills were stuck together, adding them to her kitty.

Abby rolled highest, so she started the game, moving the silver car past Baltic and Mediterranean Avenues and onto more important stuff. Deanna chose to be the battleship. Appropriate.

Deanna might have fared better at Scrabble. After the first trip around the board Abby had already picked up Water Works, one of the railroads, Pennsylvania Avenue, and Park Place. Deanna was toast.

Soon Deanna took a potty break—a long one. In her absence Abby cheated only slightly, checking out the Chance cards and placing the worst ones at the bottom. She reasoned that this was okay since she wasn't really stacking the deck in her favor. Who knew which one of them would land on Chance next?

When Deanna came back and sat down on the floor her eyes were pink and swollen again—likely post-traumatic stress from her most recent war with Brad.

"It's your turn," Abby said, pretending not to notice her sister's sniffling.

Deanna hesitated and then rolled the dice, landing on the jail square.

Abby laughed.

"I'm just visiting," Deanna said.

"No, you're only just visiting if you fork over money to get out of jail."

"Wrong," Deanna insisted. "You don't go to jail if you land on it. You only go to jail if you land on the 'Go to Jail' square."

They'd long since lost the directions, so the two of them debated until Deanna finally gave in.

"Fine, I'll be in jail."

Abby stared at her sister, speechless. Abby had never seen Deanna compromise her position on anything. And this was jail, no less!

"What's with you?" Abby asked.

"Nothing," Deanna said, her mouth open to say more. "Nothing," she repeated instead, shaking her head.

But before Abby could roll the dice, nothing became something. It always did with Deanna.

"Mom and Dad are coming home tomorrow. Dad's out of the hospital. They'll fly back in the morning."

Abby's face lit up. "Great!"

Deanna was sullen and quiet, and finally, Abby figured out what her problem was. Deanna had been kissing Abby's butt so that Abby wouldn't tell on her for slacking off.

Abby rolled and got doubles. Two sixes.

"Abby," Deanna said before Abby could move her car twelve spaces, "they're coming home because after Dad had some tests the doctors determined he wasn't a candidate for treatment. There's nothing they can do for him."

"Bummer," Abby said, sliding her car across the colored properties. So Dad would stay tired, and he wouldn't breathe well. He could live with that. Abby was glad they weren't keeping him longer at the hospital. Hospital=bad. Home=good. Dad could just keep up with his regular treatments.

Abby landed on Chance, won ten bucks for winning second prize in a beauty contest, then rolled again and scooped up Boardwalk. It was her lucky day.

EIGHT

April, Continued

Deanna had arranged for a flight back to Milwaukee that would depart a few hours after Mom and Dad's arrival, and spent the morning throwing the clothes she'd strewn all over their room into her duffel bag.

Abby sat on the edge of the bed watching Deanna scurry about and cuss about how late she was. She'd made her reservation the previous afternoon but, as usual, had put off packing until the last minute. Deanna could only function in crisis mode.

"Can I come with you to the airport?" Abby asked.

Deanna stopped packing for a moment and looked at Abby in the bureau mirror.

"Um. No."

"Why not?"

"Because Mom said . . . I just need to talk to Mom."

"Why can't I be there?"

"Just because."

So much for the bonding Abby and Deanna had done the day before. She stomped out of the bedroom and went downstairs into the living room. When Deanna hurried down, dragging her duffel bag behind her, Abby slipped her shoes on.

"Where are you going?" Deanna asked, propping the screen door open with her rear end and stuffing the bag through the doorway.

"With you," Abby said.

"No!" Deanna shouted. She dropped her bag on the front porch and walked toward Abby, letting the screen door bang shut behind her.

"Abby, come on," she said, looking Abby squarely in the eyes and resting her hands on her shoulders. Abby pulled away. "It's not that I don't want you to come with me or that Mom and Dad don't want to see you. It's just that . . ." Deanna's voice trailed off and she started to cry again. Loudly.

Deanna startled Abby by grabbing her by the shoulders and squeezing her in a bear hug, Deanna's body shaking as she sobbed. This time her sadness seemed real.

"I just need to talk to them alone," Deanna whispered as she released Abby. "You'll understand soon."

Ever since Abby could remember, Deanna had been telling her that she'd understand this or that when she got older, but the older she got, the more she realized that Deanna was full of it. Abby didn't press the issue this time. Instead she followed her sister and watched her pull the Impala around the circle driveway and onto the gravel road. Deanna stopped the car on the other side of the massive oak tree in the front yard and rolled down the window.

"I love you," Deanna croaked, her mouth turned downward like she was going to cry again.

Abby was stunned. It was the first time she could remember anyone in her family telling her that they loved her. Abby knew that they did, and they knew that Abby loved them back, but they just didn't say that stuff. Hearing it from her sister was shocking, and a little embarrassing, and scary. It was just too strange. Everything was getting so strange.

Abby waved, not courageous enough to tell her sister that she loved her, too, and Deanna sped off, leaving a cloud of dust behind her.

Leaving Abby in the dust behind her.

When Abby went back inside, Josh had just stumbled downstairs.

"Where's Deanna?" Josh mumbled.

"She just left."

Josh nodded and went into the kitchen. He'd reached his quota of words for the morning, but Abby didn't care. It was going to be a good day. Mom and Dad were coming home and neither her sister's weirdness nor her brother's indifference was going to get her down.

ABBY WAS ON THE PHONE WITH LEISE TALKING ABOUT A bunch of nothing when she heard the Impala pull into the driveway.

"Gotta go, Leise," Abby said, hopping off her seat on the kitchen counter and setting the cordless receiver in its cradle. She bounded into the living room and looked out the window. Mom parked the car in its usual spot in the circle driveway, got out, and went to help Dad out the passenger door. Abby had grown used to this kind of backwardness. Mom had become the house fixer, the snow shoveler, the cook, the house cleaner, the clothes washer, the nurturer—she kept it all together. Josh had taken over mowing the lawn, which was once Dad's job, and Abby pulled weeds and did the dishes. Dad still helped out with whatever he could, but that wasn't much anymore. Even folding the laundry wore him out.

Dad winced as he climbed out of the passenger seat and leaned against the window for support. Mom held his other arm, crouched a bit, as if she was prepared to catch him if he fell. And all five foot two, one hundred ten pounds of her, she would have. She'd have been happy to carry him around on a satin pillow.

Dad regained his posture, and so did Mom. They both stood still for a moment, gazing at the house. Mom's chest rose and fell in a heavy sigh and she shook her head. She said something to Dad and started to cry, and this time it was his turn to steady her. Dad held her tight and whispered into her ear. Whatever he said seemed to help, for she nodded, wiped her tears away vigorously with her palms, and stood up straight.

Dad clasped Mom's hand in his and together they walked toward the house. Abby ducked and scrambled away, not wanting them to know she'd seen. When the door opened Abby was lounging on the couch watching television as if she'd been doing so for hours.

"Well, hello!" Dad said cheerily, walking gingerly toward Abby and leaning to kiss her forehead. Abby pretended to wipe the kiss off, then carefully held him by the shoulders and eased him back to standing.

"Hi, punkin'," Mom said, digging through her purse as if she was searching for something. Abby knew that she was trying to hide her eyes.

Josh broke out of his Xbox trance long enough to come upstairs and say hello, and then he headed out to unload their luggage from the trunk. What a suck-up. Mom went outside to assist him, after warning Dad not to even think about it, and Dad sat in his recliner beside Abby.

"Whatcha watchin'?" Dad asked.

"No idea," Abby replied.

"Funny name for a show."

"What?"

"No Idea."

"Huh?"

"No Idea."

"Funny."

"So what have you been up to this week?"

"Nothing. Homework and stuff."

Josh and Mom walked in, their arms weighted down with luggage.

"What have *you* been up to this week?" Abby asked Josh. She'd warned him that she would tell.

"Nothing," Josh said, glaring at her.

Abby snorted. "Yeah. That's how much of your homework you got done."

"I did my homework."

"You did not."

"Whatever."

All this seemed lost on their parents. Mom climbed the stairs juggling a suitcase, and Dad had his head leaned back in the chair with his eyes closed. Obviously they weren't concerned in the least about Josh's behavior while they'd been away. They didn't care who was the good kid and who was not. Abby had completely wasted her energy all week; she'd toed the line for nada. Oh, the unfairness of it all.

Mom came back downstairs to retrieve a second load. Josh asked if he could go to Billy's. Dad's lids sprang open and his eyes locked with Mom's.

"No," Mom said, staring at Dad. "We all need to talk after dinner."

"But it's only four o'clock," Josh protested.

"We'll have an early dinner," Mom said flatly. "I'll get it started in a minute. I need you to stay here."

Josh groaned in exasperation, and Abby's excitement heightened. Revenge was sweet. Looked like Josh was going to get it after all.

THE NORTH FAMILY ATE DINNER IN VIRTUAL SILENCE, everyone sitting in their regular spots at the trestle table, avoiding each other's eyes. Except for Abby, that was. Soon after dinner the ball was going to drop on her brother, and Abby searched her parents' faces for signs. Their blank expressions held no clues, however, so Abby was forced to wait until after they'd all finished. It looked like that was going to be an eternity, the way Mom and Dad picked at their food, but Mom finally, mercifully announced that dinner was over. Abby had been much too excited to eat.

Everyone stood, and Mom cleared the table while Abby

opened up the dishwasher and deposited her rinsed dish inside. Mom set the dirty dishes on the countertop beside the sink.

"That can wait," she said dully, touching Abby's elbow and gently nudging her toward the living room. This was serious. Big-time serious. Mom never let Abby do anything after dinner until the dishwasher was loaded and running and the tables and countertops wiped down.

Abby sat on the living room couch beside Josh; Dad was in his recliner, facing them, his elbows on his knees, trying his best to suck air into his lungs. He was doing this thing with his hands—clasping them, unclasping them, clasping them again. Abby had never seen her father look so nervous.

Mom stood behind Dad's chair, resting her hands on his shoulders. When it appeared that he wasn't about to speak, she did.

"Things didn't go well at the hospital."

"That's what Deanna said," Abby replied. *Now get on with it! Off with his head!*

"What did she tell you?" Mom asked, her eyes wide. It wasn't fear, was it?

"Not much," Abby said. "Just that the treatments didn't work."

Mom nodded slowly.

"Dad wasn't a candidate for treatment," she corrected.

"The cancer has spread like wildfire. It's in his other kidney, his lungs, his bones. . . ." She fell silent and stared at the wall.

"So you're not going to get better?" Abby asked Dad.

Dad, who had been putting a lot of effort into focusing on his hands, looked at Abby and smiled softly.

"I'm going to die," he said.

Mom probably lost it then, Josh probably broke out of his teenage catatonia and spoke like a real person, Dad probably lied and said everything would be okay. But Abby didn't know. What Abby heard was a needle in the run-out groove of an old 45 on Dad's ancient record player after the song had ended.

Shh-bmp. Shh-bmp. Shh-bmp.

Abby didn't know where she went or how she got there or what it looked like, but it sounded like *Shh-bmp. Crackle. Shh-bmp. Crackle.*

Over the deafening noise Abby heard Dad's voice in the distance.

"I'm gonna kick the bucket, meet my maker, bite the dust, give up the ghost—"

"That's not funny!" Mom screamed. "That's sick! This is not a joke! This is not funny!"

Through a thick fog Abby saw Mom run into the kitchen, Dad's eyes chasing her helplessly. His gaze darted from the kitchen to them, back to the kitchen, back to them. He looked powerless and scared. Guilty.

"How long do you have?" Josh asked from somewhere far away.

"The doctors say less than six months," Dad replied. "But you never know."

Six months. It was April, so that meant that Dad would die by October. He'd be a ghost for Halloween.

Abby's senses shut down and she turned back toward the fog, now comforted by the thick blanket of nothingness that engulfed her, and rocked to the rhythmic sound of the old 45.

Shh-bmp.

nine

April, continued

Neither Josh nor Abby told anyone at school what was happening to Dad. Spence had already promised, and Leise knew only what she'd overheard in the sickroom months before and had so far upheld her secrecy oath. This indebted Abby to them for an eternity, for if they blabbed Abby would lose her lifeline—the one place she could go and be a normal girl. If anyone at school found out about Dad, Abby would become just like Jamie Thorpe.

Jamie Thorpe's brother had been killed in a car accident the year before. The Monday after he died the school administration made it a point to prove its compassion by observing a school-wide moment of silence and offering grief counseling with the school shrink, but in the end Jamie was ostracized. People didn't know what to say or how to act, so they avoided her. Kids would stand back as Jamie passed in the hallway, whispering behind her back, "That's her. That's the one."

Not everyone treated Jamie this way. Some of the popular girls decided to make Jamie their best friend—she was, for a time, a celebrity—but her fame was only temporary. As the months passed the interest in Jamie waned, and the popular girls ditched her again. Now she wasn't only ignored but humiliated. Jamie didn't come back in the fall; she'd switched to a private school. Abby never saw her again.

Abby did not want to be like Jamie. She didn't want to disappear.

Spring break came, and Josh went on a camping trip in Canada with his friend Jason and Jason's parents. Leise had flown to Georgia to visit relatives. Even Spence had gone with his mom and her boyfriend-of-the-month to Florida for the week. It seemed everyone in the world had gone on vacation but Abby and Mom and Dad. Abby was left at home with nothing to do but mess with her hair and listen to Darth. Actually she hardly heard Darth anymore, like you don't notice the hum of the furnace until the power goes out.

Mom and Dad attempted to keep Abby entertained during the break—Mom and Abby baked Dad's favorite chocolate chip cookies together, Dad and Abby did crossword puzzles—but Abby missed her friends. She envied them. They were out there somewhere having fun.

Josh came home from his camping trip early, on Tuesday morning. Jason's mom had come down with the flu, so they'd left in the middle of the night. Mom freaked out about the germs Josh might have brought into the house. She made Josh shower thoroughly and threw all of his clothes, even the clean ones, even the duffel bag, into the washing machine. Mom loaded the whole family up on zinc and vitamin C tablets, sprayed the house with Lysol, and warned Josh to stay away from Dad. Germs didn't stand a chance against Mom.

Dad didn't come downstairs that day. The painkillers weren't doing the trick anymore. The drugs left him sleepy and his eyes cloudy but did little to dull the pain. Abby didn't know where or how bad it was exactly; Dad developed a stiff upper lip when she was around.

Mom stayed upstairs most of the day, and Abby sat in her room painting her nails with a blue polish she'd borrowed from Leise. Mom always said only freaks painted their nails blue, but Abby figured she wouldn't even notice now. Dad was coughing in his bedroom. Coughing hurt him and made him groan softly, but loud enough for Abby to hear.

"I'm going to start you on morphine," Abby heard Mom say.

"No," Dad protested.

"Sam," she begged, "please. I can't stand watching this anymore. It's killing me."

"Me too," Dad said.

"Not funny."

When her nails dried, Abby crossed the hall to her parents' bedroom. She knocked on the open door and poked her head inside. Mom and Dad were sitting up on the bed in their usual spots. Dad smiled when he saw Abby; Mom did not. She never did, not anymore.

Dad commenced a lengthy coughing fit, and Abby waited until it quieted to step inside.

"Hairball," Dad whispered before taking a sip from the cup of water Mom held to his lips.

"How's it going?" Abby asked timidly.

Dad started coughing again and leaned toward the yellow bowl that they once had used for popcorn, but had now officially become the puke bowl. He shooed Abby away so she wouldn't see him vomit or spew blood. She hightailed it out of there and occupied herself in her bedroom until it was dark. With her bedside lamp switched on, Abby completed three chapters' worth of exercises from her biology workbook and wrote three essays that Mrs. Lawson had assigned as extra credit. When she'd finished she opened her old yearbook up to page sixty-seven and ogled Logan Pierce. It was hard to concentrate until the hacking died down across the hall.

At ten o'clock Abby heard Josh's bedroom door shut, and

half an hour later she figured Dad would be sound asleep, even though she didn't hear him snoring. Mom usually stayed up until at least eleven doing bills and laundry and whatnot. She wouldn't mind if Abby came down to talk.

So as not to wake Dad, Abby tiptoed to her bedroom door and opened it silently, pulling the knob upward, hard, so the door wouldn't creak. She'd lived in that house all her life and knew all of its imperfections. Her bedroom door opened without a sound.

Abby was surprised to find her parents' door almost closed. The door didn't latch, so it never shut all the way, and usually they slept with it wide open.

A dim light shone through the crack between the door and the doorjamb. Abby peered through the crack. She wished she hadn't.

Mom and Dad lay on the bed, curled into each other. His fingertips delicately traced her hairline, the slope of her jaw, her neck, her collarbone, her shoulders. Mom was smiling, kind of, but from her eye a single tear ran down the side of her face and into her short, brown curls. Dad kissed the tear tenderly, and Mom's face scrunched up in agonizing sadness.

Abby pulled away from the door ashamed, intrigued, scared, and heavyhearted. Mom could not fix Dad, but she would give him everything she had. Dad kissed her tears away to tell her that it was okay that everything was not enough. That's what he always said:

"It's okay."

"I'm okay."

"Everything's going to be okay."

Everything *wouldn't* be okay. There was nothing either of them could do to make Dad better.

They were as helpless as Abby was.

SLEEP GAVE ABBY COMFORT. SHE DID NOT DREAM, OR have any dreams she could remember, and when she was asleep she did not have to think. She was safe inside her own head.

Abby was pushed out of the foxhole, though, when her internal alarm clock rang. Before It came along she was slow to wake in the morning, but now the pain in her stomach brought her to full alertness instantly.

That particular morning during spring break, Abby tried desperately to escape back into sleep, but to no avail. She was haunted by something that she'd been chasing out of her head since It all began. She told herself that it didn't matter, that she needn't feel guilty about something she couldn't possibly have caused. Abby knew the laws of cause and effect. She knew the rules of sticks and stones. Her rational self knew all of that, but her rational self had become a stranger.

Abby lay in her bed, gazing up through the small window at the cottony clouds, remembering the incident that had happened almost two years before. Back when Josh still gave Abby the time of day.

Josh and Spence and Abby had been hanging out in Josh's room while Dad had been in his makeshift office in the master bedroom doing paperwork. Spence and Abby sat on Josh's bed; Spence on one end against the headboard, Abby cross-legged at the foot. Josh had taken a break from cleaning his fish tank to run downstairs and into the garage for supplies. Spence and Abby had stayed put. Spence must have said something like:

"You're not so fat anymore," or "You look better without that boy haircut."

Whatever he'd said was innocent enough, or so it had seemed to Abby. Didn't seem so to Dad.

Within seconds he was standing in the bedroom doorway, anger glazing his eyes. "You two—out of the bedroom!"

Spence jumped to his feet, though he didn't know what to do next. He wasn't too sure about approaching Mr. North, who was practically foaming at the mouth. Spence had never seen him that angry. Neither had Abby.

"Go home, Spence," he said in a tone only slightly nicer. Spence tore out of the room and down the stairs like he was on fire as Abby sat still, dumbfounded.

Dad glared at Abby and said, "You and Spence are not to be on the bed together. You two don't need to be in a bedroom alone at all. Period."

He'd looked as if he'd wanted to say more but couldn't, so he simply shook his head and stomped down the stairs.

Abby hadn't the slightest idea what had just happened. She had played with Spence since they were little, and they'd sat on beds together more times than Abby could remember. It had never been an issue before.

"Why?" Abby shouted, storming out the bedroom door and standing at the top of the stairs with her hands on her hips. Dad stood at the foot of the stairs, looking up at her.

"Because," Dad said, "you're eleven."

"I'm almost twelve!"

"Okay, twelve. You two are too old to be on the bed together."

"But we were just sitting there!" Abby whined.

"I don't care if you were standing on your heads! Just stay off the bed, out of the bedroom, with Spence. With any boy."

"But it was never a big deal before!"

"Well, it is now! Go play with your girlfriends!"

Abby had started to cry out of frustration. "But I don't have any girlfriends around here! There are no girls in the neighborhood!"

Dad showed no sympathy. "Well then, read a book or something. Just stay away from the boys."

Abby exploded. "You're ruining my life!"

"Good!" Dad shouted back as he retreated down the stairs to the basement.

"I hate you!" Abby screamed. He paused midway down the stairs before continuing on. Abby knew that he'd heard her, and she was glad. Her dad was suffocating her.

And now he was suffocating. Coincidence?

Now, as Abby lay in bed, remembering, she vowed to be a better person. Granted, Dad had apologized, admitting that he'd overreacted, and he'd never begrudged Abby's friendship with Spence again. But Abby had never said she was sorry for what she'd yelled at him, for what she had done. From now on she'd be good and she'd never, ever disrespect her dad again.

It wasn't purely guilt that kept Abby in bed that morning, though. An unfamiliar, cheery female voice carried upstairs into her bedroom, and there was a strange, white Taurus parked in the driveway. Another well-wisher, Abby assumed, coming to visit with Dad.

Abby had just about had it with those fakes. Everyone from Dad's grade school buddies to old neighbors to the janitor from the high school where he had taught had stopped by to tell him that if he needed anything, *anything at all*, they were there for him. Bull. After their obligatory visits, they would return to their normal lives in which the most pressing concerns were deciding what to have for dinner or where to take their next family vacation, feeling fantastic about themselves for being so kind and sympathetic to a dying man. They knew the Norths would never call them to ask for anything. Their kind gestures were hollow.

Abby was starting to feel like her house was a big top, and Dad was the star attraction. The freak show. The Elephant Man. Sad but intriguing. People couldn't help but come and take a look for themselves.

It was almost eleven by the time Abby rolled out of bed and pulled on her sweatpants. It irked her that she had to put on sweatpants just to come out of her room. People should be able to traipse around in their underwear in their own homes.

Mom was standing near the bottom of the stairs and spotted Abby before she could duck into the bathroom to shower.

"Abby," Mom said, "come on down here for a minute. There's someone I'd like you to meet."

Always. Abby trudged down the stairs, not even pretending to be happy about it. This was getting to be a dull charade.

Dad sat in his recliner reading a pamphlet, with a tall, plain, brunette woman smiling at his side. She was fortyish and built like a linebacker, dressed conservatively in khakis and a white, buttoned-up shirt. Abby figured her for one of Dad's teacher friends.

Mom did the introductions.

"Abby, this is Mary. Mary, Abby."

Mary strode over and shook Abby's hand. Her handshake was gentle for such a huge woman.

"Nice to meet you," Mary said. "I'm a nurse from hospice, and I'll be coming by to help out with your dad."

A nurse? In their house? Abby had never heard of such a thing. Not when there were three able-bodied people already there to take care of him, not to mention Aunt Fran, who came over several times a week to lend Mom a hand but inevitably wound up in tears, which was most certainly not helpful. Obviously Mom didn't think she could depend on Abby, so she'd called in a stranger. Normal life would now vanish into thin air.

"Hi," Abby said, her annoyance unmasked. "Mom, can I go take a shower now?"

Mom gave Abby a perturbed look before dismissing her.

"Teenagers," Abby heard Mom say through the bathroom door.

"I understand," Mary replied, "believe me. I've got two in college. After they left home I considered moving away and leaving no forwarding address."

Mary's voice lowered and Abby strained to hear her.

"She's awfully thin. Is she eating?"

"Abby?" Mom sounded surprised, as if she hadn't noticed. "I think so."

"Does she always sleep this late in the morning?"

"No, not usually."

"Good. Just keep an eye on her and watch for signs of depression. Kids have an especially difficult time dealing with terminal illness."

Oh, now, didn't that just take the cake. Abby turned on the shower so she wouldn't have to listen to any more of Mary's crap. Here this lady had seen Abby for less than two minutes, sized her up, and was trying to convince Mom that Abby was crazy. Who did she think she was? As if Mom weren't anxious enough already, now she had been given the additional burden of analyzing her teenaged daughter who might crack up at any second. Abby wasn't depressed, but if she had to watch her every step, knowing that her actions were being scrutinized, she was bound to become a certified schizo.

Luckily Mary was gone by the time Abby had finished showering so it was, for now, safe to go downstairs. Dad was sleeping peacefully in his recliner. Abby hadn't seen him sleep without twitching and moaning or without a grimace on his face for some time. Mom was in the kitchen preparing her daily meal—a multivitamin and a cup of coffee.

"Dad looks good," Abby said.

Mom nodded and smiled, slowly stirring powdered cream into her mug. "We started him on morphine this morning." Mom and Mary had suddenly become "we." "It should help the pain immensely."

"But I thought he didn't want to use morphine."

"He didn't originally, but the pain was getting so bad that he finally gave in. It's a low dose, so it shouldn't affect him too much."

Abby wasn't really sure what that meant.

Mom took a few sips of her coffee before heading to the back door to put her shoes on.

"I need to pull some weeds in the backyard," Mom said. "And since Dad's finally getting a good rest I could use some fresh air. Would you mind staying in here with him in case he wakes up and needs anything?"

"Okay," Abby said. Once Mom saw what a tremendous help she could be, Mary would be history.

Abby flipped to a rerun of *The Brady Bunch* and sat down on the couch beside Dad's recliner. Back in the good ol' days Abby never would have been able to hear the television over Dad's snoring. Back then it was like his nasal cavity took up all the space in his head to allow his snores to echo, to resonate.

But Dad didn't snore anymore. Abby didn't know if he didn't sleep deeply enough or what, but she missed his snoring; it was Dad's lullaby. If she awakened in the night Abby had always known her dad was there. Now she kept tabs on him via Darth.

Right at the episode's climax, when Marcia Brady got hit in the schnoz with a football (*Smack*. "Oh my nose!" *Smack*. "Oh my nose!"), Dad woke up and cleared his throat.

"Where's Mom?" he asked hoarsely.

"Outside," Abby said without taking her eyes off of the television. "What do you need?"

"Where's Josh?"

"He's upstairs."

"Can you go get him, please?"

Abby looked at her dad, waiting for him to trust her with whatever he needed. His eyes pleaded with her, so even though she was disappointed that it wasn't her that he wanted, she did as he asked, skipping up the stairs to find Josh.

Her disappointment quickly vanished when she found out that Dad needed help going to the bathroom. That job was best left to Josh, as was helping Dad clean up in the evenings. It amazed Abby that her brother was capable of caring for anyone but himself. Perhaps he was part human after all.

After Josh helped Dad up the stairs and into the bathroom, Mom came inside and stirred the vegetable soup that she'd been slow-cooking in the Crock-Pot. She looked panic-stricken when she glanced into the living room and found Dad's chair empty.

"He's using the bathroom," Abby explained.

"By himself?" her mom said, inhaling sharply and rushing to the foot of the stairs. She didn't exactly imply it, but Abby felt the sting of her mother's fear that she'd wrongfully entrusted Dad's care to Abby.

The door to the bathroom opened, and Abby and her mother looked up to catch Josh leading Dad into the master bedroom. Mom sighed so heavily Abby swore she saw the pictures on the wall sway in the breeze.

Her mother ladled soup into a bowl for Dad, and without being asked Abby fetched a couple of ice cubes from the freezer. Her mother smiled gratefully when Abby plunked them into the soup bowl to cool off the broth. She felt redeemed.

Dad was sitting upright on the edge of his bed when Mom and Abby brought the soup upstairs. Mom carried it actually, and she'd cooked it, but Abby was observing; making notes to self, determined to help.

Mom sat on the chest at the end of the bed, and Abby

pulled a tray table toward his lap. It was close to him, but not too close. There was the perfect distance between lap and tray. Abby silently commended herself for being such a natural caregiver as she sat beside Mom on the chest, waiting for the next opportunity.

Dad seemed irritable and distracted, looking at neither Mom nor Abby. His eyes were droopy, but every now and then they'd widen suddenly, darting around the room as if there was something he needed to do but he couldn't remember what. That had happened with the other pain medications, too.

As Mom dipped the spoon into the bowl, Dad held up his hand to stop her.

"Wait!" he said.

"What?" Mom asked. "What do you need?"

"Turn it over."

"What . . . the spoon?"

"No," Dad said urgently. "The bowl. You have to read the directions."

"Sam . . ."

"Turn it over and read the directions!"

Mom placed the spoon into the bowl and sighed. Neither she nor Abby knew what to say. Abby could barely think over the noise of the old 45 in her head.

Shh-bmp. Shh-bmp.

"That's not right," Dad said pitifully. "I'm sorry. I'm so sorry."

Abby wanted to hug him, to tell him it was okay. Like he was a little child.

TEN

May

In early May, the Norths' living room decor became dominated by a hospital bed. Abby wasn't sure why it wasn't set up in the bedroom—probably so Dad wouldn't feel tucked away and forgotten, or so that Mom would have easier access to him—but in either case there it was. The front door was no longer an entrance; Mom taped a note on the windowpane instructing everyone to come in and out only through the kitchen door, accessible via the garage.

The bed was big and bulky and white: white pillowcases, white sheets, and a thin, white blanket Dad never used because he was always hot. But Josh and Abby quickly figured out that the bed wasn't as forbidding as it appeared. It was fun. As soon as the guys from the medical supply company finished setting it up, Josh and Abby took turns "riding" it. When they pressed a button on the remote control, the head of the bed would rise until it was at almost a ninety-degree angle to the lower portion. Another button made the end of the bed rise almost as far as the top did. When they pressed both buttons at the same time they were sandwiched. A third button caused the entire bed to go up and down. There were more buttons, but Mom made Abby and Josh knock it off before they could test them all.

Dad stared blankly from across the room, where his recliner had been relocated. It wasn't that he looked sad, exactly, but confused, as if he couldn't remember what funny was. If he had, he would have gotten a kick out of their antics.

If Dad had still been Dad, he would have been tickled to see Josh and Abby goofing off together. It had started to seem like Josh didn't hate Abby after all. In fact, he had ceased acting like spending time with his family was torturous and was staying home and helping out more. He mowed the lawn and helped Mom fix things around the house, allowed Abby to play Xbox with him, and often pulled up a chair beside Dad's bed to read to him. It wasn't reading, exactly, only reciting the captions underneath the cartoons in his Gary Larson collection and showing Dad the pictures. Abby envied Josh; he always seemed to pull at least one grin out of Dad during their Far Side sessions.

Abby, on the other hand, spent *less* time at home. Not always by choice. There were things Dad had to do that they didn't want her to see, and the bed in the center of the house meant that Abby was frequently issued walking papers. Besides, Mary was always telling Mom in her sickeningly sweet and faux-friendly way how to take care of Dad and how to keep the household as peaceful as possible for him, so that Abby felt the only thing she could do competently was stay out of the way.

Abby sometimes hid in her room, but often she went down to the Point and daydreamed that she belonged to one of the carefree families sputtering around in motorboats or fishing from canoes. She imagined that she was one of the college girls sunbathing on distant docks, surrounded by well-tanned friends. Abby wished she could be anyone but Abby.

Spence knew where to find her. She didn't want to talk, and he didn't know what to say, so they'd lie side by side in the grass, Spence with his eyes closed and Abby gazing at the clouds, pondering heaven. People pointed to the sky when they referred to heaven, and they talked about "God above." Above where? Above the clouds? Above the clouds was outer space. Was heaven beyond outer space? Dad living among the aliens didn't sound so heavenly. Clouds were heavenly. Abby could picture Dad sitting atop a tall, white cotton-candy cumulus, looking down on her with pride. Abby hoped that's what would happen, after. She became the champion of wasting time, knowing she was wasting precious time.

Eventually Mom started trusting Abby to help with Dad more, and Abby started wishing that she wouldn't. Josh started driver's training, and while Mom wouldn't dare venture too far from the house she'd occasionally allow Josh to take spins around the circle driveway in the Impala while she clutched the panic handle above the passenger door with white knuckles, of course. Abby couldn't imagine Mom ever driving on a real road with Josh. They'd have to give *her* morphine, too.

One evening, Dad and Abby sat silently in the living room while Mom braved the driveway speedway with Josh. Abby lounged in the recliner while Dad sat upright in the bed, craning his neck and straining to keep his heavy eyelids open. As he watched his son drive his car without him, Dad's eyes seemed to cloud over.

Abby looked away, turning her attention to some educational program on PBS but too terrified to comprehend a word the narrator was saying. Dad was starting to give up. How dare he?

"Josh?" Dad said in a whisper.

"Josh?" he called again, and when Abby turned toward him she realized that Dad was staring right at her. Abby wondered if he couldn't remember her name or if he really thought she was her brother.

"Abby," she corrected, standing so he could see her better. "I'm Abby, Dad."

Dad's brow furrowed in concentration as if he were trying to remember who on Earth Abby was. Then his eyes saddened.

"I'm sorry, honey," he said. "I'm so sorry."

"It's okay," Abby lied. "Did you need something?"

"Yes." Dad's voice was dry. "I need a glass of mold."

"A glass of mold?"

"Yes. A glass of mold."

Abby wished Mom would get back inside, quick. She was much better at steering Dad back to rational thought than Abby was. Abby was apt to go along with him so he wouldn't feel stupid, but Mom had told her not to. She said that if and when Dad eventually realized the errors in his thought process, he'd also realize that his family had been playing along. That, Mom had said, would make him feel worse.

"Dad," Abby said, "you don't need a glass of mold."

"Yes, I do!" His tone was urgent, frustrated, angry. He pointed at the television where magnified microscopic mold-like images floated across the screen. "Please. Go get me a glass of mold!"

It took Abby a few moments to figure out what his morphine-afflicted mind had deduced.

"A glass of mold," Abby muttered. "Penicillin. You think penicillin will make you better."

Dad's face looked hopeful. It about killed her.

"It won't," he said, finally.

Shh-bmp.

ELEVEN

June

On the first day of summer vacation, Abby stayed in bed late, reading the notes her classmates had written in her yearbook. Some said, "Give me a call this summer!" Others jotted down dates of summer parties and sleepovers. Abby had responded to all in the same way: "See ya next year!" She couldn't let anyone come over, not even Leise. Sure, Leise knew Dad was sick, but she hadn't seen him. Abby didn't want anyone to see him, not this way. Spence didn't care what she wanted, so he would continue to pop in anyway, but summer was his busiest season. Abby's mother had signed her up for summer softball again, but since Mom wouldn't leave the house Abby had no idea how she could get to practice. She'd have to drop out. So that was that. Summer vacation would be a prison term.

Dad was having a bad day; he was hardly conscious. Abby

lounged for hours on the Longmans' hammock watching Spence and Mr. Longman put in an offshore floating dock, and when she returned in the late afternoon Dad was asleep. Josh and Abby kept quiet all evening, hiding downstairs playing Xbox. Dad slept on.

By morning Dad had yet to awaken. When Abby drowsily stumbled downstairs long after dawn she found Mom kneeling beside Dad's bed, holding his hand as if she feared he'd drift away if she didn't hold tight.

A coma, that was what Mom called it. While blood continued to flow through his veins, and his chest still sporadically rose and fell, to call Dad alive seemed a misnomer. Abby felt she had an inkling of what it meant to "walk through the valley of the shadow of death." The shadow hovered over her family and taunted her father.

Mary came to the house mid-morning. She said that a coma was often a precursor to death, so Mom anxiously watched and waited. Abby turned away.

Mom made the obligatory phone calls to Aunt Fran and Deanna, and Dad's closest friends, to announce that the end could be near. Aunt Fran rushed over first and fretted at the bedside for several hours until Mom hinted that nothing was likely to happen and Aunt Fran should go home until morning. Deanna and Brad drove in just after she left, bringing a pizza that no one ate, and after spending the evening

helplessly watching Dad, they didn't balk at Mom's sugges-
tion that they might be more comfortable staying at Brad's
parents' house nearby. Abby didn't think Mom wanted anyone intruding on what she feared might be her last moments
with Dad. Abby knew better. It couldn't end this abruptly; it
was too soon. October was still months away.

Dad slept on. His breathing was intermittent at times,
and when he took long pauses between breaths so did Mom.
She did everything she could to wake him up, talking to him
incessantly and stroking his hair and adjusting his position
from lying on his left side to his right and then back again
so that he wouldn't get bedsores. She massaged his arms and
legs, lifting and bending them to give him some sort of exer-
cise, so that when he woke up he wouldn't be stiff. She did
her best to hydrate him by gently squirting water onto the
back of his tongue with a medicine syringe and then caressing his throat to induce a swallowing reflex. If Mom could
have reached inside him to keep his heart beating with her
bare hands, she would have.

The neighbors brought meals, and a few of Dad's work
friends came by, but Mom ushered them out the door as
quickly and as politely as possible. After a while Mom stopped
being quite so compliant and simply told visitors that all the
commotion wasn't good for Dad, and none of them seemed
to take offense. They'd leave graciously, saying, "If there's

anything I can do, anything at all . . ." But there was nothing they could do.

The days passed by. Deanna and Brad tearfully left for Milwaukee, Aunt Fran caught a virus and had to stay away, and nobody else came. Abby wondered if Mom had called everyone and told them that Dad had snapped out of it, that he was just fine, that no one should give his illness another thought, and people had said, "Whew, glad that's over. We'll catch up with Sam and Helen at Christmas."

No one came, that was, except for Spence. He tidied up and swept out the garage, washed windows, moved the sprinklers around the lawn, took out the trash can on Monday night and brought it in Tuesday morning. Josh usually gave him a hand, but Spence was always reminding Josh that you have to remove the window screens to clean the windows, not just spray the Windex through and expect it to work; that the tools go back in the toolbox, not on top of the back porch picnic table; that you have to turn off the hose before unscrewing the sprinkler. One time Abby even saw Josh trying to trim the edges of the lawn without turning the weed whacker on. Lights were on in Josh's head, but no one was home. Spence was a good sport with Josh, thanking him for all his help like he'd do with a four-year-old who wanted to show what a big boy he was. But Josh wasn't a complete airhead. He'd taken over washing Dad up in the evenings, and for this he had achieved sainthood in Mom's eyes.

On Friday, Spence's friend Griffin was having a barbecue and bonfire at his house. Spence was, of course, at the Norths', helping Abby wash Mom's car, which had only become dirty because the cars on their road stirred up so much dust. Mom's car hadn't gotten any mileage in weeks.

Uncharacteristically Spence didn't "accidentally" spray Abby with the hose. Not even once. The two worked side by side, sudsing and scrubbing the car and taking turns with the hose to wash it off with more maturity than either of them had thought the other possessed. It was odd, but strangely comforting, to be with Spence and not have to talk about anything at all, to forget everything for a little while and just be.

When they finished, Spence started coiling the hose and Abby dumped the dirty water from the bucket into the garden, reasoning that she couldn't do much more damage to Mom's wilting flowers. She put everything away in the garage and turned around to discover Spence looking around, as if trying to find something, anything, to do next to make himself useful.

"Aren't you going to Griffin's today?" Abby asked, peeking into the garage fridge for something to drink. It was empty.

"Nah," Spence replied.

"Why not?"

Spence picked up a broom and started to sweep the already clean garage floor.

Abby shut the fridge door, walked over to Spence, and put her hand over his on the broom handle to still it. Spence jumped as if electrocuted.

"Stop," Abby said. "There's nothing more to do here. Go to the party."

"Abby, I don't want to—"

"You need to," Abby interrupted, removing her hand from Spence's and crossing her arms in front of her chest. "Seriously. You can come back tomorrow."

Spence smiled plaintively. "Come with me?"

Abby examined her shoes. "Wish I could." Abby didn't dare ask permission from Mom to leave. She wouldn't enjoy herself anyhow, going to a party and leaving her heart and mind at home. "Just go, okay?"

"Okay," Spence conceded. "But only if you'll take a swim with me first."

"Deal," Abby said, rushing inside for her suit. Mom was still in the living room talking to Dad, about what Abby didn't know and didn't care to hear, so she passed by quietly on the way up the stairs and back down again, peeking in just long enough to see that, indeed, Dad was still unconscious.

Down at the Point, Spence stripped off his shirt and dove into the lake headfirst. Abby followed suit, not caring that the cold water turned her into one gigantic goose bump. She stayed under a long time, listening to the muted hum of a far-off motorboat and the swooshing of the waves as they collided with the shore, feeling as if her lungs were about to explode, wondering if that was what it felt like for Dad, being unable to breathe. When a hand grasped Abby's arm and pulled her up, Abby took a huge gulp of air and the rush of oxygen flooded her lungs.

"What are you doing?" Abby spluttered, pushing her wet hair from her face and wiping her eyes.

"I wasn't sure you were going to come up again," Spence said.

Abby lay back in the water and floated face-up, with Spence alongside her doing the same. The sun was blinding, so Abby kept her eyes closed and tried to relax.

But she couldn't. She had a nagging feeling in her stomach that she needed to get home. Was this what it felt like for people who claimed to know when a loved one had passed away when they were hundreds of miles apart? Was there some sort of invisible thread that connected people together so that they could communicate, and say good-bye, without words?

Abby tried her best to ignore her feelings, for if Dad was

truly gone she didn't want to find out. Not yet. She needed this time to play make-believe, to pretend that this was just another summer day that would pass by slowly, a day when she didn't have a care in the world.

Abby had no idea how much time had passed when she started to feel the skin on her face burn. Once again she had neglected to put on sunscreen.

"You're looking pretty lobstered," Spence said at last. "You'd better get out of the sun."

Reluctantly Abby sloshed out of the water. She dried herself off and then handed her towel to Spence. He'd forgotten to bring one. Abby watched the muscles in his arms, chest, and neck as he rubbed his face and hair vigorously with the towel. A speedboat full of teenaged girls approached, slowing as it neared the Point. Spence didn't spot the girls eyeing him, but Abby did. She moved closer to Spence and glared until they sped away.

"What's the matter?" Spence asked, laughing at Abby's expression.

"Nothing." Abby ran her fingers through her wet hair to work out the tangles. "Um, the sun was in my eyes."

"I'll walk you home," Spence said, already heading up the hill.

"That's okay," Abby said. "Why don't you go on over to Griffin's? Everyone should be there by now."

Spence looked torn. "Are you sure?"

Abby nodded. "I'm sure. Have fun."

Spence started to walk toward the Fischers' house, intending to take the shortcut behind their house and around the lakeshore to his side of the bay. Suddenly he stopped and jogged toward Abby, handing her the towel.

"Thanks," he said, leaning over to give her a quick peck on the cheek before sprinting away.

Abby stood dumbfounded, unsure whether the heat rising to her cheek was from Spence's kiss or the sunburn. But the sunburn couldn't be what warmed her from the inside out and made her smile. She walked up the hill, wondering what had gotten into Spence. He'd never kissed her before, not even in the big-brother way he just had. Maybe he was just feeling sorry for her. That idea made her warm fuzzies vanish into thin air.

By the time Abby arrived home, her fleeting euphoria was gone and she was greeted with the same feeling of dread she had every time she'd walked in since Dad's coma began, wondering if she'd come home to find that his chest no longer rose and fell. When she opened the door a surge of relief always rushed through her when she heard Darth *suck-swoosh*, for Abby knew that if Dad no longer needed Darth to breathe he no longer needed to breathe at all.

Darth was still going strong that afternoon, but Abby was

also greeted with something she didn't expect: she heard Dad's faint voice in the living room.

Without closing the door behind her, Abby dropped her towel onto the linoleum and ran breathlessly into the front room. Dad sat upright with the head of the bed raised for support. He was smiling.

"Dad!" Abby shouted. "You're awake!"

"He doesn't remember sleeping," Mom said from her seat at the edge of the bed beside Dad. She was grinning from one end of the room to the other.

Josh was there, too, sitting on the couch, looking as exhilarated as Abby felt. There was life in the living room. She wanted to jump up and down. Maybe she did. She only wished that Mary were there to admit that she'd been wrong. A coma did not always lead to death. Maybe the coma was Dad's body's way of healing him, like the way you sleep a lot when you have a cold. Dad looked more alert than he had in a long time, and the shadow had lightened. For once Abby's stomach didn't hurt; it was filled with butterflies.

Abby skipped over and sat on the end of the bed near Dad's feet, studying his face. Something had changed about him, though Abby couldn't pinpoint what it was. His brow did not furrow with anxiety, his eyelids did not squint from pain, his irises were clear and free of fear. He looked relaxed and peaceful. It seemed that during his prolonged sleep some-thing miraculous had happened.

Something miraculous *had* happened.

"I want to tell you all about a dream that I had," Dad said. His voice was still hoarse and quiet, so all of them leaned forward to hear.

"I was on a raft," Dad began, "floating upon a glassy river. It was foggy and I couldn't see anything, but then I saw another raft floating toward me. Upstream. There were several people on the raft: my mother, my father, Adele, my grandmother . . . they were all calling out to me to come with them."

Despite Dad's calm demeanor, Mom looked fright-ened. Abby instinctively held her breath. All of the people on the other raft were dead. Dad's mother had died when Dad was thirteen—Abby's age—and his sister Adele had died at age twenty-one. His grandfather and grandparents had all passed before Abby was born, as well. She knew sto-ries about the people on the raft, but she'd never seen their faces. It was the first time Abby had considered that Dad had had an entire life before her that she was not a part of. He had loved people who had never loved Abby, and that seemed strange.

Dad continued. "Their raft came closer, and I was excited. I haven't seen any of them in such a long time and, you know, they all looked the same as they did the last time I saw them. I wondered how they'd recognized me.

"But then the raft stopped. It floated in place. I knelt down on my raft and paddled with my hands, trying to get closer to them. But I couldn't. Then they all waved good-bye, their raft floating farther away from me, smiling as they disappeared into the fog."

Dad was looking at Abby, but not at Abby. He looked through her, lost in the memory of his dream. The room was silent. They were all lost in the dream.

Mom was the first to speak.

"And then you woke up?"

Dad nodded.

Mom's eyes filled with tears, and her smile returned.

"You weren't ready to leave us."

Dad interpreted his dream another way. He believed that it wasn't just a dream but a warning. He thought that his family had beckoned him to follow them to where they were going but he couldn't because he wasn't *going* where they were going.

Dad was agnostic. He did not have unwavering faith in God. He wasn't altogether sure that there wasn't a higher power, but Dad didn't take the Bible as, well, gospel. He hadn't gone to church since his mother's funeral, over forty years ago.

Now he felt he'd been wrong all along. The God he'd stopped believing in when his mother was taken from him had given him a glimpse of His world. She was all right, as were his sister and the others, and they were waiting for him in another place. But Dad thought he might not get there if he didn't profess his new beliefs. God had told him to shape up or ship out.

So that very evening Mom called in their neighbor, Reverend Stover, a retired minister. He was about two hundred years old, so apparently his religious devotion had earned him brownie points. Dad was only fifty-five. *Sucks to be agnostic.*

Reverend Stover sat in a folding chair next to Dad's bed while Mom looked on from the opposite side. The three of them were quiet and solemn, with only the reverend reading from the ancient Bible he held. He read a passage and then announced, "Let us pray."

Abby was in the kitchen, but she bowed her head and closed her eyes anyway. She couldn't comprehend much of Reverend Stover's prayer other than "Dear God" and "save his soul." It was all so foreign to her. The only time Abby had ever attended church was for a couple of weddings and on Christmas Eve and Easter Sunday with Aunt Fran. But Abby hadn't learned anything there about God or prayer; it simply taught her that church people sure knew how to have a party.

There were flowers and crepe paper and singing choirs and, afterward, all kinds of desserts. Abby had wished her parents would take her to church more often.

What was happening in her living room was much different. There were no decorations, no hallelujah choir. It was serious. It was desperate. Mom cried, so it must have been sad.

The intensity of it all was exciting, but unnecessary, Abby thought. It was nice that Reverend Stover had come to provide Dad with a safety net, just in case, but Dad wasn't going anywhere anytime soon.

His family of origin had waved him on and he'd come back home.

TWELVE

June, Continued

The morning after Dad's awakening, the phone rang early. Mom, who had fallen asleep on the hospital bed, curled around Dad, picked up before the second ring. Abby rolled over and tried to go back to sleep, but soon Mom came into her room and shook her shoulder.

"It's Jenna," Mom said, handing her the phone.

Abby opened one eye.

"Who?"

"Jenna Foley."

Oh, Foley. From softball. No one had called her Jenna since T-ball, and she'd been on Abby's team every year.

Abby rubbed her eyes and placed the phone to her ear without raising her head from the pillow.

"Hey, Foley."

"Hey. Practice is at ten, right?"

Abby's heart sank. This would be the one and only practice session before the summer's first game, neither of which she could attend.

"I don't know."

"Well, I think it is." Abby heard paper crinkling on the other end. "Yeah, ten. Can you bring your extra mitt with you? My dad cleaned the garage and now I can't figure out where he put mine."

Abby sat up in bed. "You can use my mitt if you want to, but I'm not going to practice."

"Why not?"

Mom stared out the window, her hands on her hips and her lips pursed. Abby didn't want to make her feel any worse than she already did. It wasn't her fault that she couldn't get Abby there. Besides, Abby didn't really want to leave now that Dad was conscious.

"I just can't. If you want to borrow my mitt, though, you can stop by and grab it. I'll meet you in the driveway."

"My mom can drive you," Foley suggested.

"Thanks, but—"

Mom was waving her hands frantically to get Abby's attention.

"You should go," she whispered.

Abby placed a hand over the mouthpiece.

"Mom, I can't."

"Yes, you can."

"No, I . . ."

"Abby?" Foley said. "My mom says she can pick you up in half an hour."

Mom was nodding like a maniac.

"Um, okay," Abby said. "Thanks."

She clicked the OFF button and stared at the phone, torn between excitement and guilt.

"You'd better get dressed," Mom said, smiling. Abby noticed that color had come back to her cheeks.

"But Dad—"

"Is sleeping." When Abby's eyes rounded, her mother held up a hand. "Just sleeping." She pulled Abby out of bed and wrapped her arms around her shoulders. "And when he wakes up, he's not going to be too pleased if you've skipped practice. So get moving."

Foley's mom picked her up at a nine thirty. Abby met them at the end of the driveway.

On the way to the middle school, where all of the Hi-White league's games and practices were held, Mrs. Foley asked after Abby's parents and Abby said they were doing great. It was true. When Abby had left for practice Dad was beginning to stir and Mom sat in a chair beside him, coffee mug in hand, her hair wet and curly and her cheeks still rosy from a shower. Josh was in the kitchen fixing scrambled eggs and cheese, Dad's favorite breakfast. Abby had said good-bye, and though her father was still foggy from sleep, he'd smiled back at her. None of them could stop smiling.

When she approached the field, Skip DelProposto, her coach for the last three years in a row, nodded his head and flicked the bill of his baseball cap. He jerked his thumb toward the bench where her fellow Cyclones awaited his pre-practice briefing.

"I heard Skip picked you fourth this season," Foley whispered as she and Abby ambled toward the bench.

"Really? Where'd you hear that?"

"My mom was in charge of the draft. Teri was automatically on the team 'cause she's his kid, so besides her he picked me first, Tamika second, Kelly third, and then you." Foley grinned and punched Abby in the arm before finding a seat on the bench and turning to chat with a couple of other teammates.

Abby sat on the edge of the bench in quiet disbelief. She had never been privy to the order of the draft picks in previous seasons, but had always assumed she'd been chosen close to last. It didn't matter to Abby why she was chosen fourth; she was just proud that Skip thought she was semi-valuable. She vowed to show him her best stuff that season and prove that he hadn't made a mistake. Next season he might even pick her third.

Coach Skip led the team through the usual exercises: the girls warmed up by playing catch, then Skip hit grounders, pop-ups, and line drives to them while they rotated positions from outfield to infield. Batting practice followed, and each team member took a turn at the plate while the others assumed loose positions in the field.

That day Abby was on fire. Her throw was exquisite, not a ball got by her, and her batting was flawless—she nailed every pitch and kept her teammates on their toes. She would hit the ball to left field and then she'd do it again, and just when the center fielder had moved left and the girl at third had backed up a few feet she would slam a ball out to right field, followed by a line drive to shortstop and then a bunt. She was having a blast.

After practice had ended, and as Foley and Abby followed Foley's mom to the parking lot, Foley said, "Man, you were awesome! What happened to you?"

"I don't know," Abby said. But she knew. It was a miracle.

When Abby got home from practice Mary was there and Mom was crying. Dad had withered again and his pain was as intense as ever, so they'd doped him up again. It wasn't fair. Abby wouldn't get to gloat to him about softball practice; he wouldn't understand. His visit had been too short; Abby hadn't crammed all of her unspoken feelings into Dad's one coherent evening. She hadn't told him that she loved him.

She consoled herself with the belief that he'd be back. She just had to be patient. Good things came to those who waited.

Abby waited. And she waited, while Dad continued to deteriorate. He wasn't comatose, but to call him alive seemed wrong. He couldn't sit up—the head of the bed was raised just enough so that he wouldn't choke on his saliva—and he couldn't eat. Dad didn't speak, he only whispered in an unintelligible mumble that sounded like some ancient language, and he rarely seemed to know that any of them were there. His eyes were open, but he stared blankly at the ceiling. Every now and then his face held a brief expression of surprise or worry or sadness, and Abby wondered if he was in limbo again—half in this world and half in another where his "old" family still floated upon a raft and beckoned him to join them. Abby hated every one of them.

The rain was a sucker punch. It showered for ten days straight, so often and so heavily that Abby's weekly softball practices and her first game—her only outlets to sanity now that school was out for the summer—were canceled. She continued to function on autopilot, trying to be as helpful as she could, hoping to break through the force field that surrounded Mom, though at the end of each day she found she couldn't remember anything that had transpired since waking in the morning.

The rain finally ceased, and that Saturday Abby's

softball game went on as scheduled. It was a gorgeous summer day: warm, but with little humidity, and with enough
benign clouds to shade the team from the sun, keeping it
from blinding them as their eyes followed the softball sailing
through the sky.

Foley's mom and dad drove Abby to the game, and as she
and her teammates tossed the ball around the field to warm
up, Abby watched the Foleys take their usual places, setting
up their lawn chairs directly behind the backstop where they
could scrutinize the umpire's calls for balls and strikes with
an almost straight-on view of the plate. Abby didn't know
why they even brought chairs; they were always on their
feet, rooting the team members on when they succeeded
and shouting consolation when they goofed up. Foley's parents never missed a game and were invariably the loudest
cheerleaders.

Abby's mom and dad had never missed a game before,
either. They weren't as loud as the Foleys, but were just as sup-
portive with their quiet smiles and thumbs-up and applause.
They normally sat only a few feet from Abby's team's bench,
on the opposite side of the fence from first or third base
depending on whether the team had been assigned home or
away. So as not to break Abby's concentration, they wouldn't
speak to her as she waited at first base for her opportunity
to run to second or as she crouched with her hands and mitt

on her knees waiting for the batter up to knock one toward third, but when Abby succeeded they said, "Good job," and when she screwed up they said, "Nice try." Abby didn't compare their encouragement to the loud, boisterous cheers of the Foleys. She knew that Mom's and Dad's attention was focused on her, and her entirely. It was nerve-wracking. It was magnificent.

On the Saturday of Abby's first game, someone else's parents sat in Mom and Dad's usual spot. Abby wanted to slug them.

Skip had placed Abby fifth on the batting roster, but she didn't take offense. Many coaches put all of their best hitters to bat first, but not Skip. He mixed the sure hitters up with the inconsistent ones; Abby figured he pulled names out of a hat and wrote them down. Their team had won second place in their age division the last two years in a row, so maybe there was a method to Skip's madness.

That day Abby questioned Skip's logic, though. He'd put Laura Briggs and Chelsea Farnsworth to bat first, and everyone knew that they rarely made it on base. Today was no exception. Laura struck out and Chelsea hit a wimpy grounder straight to the pitcher, so *boom-boom*—there were the first two outs.

The next two batters fared better. Kelly Kutcher sailed one over the shortstop's head that hit the ground between shortstop and right field. The right fielder scrambled to retrieve it, but Kelly made it to second base before the ball did. Natalie King was next and she hit a line drive past the player on third base. The ball was scooped up by the left fielder, but not before Natalie had made it to first successfully and Kelly had slid into third.

Then Abby was up. She'd been slicing the air with her bat while on deck and was ready to knock the ball straight out past the fielder's heads. She was going for a home run.

Abby squared up to the plate prepared for greatness. The first pitch came in low but she swung anyway and missed. Strike one. The next pitch was almost perfect, but Abby swung like a samurai and missed again. Wasn't even close.

"Don't need to murder the ball, Abby," Skip called from the bench. "Just take it one base at a time. Wait for your pitch—it's gotta have your name on it."

"Be patient," Mrs. Foley hollered from behind the backstop. "Wait for your pitch."

"Don't swing at 'em all," Mr. Foley yelled. "Wait for your pitch and get a piece of it."

Wait for my pitch. Wait for my pitch. Wait for my pitch. Gotta have my name on it.

Abby waited, and the pitcher threw in four stinkers. Abby didn't swing at any of them. Chucking the bat beside home plate, Abby jogged to first base, earning it the loser's way.

As she stepped onto first base the people behind her, the creeps sitting in Mom and Dad's spot, said: "Good eye! Good eye!"

Who did they think they were, talking to Abby? Didn't they know they'd stolen her parents' spot? Abby would have rather seen a gaping hole there than those jerks. Couldn't these people even let her imagine that her parents were there?

But they weren't there. Abby was suddenly overcome with anxiety. What if while she was away Dad had fallen into another coma? What if he'd slipped away completely?

"Go! Go! Go!"

Abby was startled by the harried shouts of her teammates on the bench and the spectators behind them and realized that she'd been lost inside her head. She hadn't even seen Tamika Jakubic step up to the plate, much less heard the crack of the bat when it connected with the ball. Abby looked around, stupefied, and saw Tamika approaching her, fast.

"Run!" Tamika screamed angrily, and Abby did, but not soon enough. She barely had time to jump off first base before being pummeled by Tamika, and when she started to run toward second she saw the second baseman, with one foot on the base, catch the softball snugly in her glove.

That was it. Last out. End of inning. Abby stood still,

stunned and embarrassed, as the Hurricanes jogged past her toward their bench, chuckling. Tamika didn't even look at Abby as she stormed off to grab her glove.

Eight innings remained, but Abby wanted nothing more than to head for the parking lot. She couldn't face her teammates and, besides, she had a compulsive urge to go home to check on Mom and Dad. The Foleys weren't leaving until the game was over, so Abby had no choice but to try to pick herself up and get her mind in the game.

Abby trudged toward the bench with her head hanging low, but Foley jogged toward her before she got there, tossing Abby her glove.

"Right field," Foley said.

Abby nodded and turned toward the outfield. If they weren't short two players already Abby would have asked Skip to let her sit on the bench. She wasn't doing her team any good and he knew it. The slackers were always sent to right field.

"What was that?" Foley asked as she walked alongside Abby until she reached her spot at second.

"I dunno," Abby said. "Sorry."

"Get your head out of the clouds!"

Abby continued on, comforted by the knowledge that nothing was likely to come her way. If she couldn't snap out of this fog she'd have to insist that Mom let her drop softball for the season. Abby would be doomed if one of the high school coaches decided to watch a game to scout out players for the freshman team and saw her one-girl comedy of errors.

As Abby loitered in right field she attempted to pay attention to the game. She chanted along with the other girls, "Ay, batta, batta, batta, batta . . ." until something caught her eye. A cluster of pine trees stood beside the field, behind the bench and the spectators, and through a clearing Abby caught sight of a couple walking hand in hand toward the fields on the farthest edge of the middle-school grounds. The two people were adults—the man had a medium build and short, dark hair and a beard; the woman was petite with curly brown hair. As they strolled, a kid in a yellow-and-white uniform rushed up behind them and leapt onto the man's back. The man released his partner's hand and spun around with the kid laughing on his back. They were all smiling; they were so happy.

"Abby!" Jodi Lange, the center fielder, screamed as she sprinted in Abby's direction. Abby looked up to find the softball in the air, traveling past her. Abby turned and ran toward the ball with her glove in the air, hoping to snag it if she could just get her sluggish legs to move fast enough. She wouldn't make it. She'd never make it. But she'd try.

"Got it!" Jodi yelled from behind her, and Abby heard the softball smack into Jodi's glove.

The crowd cheered as Jodi threw the ball to Foley, who in turn tossed the ball to the pitcher's mound.

"That was yours!" Jodi snarled as she trotted back to center field.

Abby nodded an apology. It was hers. But she'd let it slip away.

THIRTEEN

June, Continued

Four days after her disastrous ballgame, on Mom's forty-eighth birthday, Dad slipped into another coma. It hardly seemed appropriate to wish Mom a happy birthday, so neither Josh nor Abby did.

At noon the doorbell rang, and Abby stepped in front of the window on the front door to motion to the visitor to enter through the garage. There was a white van in the driveway with the logo for Lawry's Florist printed on the side. The deliveryman did as he was told, waiting by the kitchen door until Abby opened it.

"Helen North?" the man said dully. He was holding a cone-shaped sleeve of violet paper.

"No. That's my mom."

"Is she here?"

"Yes, but she's busy. Can I take this for her?"

The man shrugged and handed it over, then left without a word.

Abby shut the door and carried her load to the living room, peeking inside to find a bouquet of daisies in a dainty glass vase. Abby almost dropped them. Dad knew Mom had a weakness for daisies; the garden was full of them. Mom said that daisies portrayed innocence and purity and loyal love, things the world had too little of. When they were first married Dad had sent Mom roses a few times, but he had long since learned that nothing brightened her day more than daisies, and had given them to her on every subsequent birthday and anniversary. "Who was that?" Mom asked as Abby stepped into the living room. When she saw the still-wrapped flowers she grabbed the bedsheet that lay over Dad's lap and tightened her fist, crumpling it. Her eyes were squeezed shut, her knuckles white, and Mom bit her bottom lip so hard Abby thought it might bleed.

"Here," Abby said, unwrapping the vase and placing the daisies on the coffee table beside Dad before tiptoeing away.

This wasn't a moment she was part of.

Josh was downstairs playing a video game. Abby told him about the flowers, and he said he knew all about them. Dad had asked him to order them weeks before, just in case. In case of what they both knew.

Mom spent the remainder of the day in stunned silence on

the couch, staring at her daisies, while Josh feverishly read the *Far Side* book at Dad's bedside. Josh feigned laughs as he read the one-liners under the cartoons and then turned the book toward Dad. When Dad showed no sign of having heard, Josh would read more urgently, laughing louder, explaining what was happening in the sketches. Abby leaned against the piano, giving him nods of encouragement when it looked like he was about to call it quits.

Don't give up. He'll be back again. Just like before.

Aunt Fran came with her suitcase. Abby wanted to pack hers and hightail it out of there.

Now not only did the Norths have that know-it-all Mary barging in day and night, they also had Abby's aunt moving in. She took over Abby's room, and Abby was told she'd bunk with Mom until Aunt Fran went home. When that would be wasn't clear, and Abby didn't ask.

While having Aunt Fran stay at the house wasn't exactly at the top of Abby's wish list, she didn't mind sleeping in her parents' bed. Mom had been sleeping on the couch beside Dad since he'd become living room furniture, but at night she would lie down with Abby while Aunt Fran watched over Dad in the living room. Mom and Abby would lie back-to-back on the king-size bed, both of them curled into the fetal position. Abby's stomach didn't hurt so badly when Mom snuggled in bed with her, and she fell asleep more quickly.

When she awakened, Mom would be gone, sleeping with one eye open beside Dad downstairs, but her warmth would remain on the sheets. Her smell was there.

It turned out that having Aunt Fran stay wasn't nearly as horrid as Abby had anticipated. Aunt Fran was decent to Josh and Abby, helpful and kind to Mom, and distraught over Dad. She'd seen him deteriorate into this unconscious state before, but she hadn't seen him bounce back. She didn't know that's just what happens with cancer. She had no experience. She wasn't part of the team. Poor Aunt Fran.

One night, Abby couldn't go to sleep. Her stomach hurt something awful, and she was worried. Mom was slipping further into her own world, and Abby feared that she might awaken the next morning to find both of her parents comatose in the living room. Abby wanted Mom in bed with her so that she could keep watch over her.

As always, though, Darth's drone eventually lulled Abby to sleep.

Her eyes opened wide soon after. Abby wasn't normally one to wake during the night unless she had to pee, and even then her eyes would remain glued shut as she begged her bladder to cool it until morning. But it wasn't physical necessity that woke her that night. In fact, she felt nothing at all.

Abby felt no fear, no sadness, no worry, no loneliness. Her stomach didn't hurt. Her soul seemed detached from her body. Abby could not feel the mattress below her, or the pillow under her head. It was as if she were floating in a bubble, safe and warm.

The bedroom window above the bed was open, and though Abby felt no breeze, a chorus of rustling leaves and chirping crickets and belching bullfrogs drifted through the screen and filled the room. The Stovers' porch light projected through the window and onto the ceiling. The limbs of a shade tree between the houses swayed back and forth, the shadows of its leaves dancing in this soft light.

"Go to sleep," coaxed a voice in her head.

And Abby did, experiencing God's ballet in complete peace as she drifted into dreamless sleep.

THE SUN SHONE BRIGHTLY INTO ABBY'S PARENTS' BEDROOM the next morning, and already, sounds of life drifted in through the open window. Motorboats whirred around on the lake, lawn mowers buzzed, someone was chopping away at a tree, or hammering something, it was hard to tell. Abby rolled over to look at the alarm clock on the nightstand and was surprised to find that it was already ten o'clock.

Abby had stayed in bed way past ten in the previous months, but never before had she slept that long or that soundly. Being completely rested felt great and made her realize that she, too, had been living in a fog.

She hopped out of bed, and as she reached for the bedroom door she heard Deanna's voice. She pulled her hand away from the doorknob as if it had given her a shock. Abby hadn't gotten word of any plans for Deanna to come home; she must have flown in overnight. Deanna wouldn't wake for anything before dawn, much less get on an airplane. Not unless . . .

Shh-bmp. Crackle. Shh-bmp.

Abby opened the door and stepped into the hallway. From there she could see half of the kitchen and living room. Deanna sat in Dad's recliner. The curtains had apparently been opened, for the house was brightly lit.

The shadow was gone.

Darth continued its *suck-swoosh*, but Abby didn't buy it for a second.

"Good morning!" Deanna shouted too loudly when she spotted Abby. It wasn't a greeting; it was an announcement.

Skipping a hello, Abby ducked into the bathroom, bracing herself with her hands on the counter. Staring at her reflection in the mirror she thought to herself: *this is it.*

Abby hadn't bothered shutting the bathroom door, knowing that Mom would come knocking within seconds.

Sure enough, there she was.

"I need to talk to you," Mom said, and Abby silently followed her back to the master bedroom. Mom shut the bedroom door, sat on the bed, and patted the mattress beside her. Abby obediently sat down.

Mom opened her mouth to speak but shut it again before the words could come out. Mom looked like a glass figurine. She was so white she was almost transparent.

She placed her hand on Abby's knee, opening her mouth to speak again, but only one word came out.

"Dad . . ."

Abby didn't make her finish.

"I know, Mom," Abby said, placing her hand over her mother's. "I know."

Mom didn't have to tell Abby that Dad had passed. He'd told her himself on his way out of her world.

Abby held Mom as her tiny body quaked for what seemed like an eternity. Abby wasn't about to let go of her until Mom was ready. Abby couldn't cry; a gallon of tears were stuck in her throat but wouldn't come out. She was sad, but a bigger part of her felt something more horrible.

Relief.

Dad wouldn't hurt anymore. There was nothing else It could do to him.

Abby could not tell her mother how she felt, nor could she tell her that she'd felt Dad leave. Mom wouldn't believe what Abby had experienced unless she'd felt it herself. What if she hadn't? Mom needed to feel Dad's peace more than anyone.

The sobs that jolted her mother's frame as it pressed tightly against Abby's told Abby that she hadn't.

When Mom finally released Abby, she dabbed her bloodshot eyes with a soggy Kleenex.

"Let's go downstairs and call Coach Skip."

Her softball game—Abby had forgotten all about it. Abby almost wished she could go, so that she could pretend that none of this was happening. She didn't want to go downstairs, yet she followed Mom down into surreality.

The hospital bed was still there, the sheets and blanket pulled up and tucked in neatly, and in place of Dad a single red rose lay with its petals resting on the fluffed pillow. Atop the piano, amid the standing cards from well-wishers, a votive candle burned, its flickering flame unnecessary in the bright, sunny room.

It was as if Dad had simply vanished.

Mary was there, standing beside the piano. Abby assumed she'd done the decorating. Mary smiled at Abby sympathetically and turned to Mom. "Are you ready, Helen?"

Mom closed her eyes and nodded.

"We didn't want to wake you," Mom half whispered as Mary ceremoniously reached down beside the bed and switched off the oxygen machine. Now Darth was dead, too.

The room was eerily quiet, aside from the *shh-bmp* of the 45. Until Mom wailed.

"Oh, God!"

Mom filled the silence with her grief, sobbing uncontrollably. Deanna rushed in from the kitchen and wrapped her arms around Mom, whispering and shushing and trying to soothe her. It didn't much help when Deanna started bawling, too, making the sadness in the room chaotic and overwhelming. Abby backed into the kitchen and bumped into the counter. "Hey," Josh said. Abby turned to find him hunched over the kitchen table.

Josh and Abby looked at each other with unspoken confusion and disbelief. Their eyes held the same question:

So now what?

It was then that Abby realized that her brother was as ignorant as she was. He'd been there all along, he'd known it was coming, but had never really believed it would happen.

They had never thought Dad would really die.

Abby did what she'd come into the kitchen to do. Coach Skip's line was busy, so Abby called Foley and told her why she wouldn't be at the game. Foley cried. Abby apologized. She didn't know why she did that.

After hanging up, Abby tried to imagine what a person would normally do next. Mary was preparing to leave in the next room, and Abby did not plan to see her off. As much as Abby had abhorred Mary's visits, her pending absence seemed so final. Mary would move on to another disintegrating family; she was done with the Norths.

Breakfast. People have breakfast in the morning.

Abby pulled a box of cornflakes from the kitchen cabinet and found a gallon of milk in the fridge. She poured some of both into a cereal bowl and put the carton and box away. She took a bite, but the cereal tasted like cardboard so she dumped the rest in the trash, forgetting that you can't dump milk into a trash bag. It leaks and gets all over.

As Abby started to clean up the mess, Mom came into the kitchen.

"I'll get that," she said.

"No, Mom, I'll get it. I'm sorry."

"Don't worry about it. Leave it. I'll get it."

Abby got the feeling that Mom truly wanted to clean it up. Cleaning would keep her busy. She needed to be busy. Deanna walked into the kitchen and opened the cereal cabinet, finding the gallon of milk there. The cornflakes box was in the fridge. Deanna relocated them and Abby laughed nervously.

"Oops."

I'm okay, Abby told herself. *Everything will be okay. Everything has to be okay.*

PART TWO

After

FOURTEEN

Since Abby's wardrobe pretty much consisted of jeans and sweatpants, and nothing black, on the afternoon of Dad's death, Mom and Josh and Abby went to the mall so she could get a dress for the visitation and funeral. Something told her that shopping wasn't what normal people would have done, but she wasn't concerned with what normal people did anymore.

The ride to the mall was just . . . odd. Abby couldn't remember the last time the three of them had been out together. Mom jerked the wheel and slammed clumsily on the brake and accelerator as if she'd forgotten how to drive. When they arrived safely, they let out a collective sigh. And Mom cried.

Josh's shopping came first, and didn't last long. He picked up dress pants, and a shirt and tie from the men's department at JCPenney, which Mom bought without even making him try anything on. He found leather Oxfords directly across the aisle in Shoes, and was ready to get out of there.

But now it was Abby's turn. Instead of heading straight for the women's department at Penney's, Mom let her decide where to shop for a dress. Abby suggested Macy's, and was surprised when her mother didn't object. Mom was quiet and distracted. Lost. Lack of money apparently wasn't an issue in Catatonia.

Josh sat in an armchair near the fitting room. Mom stood beside him, staring at the wall, her face absent of expression and color, like frosted glass. Each time Abby came out in a different dress, she simply nodded absentmindedly. Abby could have worn a micromini, stilettos, and fishnet stockings and gotten the same reaction.

When she tried on a simple black sundress, Mom managed to speak. "Very pretty."

Josh offered his unsolicited two cents. "The skirt's kind of short."

"She's got the legs for it. Let's get it. And the one with the white flowers." Her mother had been paying attention after all.

After getting her a new pair of sandals, too, they were all set. Time to go home.

But when they reached the row of glass double doors that opened on the parking lot, Mom stopped in her tracks.

Her eyes were wide, her mouth open as if she was about to wail. Abby checked to see if anyone was watching—but not because she was embarrassed or concerned with what strangers thought. She was looking for someone who appeared stable enough to help. If Mom broke down, how would they get her home? They could carry her to the car, but who would drive? Josh didn't have his license yet.

"Come on, Mom," Abby coaxed, afraid to touch her mother. Mom closed her eyes, pushed open the door, and slowly crossed the threshold. Once outside, she took a few steps and then stopped, turning and staring through the glass doors as if the mall were Mecca.

"I want to go back in." Her mother's voice was uneven and desperate.

"Why?" Josh asked.

She covered her face with her hands and shook her head.

"What is it, Mom?" Abby whispered.

"He held my hand," Mom managed. "From the moment we walked into the mall, he held my hand. He didn't let go the whole time. I knew that when we walked out the door he'd be gone. I shouldn't have left. Why did I leave him? Oh, God. How could I have left him? I'll never feel him again!"

She wept quietly as the two of them looked on, dumbfounded. She didn't turn to go back in, though. When other shoppers started looking at her strangely, she headed toward the car, still sobbing.

The look on Josh's face made it clear that he feared their mother had gone around the bend, but Abby knew better. Dad had come to say good-bye to Mom, too.

THAT EVENING AUNT SHIRLEY, MOM'S SISTER, FLEW IN WITH her husband, Dub, from Duluth, and Grandpa Warner, Mom's dad, flew in from Florida. Abby's maternal grandmother had died when Abby was a baby. Grandpa had been living alone as long as Abby could remember. Other members of Mom's family—Aunt Shirley's kids and Aunt Marlene, and her family—would drive in the next day. They'd all stay at the Holiday Inn Express in Waterford, but for tonight Shirley and Dub and Grandpa would stay with the Norths. Mom had made up the foldout couch in the lower level for Grandpa, while Shirley and Dub shacked up in Abby's room. Abby would sleep with Mom.

The visitors spent much of their time in the living room, where Dad's empty bed remained, commiserating.

"He was so young."

"Such a tragedy."

"Poor Helen."

"You know, everything happens for a reason."

Abby was disgusted. Was that all they had to say?

At her first opportunity to escape, she ran down to the Point. She wanted to jump into the lake and swim to the other side, and though it was a good three-quarters of a mile, that night she could have done it. Something buzzing and angry and fearful and wild stirred inside her. An all-out swim would have helped, but it was growing late and dark, so instead she collapsed onto the grass and took the deepest breath she could. She exhaled slowly and inhaled again, but nothing changed. What was wrong with her? Why couldn't she just feel sad like a normal person?

It was a beautiful night. The sky wasn't completely clear—dark purple clouds threatened rain—but a warm breeze embraced her, calming her just a little. A single bright star shimmered overhead.

Is that you, Dad? If that's you, give me a sign.

The star didn't dance or shoot across the sky. So maybe Dad wasn't a star.

Another warm gust of wind tousled her hair, and Abby closed her eyes.

Is that you, Dad? If that's you, blow harder.

The wind died down and the air seemed even more still than it had before.

Okay, so maybe Dad wasn't the wind.

Abby squeezed her shut eyes tight and asked Dad for just one sign. She opened them and searched the dark world around her, but nothing miraculous happened. Abby sighed in disappointment. She wondered if there really was a heaven, after all. Surely Dad would have given her a sign if he could have. Or maybe he was so happy to see his old family again that he'd already forgotten the one he left behind.

FIFTEEN

Visitation at the funeral home started at five o'clock, but they arrived early to have "family" time. It was just after four when they pulled into the parking lot, with Deanna in Dad's Impala behind them. Aunt Fran's minivan was the caboose.

The five of them gathered near the door of the funeral home, a white Georgian-style mansion that looked out of place among the strip malls and fast-food joints of Waterford, which was a good thirty minutes from Highland. Mom would have picked Lynch & Sons in Milford, since it was closer to home, but Dad taught in Waterford and had chosen a location convenient for his colleagues. He'd made his own arrangements months before, so Mom wouldn't have to.

They walked through the double doors and into the dark foyer. The carpeting was burgundy and black, and the walls

and furniture matched the carpet. Two big, ornate chande-
liers were dimly lit, giving off enough light that you wouldn't
be completely blinded by gloom. Abby knew where the
shadow had gone.

A balding man in a black suit approached Mom.

"Mrs. North," he said, taking Mom's hands in his, "I'm
very sorry for your loss. Please let me know if there is anything that you need and I'll do everything I can to make this
experience as comfortable as possible for you."

"Thank you," Mom said, pulling out of his grasp. Abby
didn't think her mother wanted anyone to touch her hands,
to wipe away whatever trace of Dad's ghost might remain on
them.

"Your services will be held in Room Two." The man
pointed to a room at the other end of the expansive foyer.
Short, squat pedestals holding white candelabra and tall
vases with white orchids stood sentry outside the French
doors. The white stuff was probably chosen to look heavenly,
but it contrasted just a bit too much with the rest of the place.

As they passed Room One, Abby peered inside. There
were rows of seats and what looked like a stage in front.
She'd never been to a funeral before, but she figured that
people stood on the stage to talk about the dead person.
This thought got her sweating. Abby wouldn't be expected
to say something, would she? She hated talking in front of

large groups; nearly passed out when she had to read aloud at school. And to talk about Dad? Why hadn't anyone prepared her for this?

"Room One is unoccupied today," the man said. "You'll have the place to yourselves."

There was a sign outside the first set of French doors at Room Two, and white letters had been stuck on the black background reading SAMUEL LEE NORTH.

It was strange seeing Dad's name announcing the gathering he wouldn't attend. As she stepped through the open doors of Room Two, Abby caught sight of something she hadn't seen in Room One. Something she didn't expect.

Dad was there, in a polished cherrywood coffin in the front of the big, empty room. All alone.

Lava boiled inside her, and Abby erupted. She lost control, screaming and running back down the hallway. She stopped for a moment at the doors and turned to find her family gaping at her in horror, then bolted. She didn't stop running until she made it across the parking lot to a fence on the other side. There was nowhere to go. She could go nowhere but back into that place where Dad's body lay on display for all to gawk at. It was sick, ghoulish.

She couldn't look at her dad, knowing his chest no longer rose and fell. It was him; it wasn't him. He appeared to be sleeping. He wasn't sleeping.

She paced near the fence, panting, unable to catch her breath. Deanna ran outside, crying hysterically. Abby held up her hand to stop her from coming closer.

"Stay away from me!" Her voice was unrecognizable, a shriek; it abraded her throat. "I'm not going back in there! You can't make me go back in there!"

Whether or not Deanna came closer Abby did not know. Her eyes were camera lenses zooming in and out, in and out. Deanna was trapped in a carnival fun house; her face was mangled, her body warped.

Somewhere in the distance was her mother, a blurred vision of her brother following close behind. They were foreign objects, familiar yet unrecognizable.

Hot tears burned Abby's cheeks. A fire blazed in her stomach.

"Why didn't you tell me he'd be in there?" she screamed to no one in particular. They were all to blame. They all knew what was going to happen and had left her in the dark.

"We thought you knew," Deanna sobbed.

Abby turned away and sprinted back across the parking lot toward the busy road. She didn't know what she'd do once she got there; maybe she'd walk home, maybe she'd hop on a bus and take it as far as it would go. Abby was leaning toward option two. Her home was full of strangers; home wasn't home anymore.

Heavy footsteps approached, fast, and she turned to tell Deanna to leave her alone. It wasn't Deanna, though; it was Josh.

"I'm not going back in there!" Abby yelled, walking faster.

Josh didn't make her stop. Instead, he fell into step beside her. "Where are you going?"

"I don't know," Abby said, no longer shouting. "Anywhere but in there. I want to go home, I guess."

"You can't walk home from here."

"Watch me."

"Wait." Josh stopped. Abby halted three paces ahead of him. "Maybe Mom will let Deanna drive you home."

"She won't."

"Maybe she will. Do you think seeing you like this makes her happy?"

Abby cringed. She was so selfish, so consumed by her own suffering that she'd forgotten about Mom's. Balling her fists, she dug her nails into her palms, focusing on the pain in her hands to distract herself from the pain in her gut and in her heart.

"Come talk to her," Josh begged. "Please?"

When Abby didn't respond, Josh looked away. Her brother turned away and slowly backtracked the way he'd come, heading toward the funeral home.

"Don't leave me!" she wailed, crumpling onto the pavement and crying into her knees.

Josh approached her and held out his hand. "Then come with me."

Abby looked up at her brother and let him help her to her feet. Then she followed him. At that moment she would have followed him anywhere.

They returned to where Mom stood near the funeral home entrance. She wasn't crying—her body had probably run out of tears—but she looked anxious and careworn.

"I'm sorry." Abby stared at her feet.

"Oh, honey," Mom said, wrapping her arms around her and holding tight. "Don't be."

"I don't want to go in, though." Her mother sighed and shook her head.

"Can Deanna take her home?" Josh suggested.

"No," Mom said, kissing Abby's tear-streaked cheek. "I need you all here."

"Well, maybe she could stay outside," Josh said, "or sit in the parking lot. I could stay with her." Josh had become Abby's chief negotiator.

"It's ninety degrees out here." Everyone was silent. They'd reached an impasse.

Abby finally relented. "I'll go inside, but not into that room. I'll stay in the waiting area."

Mom nodded quickly, accepting the compromise. So back inside Abby went, immediately plopping down on a plush bench beside the door before anyone tried to renegotiate.

Once visiting hours were underway, Grandpa and the Warner aunts came, all visibly puzzled at her chosen seat. After Mom whispered in their ears, they nodded and looked at Abby pityingly. She averted her eyes, ashamed, wishing she could be stronger, like Josh, who had stayed by Mom's side as she mingled with guests. She knew she was letting everyone down.

Leise showed up with her parents. After offering their condolences, Leise's mom and dad stepped into Room Two to see Mom, and Leise eased onto the bench beside Abby and hugged her tight.

"Abby, I am so sorry."

Abby shrugged. "How did you find out?"

"I called your house earlier and your grandfather answered the phone. He told me what happened." Leise released Abby and tried to look her in the eye. Abby wouldn't let her. "I'm your friend, Abby—you can tell me anything. I knew your dad was sick, but I didn't realize . . . Why didn't you tell me?"

"I didn't know."

Leise gasped. "Your dad didn't know his cancer was terminal? Oh my gosh, that has to be so hard . . . that it happened so unexpectedly, I mean."

"No," Abby said, her eyes following a daddy longlegs crawling along the base of the wall, "we knew the cancer was terminal."

Leise sat in silent confusion.

"I knew my dad was going to pass away," Abby tried to explain, knowing Leise would never understand. "I didn't know he was going to be dead."

DAD HAD ALWAYS SAID THAT ABBY WAS SO STUBBORN that the Great Wall of China would cave more easily than she would, and that evening she proved it. After Leise and her parents left, Abby moved to the bottom step of a curving staircase on the other side of Room Two where she'd be less noticeable to the comers and goers who'd wanted to get a good look at the dead guy.

Occasionally Mom would beckon from the hallway out-side Room Two, and she'd have to make nice with distant relatives and strangers who said that they'd known her since she was knee-high to a grasshopper or that they used to change her diapers or some other crock, and of course they'd say, "I know how you feel. I lost my [fill in the blank] when I was younger, and it was hard. But this too shall pass."

Every now and then during these strained conversa-tions Abby's eyes would wander into Room Two where Dad still lay in his coffin, his hands still resting upon his stomach, his expression still non-expressive. She'd quickly return to her station. In a way, it was like playing peekaboo with her little cousin Krissy when Krissy was a baby. When Abby had put her hands over her face, Krissy's attention would wander, as if Abby's hiding her eyes hid all of her. Then, when Abby uncovered her eyes and said, "Peekaboo," Krissy would squeal with delight, so glad to see Abby again. Abby sat on the stair, avoiding Room Two as if she herself was six months old. If she didn't see Dad's body, it wasn't there. He was somewhere else: not gone, just away.

Two hours in, Spence came through the door, red faced and sweaty. Abby hurried to greet him, but before she could, his arms were already around her.

"Are you okay?" he asked, his voice catching.

"You stink," Abby replied.

"Sorry," Spence said, releasing her. "I rode my bike."

"From Highland?"

Spence shrugged and turned his face away. When he did, he caught sight of the coffin and swayed on his feet.

"Sit down," Abby ordered, pointing to her stair. Spence did as he was told, and Abby sat beside him, pretending not to notice that he was choking back sobs.

"You rode your bike all the way here," she said in awe.

Spence cleared his throat and took a deep breath. "My

mom wasn't home. I probably could have found someone else to drive me, but I . . . I just wanted to ride. You know?"

"Yeah, I know."

"Where are your mom and Josh?"

Abby jerked her thumb over her shoulder toward Room Two. "They're in there."

Spence wiped sweat from his brow. "I bet I look pretty gross, but I want to go see your mom anyway." He grasped her hand. "Come with me."

Abby pulled away. "Uh-uh. You go ahead. I'll be right here."

Spence didn't ask why. He simply nodded and stayed put. "I'm sure they'll be out here soon enough."

So they sat for hours in near silence, watching people come, watching people go. At the end of the evening, the only person left besides the Norths was Spence.

Josh stuffed Spence's bike into the back of the TrailBlazer and Mom drove him home. Abby had wanted him to stick around a while to keep her company, but when Mom pulled into the Harrisons' driveway she was afraid to ask. The lights were out inside the house, as usual.

Mom waited in the driveway while Abby walked Spence to the door. He fished the key out of the way-too-obvious plastic rock in the garden and fumbled with the lock. When he finally got the door open, Abby gave him a quick hug before starting back toward the car.

"Anything I can do to help out tomorrow?" Spence called. "I can mow the lawn in the morning, or, I dunno . . . I can spray for mosquitoes. I know you'll have company after the funeral."

Abby turned around. "I don't think so. Thanks, though."

Spence's voice turned desperate. "There's got to be something I can do. . . ."

Abby's mouth twitched, a feeble attempt at a smile.

"No, Spence. You can't fix this."

Grandpa Warner and Aunt Shirley and Uncle Dub were already at the house. Aunt Shirley had fixed a late snack of crackers and cheese and beer, and Mom tried to appear grateful, but Abby knew she wanted nothing more than to hide with her grief. Abby and Josh skipped the snack—though Josh took a longing look at the beer before heading to his room—while their mother stayed downstairs. Abby went to the master bedroom, where she rolled from one side of the bed to the other so that the whole mattress would be warm for Mom when she climbed in.

An hour and a half later Abby heard her bedroom door shut and a blanket of quiet settle over the house. Expecting Mom to come up any minute, Abby closed her eyes and pretended to sleep. The last thing her mother needed was to think she had to talk any more.

After another half hour, she still hadn't come upstairs.

Abby was worried. Mom didn't need to talk, but she shouldn't be left alone, either. She quietly opened the bedroom door and crept down the stairs to check on her.

There was someone curled up on the hospital bed. For a moment she imagined that Dad was still there, that his death had just been a bad dream. But then she heard Mom's hiccup and fretful sigh.

Inching closer to the bed, Abby saw that she was asleep, lying atop the bed fully clothed. She was hugging herself, and the pillow was wet with tears. Stretching out on the couch beside her, Abby was able to reach out and place her hand over her mother's. They both needed something to hold on to.

SIXTEEN

June 30

For the funeral Abby was expected to sit front
and center with her family. She did, for hiding was no longer
an option. The image of Dad in that coffin was permanently
branded on her brain, kind of like what happens when you
stare at a light for too long and you see dark spots when you
close your eyes. It was there forever, or at least until it faded
with time. Thankfully no one insisted that she get up and
speak.

Dad had asked their neighbor Reverend Stover to officiate.
As he stood at the podium, dabbing his brow with a hand-
kerchief and riffling through his notes, Abby looked over her
shoulder at the growing crowd. Every seat was filled, mostly
with people she knew, but some of whom she couldn't recall
ever having seen before. Mary sat a few rows back, smiling
sympathetically. Abby smiled back weakly and looked past

her at the dozens of people left with standing room only. Leise was there with a couple of girls from school, and Foley, along with half the softball team. She saw Billy Mohr with a handful of Josh's buddies, including Logan Pierce. He gave Abby a half wave. For once, his cuteness didn't register. Maybe he wasn't there at all. Maybe this was all just a bad dream, like those nightmares you have when you're walking down a busy street and suddenly realize that you don't have any clothes on. Only she felt like she'd been skinned alive and her innermost parts were exposed for everyone to see.

Spence stood against the far wall, talking with a couple of the neighbors. Abby almost didn't recognize him in a shirt and tie. She looked around for Spence's mom, and when she didn't see her Abby wasn't surprised—but she was still furious. Mrs. Harrison had only met Dad once or twice, and half the time couldn't remember Abby's name, but she obviously had no idea how much Spence cared for Mr. North, or it just didn't matter to her. Spence finally looked over, and she gestured for him to come share her chair, but when Reverend Stover cleared his throat and asked for those who could find a seat to please be seated, Mrs. Beasley slid an arm around Spence's waist. He wasn't alone. Abby turned around to listen.

Sitting no more than ten feet away from Dad—Dad's body—Abby listened to the reverend talk about the glory of death. He made dying sound pretty great: it provided an absence of pain, a new life in heaven, and all that. This should have made her feel better about being relieved that Dad no longer suffered, but it didn't. An absence of pain was an absence of everything.

Mom didn't seem to be consoled by the sermon, either, nor by the words of sympathy after the funeral.

"This too shall pass," people said, or, "Everything happens for a reason."

Mom flinched each time some moron uttered one of these stupid clichés, and Abby half expected her to deck the next person who used them. She didn't.

When the funeral was over, everyone flocked to their cars, which had been marked with small, orange flags stuck onto the hoods with suction cups. Everyone, that was, except for Abby and Josh and Deanna, Mom and Aunt Fran. They stayed behind to say their final good-byes.

Aunt Fran went first. Everyone else stood back as she said a few tearful words to Dad, touched his hands, and kissed him on the forehead. Deanna followed suit. Then Josh was up.

"Bye, Dad," Josh said, tucking the *Far Side* book into the coffin. Mom started crying again.

Josh stepped aside and looked at Abby. It was her turn. Josh smiled at her, giving her the encouragement she needed to step up to the coffin. She stood beside Dad, feeling bad that she hadn't thought to bring him a present, too. At least she'd say good-bye the way she was supposed to.

Seeing her father's face up close Abby could tell that he was wearing makeup: foundation and blush. He looked like he was wearing a mask. It was a body wearing the mask of Dad.

No, it was no mask. Abby could tell from the dark mole on his cheek and the familiar smile lines, crow's feet, and forehead wrinkles. Part of Abby knew he wasn't in there; he was somewhere else, looking down on his former shell, disgusted that his hair had been parted on the wrong side.

Another part of Abby, though, the part that was his child, the one who had sat on that lap and had been held in those arms and had ridden piggyback across the backyard on that once-sturdy frame, yearned to shake him, to pour cold water on his face, to pump his chest with her hands until he awoke, startled, wondering what he was doing lying there in his best suit.

Oh, Dad, what happened to you?

Abby touched Dad's right hand, which had been placed over his left, and was taken aback at how cold it was. And tough; his skin felt like rubber. Chilled Silly Putty. Abby was sad for him; he needed a blanket. She leaned down to kiss his forehead, which seemed even colder than his hands, if that was possible. Since she was little, Dad had done the kissing, while she'd chased him away. And now for the life of her Abby couldn't figure out why.

The game wasn't funny anymore. The game was over.

"G'bye Dad." She tried to say "I love you," but the words didn't come out. Her family didn't say stuff like that.

Aunt Fran, Deanna, Josh, and Abby left Room Two to give Mom a few minutes alone. Abby craned her neck as they walked out, staring at Dad until she rounded the corner, wishing she'd forced herself to look at him, really look at him, over the past couple of days. Now she'd lost her chance.

Once outside Room Two the four branched off: Aunt Fran sniffled all the way into the ladies' room, Deanna hustled out to the parking lot, and Josh joined the pallbearers congregated near the back door. Spence was one of them. He stood with his hands shoved deep into his pockets, staring at the floor. Abby went to him and touched his arm.

"Spence," she said, "tell me you didn't have to ride your bike today."

"I didn't. Hitched a ride with the Beasleys."

"Good." Abby nodded slowly. "Well, thanks for being here." Abby squeezed his forearm and started back toward Room Two, to wait for Mom.

"Abby?" Spence said, grasping her hand. Abby turned to look at him.

"What?"

"I'm sorry."

"Me too." Abby eased into Spence's arms. She bowed her head against his warm shoulder, closing her eyes and focusing on the rise and fall of his chest, synchronizing her breaths with his. At any other time, it would have felt awkward; she and Spence had never embraced. But all the rules had changed now; nothing would be the same as it was. He felt familiar. Safe. She wondered, *Was this how Dad made Mom feel?*

Her mother's sobs pulled at her. Abby drew back as the funeral director approached the pallbearers. It was time.

Mom, Josh, and Abby followed the hearse to the cemetery in a limousine. She linked arms with Mom as they walked toward the graveside, watching silently as the pallbearers carried the coffin from the hearse to a pedestal underneath a blue canopy, and they stayed that way through the short burial ceremony. Mom was a mess, but Abby didn't cry. Now that the casket was closed, *anyone* could have been in there. Her mind allowed her to pretend that it was empty. God had come down from heaven to carry Dad up Himself.

Afterward, most people headed back to the North house

for what Mom called a "wake." She said it had been Dad's wish to get friends and family together to share stories and toast his life, not mourn his death.

Once everyone else had gone, Deanna and Brad, Josh and Abby lingered, watching as Mom kissed her fingertips and touched the coffin, then leaned down to whisper softly, talking to Dad for the last time. She embraced the casket and lay her head down. She stayed there for a long time, completely still, like a human shield. She'd asked the funeral director to arrange for the casket to be lowered into the ground after the family had gone. If she refused to budge, Dad couldn't be buried.

Finally Deanna tiptoed toward the casket and guided their mother away, soothing her with hushed words as she led her to the limousine and helped her inside. As much as she wanted to leave, Abby couldn't move. Josh stood beside her.

"It's time to go," he said after a while.

Abby's heart thudded in her chest. "We can't just leave him here alone."

"He's not alone," Josh offered. She knew he was talking about Dad's reunion with his loved ones on the other side, but she couldn't tear her eyes away from the scruffy-looking guys loitering near the backhoe parked at the back of the cemetery. She turned abruptly and quickly climbed into the limo.

As the driver pulled away, Mom swiveled in her seat to keep her eyes on the casket, placing her hand on the back windshield so that it appeared to still touch the coffin. When the limo turned and the coffin was out of sight, she turned away and rested her head on Josh's shoulder.

Back at the house, Abby did her job and made small talk with the people she'd already had enough of, keeping one eye on her mother. Mom was talking with their visitors—mostly listening, actually—nodding and trying to appear interested, but her lips were pursed, her eyes flat. She was a walking statue.

The visitors had the decency not to stay too late; most of them were gone by seven, and the last few straggled out by nine o'clock. Spence was the last to go, reluctantly leaving the house to Mom, Josh, Abby, and Deanna alone. While Deanna rearranged the refrigerator, attempting to find space to stow the leftover food, Josh gathered cups from the backyard and stowed returnable bottles in the garage. Abby loaded the dishwasher and wiped everything down. Mom got the vacuum out, even though it was ten thirty, and cleaned the floors before grabbing the toilet brush and Comet from under the sink and attacking the bathrooms. Abby wondered if the house would be spit-shined by morning.

Eventually Mom collapsed in a heap on her mattress and cried herself to sleep. Abby lay beside her, inhaling the scent of Windex and Comet and sweat. She was hyperaware of any movement in the air around her, wondering if her father might appear. Her eyes swept the room. The very still room.

Dad? Are you here?

Nothing. Maybe ghosts couldn't read minds.

"Dad?" she whispered. Mom whimpered, but didn't wake.

Abby let her eyes fuzz over and stared at the dormant ceiling fan, waiting. And waiting.

Eventually her heavy eyelids closed. She dreamed she was bobbing on a raft in the middle of an ocean. Far off in the distance, a crowded boat floated in the other direction, until it disappeared around the curve of the earth.

Mom woke at dawn the next morning with a sharp cry, and hurtled out of bed and down the stairs. Abby found her in the kitchen, rifling through the medicine cabinet. Suddenly she stopped, bracing her hands on the counter.

"What's going on?" Deanna asked from the top of the stairs.

"Nothing," Mom said, reorganizing the bottles and shutting the cabinet door.

"Are you okay?" Abby asked, inching closer.

Mom nodded, looking at the empty bed in the living room.

"I thought I'd forgotten," Mom murmured.

"Forgotten what?"

"Dad's morphine . . . I thought I'd messed up the schedule."

Mom shook her head and went upstairs, locking herself in the bathroom. Her choking sobs echoed through the house.

That afternoon, a couple of guys from the medical supply company came to haul the hospital bed away, and by the end of the week, Deanna and Brad and Grandpa Warner and Mom's sisters and their families had gone home. The stream of visitors slowed to a trickle, finally drying up completely. For everyone except the Norths, the event was over. They'd done their thing, wished them well, and could now move on with life as usual. The house was eerily quiet. No more mind-numbing chitchat, no more phone calls, no more Mary, no more Darth. Mom turned fans on for noise, but that did little to drown out the deafening silence. The house was dead.

Abby continued to sleep beside her mother in her parents' room. Dad's room. His clothes still hung in the closet, his spare change remained scattered all over the top of the dresser, and his books were in a teetering stack beside the bed. The room expected him to return any time. She hoped her mother would never, ever change a thing.

But his belongings didn't bring much comfort to Mom. Mrs. North roamed aimlessly from room to room trying to find peace, but instead found Dad's toothbrush in the ceramic holder, his reading glasses atop the piano, his WORLD'S GREATEST DAD coffee mug in the cabinet. When Mom thumbed through the mail, filled with a seemingly endless array of pension and life insurance forms she had to sign and sympathy cards she didn't want to read, she'd toss them aside and sit at the table with her head in her hands, breathing deeply in and out, in and out. She was falling without a parachute, too fast for Abby to catch her.

At the end of the week, on the Fourth of July, Mom woke Abby with a soft whisper in her ear: "Let's get out of here."

SEVENTEEN

July

After the funeral, Aunt Marlene had invited
the Norths to their house in Curtisville, a small rural town a
few hours north of Highland. Mom had declined, saying she
needed a little time to herself, but she called Marlene up that
morning to tell her she'd reconsidered. There wasn't much
for Abby to do in Curtisville but play with her four- and five-
year-old cousins, Katie and Krissy, and take walks in the
woods. Abby wasn't too thrilled at the prospect of visiting
family—she'd had enough of that to last a year, at least—but
it would suffice. Getting away was all that mattered.

Abby and Josh quickly packed and hopped into the
TrailBlazer. Josh sat in the passenger seat; Abby was in
the back. It didn't much bother her that Josh had assumed
he automatically rode shotgun; she enjoyed having the
backseat to herself. Mom didn't even protest when Abby

loosened her seat belt, stretched her legs out, and relaxed.

Relaxation didn't come as easily to Mom. In fact, it didn't come at all. She made her best attempts at conversation at first, asking about school and softball and their friends and whatnot, feigning excitement over her upcoming return to work, but about an hour into the trip she fell silent. Abby attempted to keep up the light banter, but after receiving countless replies like "Mm-hmm" and "Uh-huh," she gave up.

When they were less than twenty miles from Curtisville, Mom stopped for gas. While Josh filled the tank, she sighed and said, "I want to go home."

"But, Mom," Abby protested, "we're almost there."

"This doesn't feel right." Mom covered her face with her hands. "Nothing feels right."

Abby leaned forward and rested her chin on the back of the seat, placing her hand on Mom's shoulder as she wept.

Josh paid for the gas with the fifty Mom had given him, and when he climbed into the car to find her crying, he glared at Abby.

"What did you say?" Josh barked.

"Nothing!"

"She didn't say anything," Mom said. "It's not her fault. I just want to go home." She sounded like a homesick kid.

Abby felt homesick, too, yearning for the old days when she used to believe that her parents were omnipotent. They were the shield she could hide behind when the world got scary, but now a whole piece of the shield had been torn away, and the rest was cracked.

Using his now fine-tuned negotiation skills, Josh was able to convince their mother to continue on to Aunt Marlene's. If, after they got there and said hello, she still wanted to go home, they'd leave without argument. Spending another three hours in the car only to turn around was without a doubt the last thing Abby wanted to do, but she didn't have a seat at the bargaining table.

They made it in time for lunch. Uncle Bob fixed burgers on the grill while Aunt Marlene boiled corn on the cob and whipped up a tuna salad in the kitchen, filling the room with nervous chatter about this, that, and the other thing. Like everyone else, she didn't know what to say, but her way of dealing with it was to say anything and everything that popped into her mind. Aunt Marlene and Uncle Bob bent over backward to avoid talking about Dad. But ignoring the void didn't fill it. If anything, it made it worse.

Josh and Abby played with Katie and Krissy in the family room. They were able, for the most part, to drown out Aunt Marlene's babbling. But then the voices lowered, and Abby knew Aunt Marlene had broached the subject of Dad. Abby heard her say:

"Everything happens for a reason."

Josh and Abby glanced at each other, waiting for Mom to explode. Instead she silently left the kitchen and retreated to the back porch.

"What did I do?" Aunt Marlene asked, starting toward the door. Abby held up a hand to stop her.

"Hang on a sec." She slipped on her flip-flops and went out on the porch.

Her mother was already walking toward the wooded trail behind the house. At first her pace was swift and determined, but she soon slowed enough for Abby to fall in step beside her.

As they followed the trail through the hardwoods, birds sang, fat black squirrels scurried across the path in front of them, and they even spotted a doe and her fawn. The doe stared them down as her baby munched on berries that had fallen from a wild blackberry bush. Though she didn't take her eyes off them, she didn't run.

Each time Abby heard leaves rustling or the snap of a fallen branch, she half expected a glowing vision of Dad to come strolling out of the forest, smiling and taking Mom's hands and telling them that no matter where they were, he'd always be there.

Is that you, Dad?

Mom and Abby walked in silence for half a mile, their only communication when Mom slipped her fingers between Abby's.

"I miss him," she said finally. She tightened her grip. Abby nodded, flexing her fingers, trying to get Mom to ease up. "This isn't fair." Mom's voice was louder and uneven. "This just isn't fair."

Abby nodded again. She shook deep inside.

"I don't want to be here," Mom said through clenched teeth, even more loudly. Abby got the feeling that she wasn't talking to her at all.

Mom released Abby's hand and stopped walking. "I can't do this by myself!" she shouted angrily. "I don't want to be here alone!"

"You're not alone—" Abby started to say, but Mom didn't let her finish.

"You're supposed to be here!" she screamed at the sky, both fists in the air. "Damn it, Sam! You're supposed to be here!"

Mom dropped to her knees, sobbing fiercely. Abby wondered if anyone back at the house could hear. Unfortunately no one came to the rescue.

"Mom." Abby knelt down beside her. "I'm still here."

Her mother looked at her hopelessly. "I know. But one day you'll go off and have your own life. I need Dad."

"I'll never leave you," Abby promised. And she meant it.

Mom tried to smile. "Yes, you will. You're supposed to. Dad wasn't supposed to leave."

Then she dissolved into more tears, turning away when Abby tried to comfort her.

"Dad wasn't supposed to die!"

Abby sat down beside her, doodling in the dirt with her index finger. She didn't know how to help. She was useless. The shadow remained.

And, that night, it followed the three of them back home. The fireworks on the lake went on as usual. Abby and Josh asked Mom if she wanted to go down to the Point to watch, but she refused. She sat on the couch and cried as the world boomed around them and people cheered in the distance.

Abby and Josh walked out into the driveway just in time to catch a glimpse of the grand finale over the neighbors' rooftops. The pyrotechnics lit up the sky as they exploded one after another. The show ended abruptly, leaving the sky dark, even the stars hidden by a gray cloud of smoke. The air was heavy and quiet, with only the exuberant, faraway voices of celebrating spectators breaking the silence. Soon the voices had drifted away, too.

Mom went to bed. Josh ran down to the Point to see if Billy Mohr or any of his other friends were still there. Abby didn't want to see anyone, not even Spence. The way she was feeling, she wouldn't be the best company.

Climbing up the stairs and into her room, Abby grabbed

her trusty 8 Ball and sat down on her bed to have a conversation with God.

Abby: Is Mom going to get over this?

God: OUTLOOK NOT SO GOOD

Abby: Is Dad in heaven?

God: CONCENTRATE AND ASK AGAIN

Abby closed her eyes tight and shook the Magic 8 Ball vigorously.

Abby: Is Dad in heaven?

Opening her eyes, Abby glanced hopefully down at the circular window. Just a white line was visible. The pyramid was stuck between two replies, and no matter how hard Abby shook it, the pyramid would not budge. *Okay, new question.*

Abby: Will we ever be happy again?

God: DON'T COUNT ON IT

Oh, God.

Abby squeezed her eyes shut and tried to summon Dad.

I won't be scared, Dad. I want to see you, just this once. I promise I won't be scared.

She slowly opened one eye and then the other. Her father wasn't there.

He was the one who was dead, but she lived with the ghost of her mother.

EIGHTEEN

September to December

"Welcome back to Lake . . . side . . . High!" Principal Patronis yelled with a fist pump, proudly displaying his school pride along with his pit stains. The crowd roared wildly, drowning out whatever else he was trying to say. The seniors started chanting first: "Sen-iors! Sen-iors! Sen-iors!" followed by the almost-as-rowdy juniors: "Jun-iors! Jun-iors!" The sophomores made a feeble attempt— "Sophmerssophmerssophmers" was barely audible. The freshmen clapped and cheered along, but didn't boast about their lowly status. That would just be embarrassing.

The music pumped through the speakers hung around the gymnasium, making the entire gym throb and buzz. The bleacher underneath Abby in the freshman section vibrated with the stomping of feet and the bass of "Boom Boom Pow." An oversize eagle wearing Lakeside's silver, blue, and white jersey exploded through the gym doors and boogied at center court. You'd think a rock star had entered the gym, the way everyone went nuts. The eagle was the LHS mascot—a poorly constructed one at that, its head way too large for its body, its beak way too short for its face, the entire thing in dire need of re-feathering.

And then its head popped off, revealing what all the fuss was about. Justin Elway, last year's junior class president, now a senior, tossed the eagle head into the senior section of the bleachers, then howled at the ceiling, pounding his fists on his chest like King Kong.

"Isn't this awesome?" Leise screeched. Abby covered her ears and nodded. She had to smile when the previous year's student government jogged through the doors and joined their leader. There was Josh, the incumbent vice president from last year's freshman class. While everyone around him danced, Josh stood with his hands in his pockets.

Erica Nichols nudged Abby from behind. "There's your brother!"

"Oh, yes." Abby snorted. "Mr. Charisma."

"Hey," Erica said solemnly, placing a hand on Abby's shoulder. "Sorry to hear about your dad."

Abby squirmed. *Here we go.* "It's okay."

Kailyn Romczik, on the bleacher in front of Abby, spun around. "What happened?"

"Her dad passed away," Erica reported.

Kailyn's hand flew to her mouth. "Oh my gosh! When?"

Abby shrugged. "A couple of months ago." Seventy-one days, seven and a half hours. Give or take.

"You all right?" Kailyn asked.

"I'm fine," Abby replied. No big deal; you win some, you lose some; *c'est la vie*. Right? The recorded music faded and the marching band began to play "Eye of the Tiger."

"Look!" Erica pointed over Abby's head at a cluster of boys entering the gym. "The football team!"

Everyone rose to their feet, leaving Abby feeling like a stump in the middle of a forest. She realized that Jamie Thorpe would have fared better at the high school; people were so wrapped up in their own stuff that everyone else's business would play second chair. They would soon forget that Abby's dad had died. And that would make it so much easier for Abby to pretend that she'd forgotten, too.

When Abby stood, Leise elbowed her.

"There's Lo-gan!" she sang.

Abby squinted at the throng of gigantic, hairy, muscled, thick-necked boys. No, not boys; guys. They waved coolly at the masses, like gladiators ready for battle. She finally spotted Logan, a head shorter than many of his teammates, somewhere in the middle of the junior varsity. Most of the guys were stone-faced. Logan wore his cocky grin. Still cute as ever.

The varsity cheerleaders came next, bouncing and squealing, waving their pom-poms in the air. These girls were so different from the cheerleaders at White Lake Middle School. They were chesty, curvy, confident. Abby felt herself shrink.

The crowd hushed as the varsity captain boasted about how awesome their team was, and how they were going to kick the crap out of Milford on Saturday. More cheering. He said some other stuff, but Abby wasn't paying attention. She had her eye on another group of boys gathered near the gym's entrance. The hockey team. There was Spence, looking so proud he glowed—he'd made varsity as a freshman. As the football team made its way off the court, Logan Pierce and a couple of the other football players joined the hockey guys. Logan stood next to Spence. Spence wormed his way to the other end of his pack.

Erica pinched Abby's side. "I see your boyfriend!"

"What?"

"Spence Harrison!" Erica said. "Leise told us you guys are going out!"

Abby glared at Leise and punched her lightly on the arm. Leise held her hands up in defense. "I did not!" Leise insisted. "I just said you're with him all the time!"

"We're friends," Abby corrected. How could she explain to Leise and the other girls that she couldn't leave home much and Spence was the only person in the world who understood why? When Mom saw Abby off for an infrequent outing, she would hug her tight and refuse to let go, and after Abby pried herself loose, Mom would study her like she thought she'd never see her again. She'd be smiling, but Abby knew that smile. It was the one she painted on just before hiding somewhere to explode in grief. Spence didn't mind coming over and doing nothing, just so Mrs. North wouldn't be lonely.

"Just friends, huh?" Kailyn purred. "Well then, I'll take him. He's hot!"

Abby laughed, but she felt like the wind had been knocked out of her. What if Spence got a girlfriend? She looked at him through Kailyn's eyes. He was taller than most of the other boys, and while they put on their tough-guy faces, Spence smiled with his chin held high. He deserved his varsity spot more than anyone. He'd trained hard to hone his skills, and worked his tail off to earn enough money to pay for the team fees and equipment—he might have been one of the youngest on the team, but he was more of a man than any of the rest of them.

And Kailyn was right. Spence *had* developed a certain hotness. Would he figure that out soon and realize that there was much more to life than sitting around Abby's house playing cards with her mother? What then?

Spence was searching the crowd, and when he caught sight of Abby he beamed and waved. Abby smiled and waved back.

"Yeah, just friends," Leise teased. "Whatever."

The pep rally ended and everyone was sent back to class. Jostled on all sides in the hot, pulsating swarm of people, some kids got annoyed and shoved. Abby, on the other hand, felt lighter than she had in a long time. She was part of this machine.

By mid-autumn Mom's complexion had changed from transparent to buttermilk, she smiled on occasion, and every now and then she laughed. Most days they were able to make it all the way to the Dairy Barn during their after-dinner walks without Mom losing it. A couple of times she went out to dinner with friends from work, and came home looking fresh and alive. Mom slowly packed some of Dad's things away, though refusing to throw anything out, including his frayed toothbrush or the folded pieces of toilet paper he'd used as bookmarks. But it was a start.

She hung a pencil drawing of Dad that she'd done before he got sick over the spot where his hospital bed had been. Abby loved that picture, and she knew what it meant— though pieces of Dad were disappearing from the house, he'd always be a part of home.

Josh seemed to be handling things wonderfully; he went on as if It had never happened at all: training for soccer, serving a second term as class VP, hanging out with friends after school, and going to field parties (though telling Mom he was staying the night with a friend to work on a class project—puke).

Abby followed suit, firmly deciding to leave Dad be, to let him enjoy his heaven and to spare him the agony of watching her feel sorry for herself. She appointed him her guardian angel, and for a while he did his job remarkably well. She and Leise had three classes together, she figured out how to do her hair and makeup without Leise's help, and a couple of times Abby caught stray, curious glances from cuteish upperclassmen in the school hallway. She imagined her father and God, both lounging in beige corduroy recliners, partners in making her life better.

But the shadow lingered.

Mom still cried in the shower every morning, and from the way she had to apply extra mascara to draw attention away from her bloodshot eyes and smooth on concealer to mask the puffiness, Abby could tell she'd cried herself to sleep, too. Sometimes she even called out Dad's name in the middle of the night.

Abby still woke as an amnesiac, having forgotten, looking out her bedroom window before the sun rose each day, watching for Dad to drive around the semicircle driveway and down the gravel road on his way to work. She still accidentally placed four plates and glasses on the dinner table.

She continued to refer to "Mom and Dad," instead of just Mom. She couldn't help but wonder how Dad would feel about his family adapting to their new life in this odd, three-legged fashion. Surely he would have wanted them to go on without him, but did it make him sad?

In late fall, Lakeside initiated a program dubbed "Grief Group" for kids who had "lost a loved one." Abby thought it might as well have been called the "Woe-Is-Me Hour." In Grief Group, kids were supposed to "talk about their feelings," to open up their darkest places for all to see. Abby went for a while, mostly to get out of class for an hour once a week, but she was not exactly an active participant. She wasn't about to bring the shadow to school.

Some kids cried during Grief Group. Abby pitied them. They were weak, unable to deal with reality, stuck in the past; they couldn't move on.

Abby envied those who cried.

Abby did not cry. She could not cry, but she did take a stab at grieving. She poured her heart out on paper, mourning via the poems and essays assigned by her English teacher, Mrs. Parker. Words were her tears.

And old Mrs. Parker ate that stuff up—Abby swore she could see tearstains on the paper when they came back graded A+, with heartfelt messages written in red ink at the bottom:

Beautifully written. It may not seem so now, but remember that in time this, too, shall pass.

At mid-semester parent-teacher conferences Mrs. Parker suggested that Mom get Abby into therapy to "help her find closure."

Abby never wrote about Dad again.

NINETEEN

December

Mom wanted to skip celebrating Christmas altogether. She'd tried to get time off from work so that they could fly down to Florida to visit Grandpa Warner. It always snowed on Christmas in Michigan. It never snowed on Christmas in New Port Richey. Normally Abby would have been thrilled at the prospect of taking a vacation, but a Christmas without snow wouldn't be Christmas. For Mom that was the point.

Turned out it was a nonissue. Mom couldn't get the time off.

Aunt Fran invited them over for Christmas Eve, but Mom turned her down. "I've tolerated your aunt for seventeen years, for your father's sake," she said, "but now there's no reason to make nice." So much for the Christmas spirit.

In years past, the whole family made an event of going to a Christmas tree farm to pick out the tallest, fattest tree they could squeeze into the living room. This year Mom tried to get away with not putting up a tree, but Abby insisted, so a week before Christmas they spent an evening sticking the plastic branches into the metal pole of a fake pine and hanging decorations. Mom didn't want to go through the hassle of rearranging the living room furniture, so they put it up in a corner of the basement, right next to the easel Mom had once used for painting, but that had now been put into service drying sweaters. And the lights didn't work. She promised to stop at Walmart, but conveniently forgot to do so. At night, shoved off into a dark corner, the tree was downright scary. Abby's heart jumped every time she passed through the kitchen and caught sight of it.

Mom treated December 24 like any other day, cleaning house and fixing tacos for dinner. After dinner Josh took off for Billy's, and Mom and Abby played Scrabble on the living room floor. It was fun, especially when Abby had to correct the spelling of the words her mother laid out. And Mom didn't get mad; she just laughed. She knew she didn't stand a chance.

At ten o'clock she announced that she was going to bed. She looked exhausted, but triumphant. She'd made it through the day, but was ready for it to be over as early as possible.

"Will you be all right down here by yourself?" Abby

couldn't tell whether Mom was really concerned or if she wanted company in her big, empty bed.

"Yeah. I'm just gonna watch some TV and then go to bed. I don't want Santa to skip our house because I'm still awake."

Mom smiled and kissed the top of her head.

"All right, just come wake me up if your brother doesn't make it home by eleven."

"Okay," she promised, though both of them knew she would do no such thing.

After Mom went upstairs, Abby channel surfed, hoping to find *Frosty the Snowman*, *Rudolph, the Red-Nosed Reindeer*, or *How the Grinch Stole Christmas* but that stuff was on early in the evening when little kids were still awake. Instead, the networks played hokey old black-and-white movies like *It's a Wonderful Life* and *White Christmas*. Abby tuned into *Miracle on 34th Street*, settling onto the couch and watching Natalie Wood do her scowl-and-pout thing. Natalie Wood was dead now. Abby wondered if the other actors were dead, too. It would have been nice if Dad had been a movie star; she could pop in a DVD and see him come to life whenever she wanted.

She remembered the old home movies that sat collecting dust somewhere in the basement, and for a brief moment considered digging them out. But it would take forever to figure out which tape was which, and besides, Dad wasn't in most of the footage anyway. He was the cameraman. The only traces of him were the wisps of cigar smoke that floated across the camera lens as he filmed.

Josh wandered in just after eleven, kicking his snowy boots off near the front door.

"Merry Chrishmish!" he slurred. "Izh Mom shtill up?"

"Have you been drinking?" Abby asked.

Josh smiled mischievously, reaching into his deep coat pockets.

"I brought you an early Chrishmish prezhent," he said, plunking two cans of Bud Light on the coffee table.

"Gee, thanks," Abby said, sitting up. The very smell of beer made her gag.

Josh whipped off his coat, chucking it onto the living room floor, and sat down on the couch. He snapped open the tabs of both beers and handed one to her.

"Here's to Chrishmish," Josh said, tapping his can against hers. Beer dribbled onto the carpet. Josh wiped the mess up with his bare hand, spilling more in the process. Mom had a nose like a beagle; they'd both be toast in the morning.

Josh slammed his beer, gulping down the entire thing without stopping to take a breath. Abby took a sip and wanted to spit it out.

Josh belched heartily and flipped the TV to *David Letterman*. Seconds later he was asleep with his head tilted back on the couch, snoring lightly. Abby had never heard Josh snore before. He sounded like Dad.

She eased the empty can from his hand, and took it, along with her own, into the kitchen. Then she dumped whatever was left down the sink and turned on the water to get rid of any lingering smell. Tucking the cans into a Ziploc bag, Abby hid them in the garage behind the lawn mower. She had until spring to get rid of them.

When Abby reentered the living room Josh was snoring louder. She grabbed a throw pillow, lay down on the couch beside him, stuffed the pillow under her head, and inched closer and closer until the crown of her head nearly touched Josh's leg. Her eyes grew heavy and soon closed, and Abby was lulled to sleep by the familiar lullaby.

Abby awoke late Christmas morning still on the couch, stiff and sore from sleeping cockeyed. Josh was gone; he must have drifted up to his room in the middle of the night.

She stretched and got up to find Mom. On the way to the kitchen, she glanced downstairs. There were two neatly piled stacks of presents under the tree, but no "biggies." Dad had always thought that bigger was better, and every year without fail there had been something that was too large or cumbersome to wrap: a giant piggy bank, a life-size doll, beanbag chairs.

This year, however, the gifts were small. Santa's tastes had changed.

Abby didn't see her mother downstairs, though, nor was she in the kitchen. The shower wasn't running. The clock on the stove read nine thirty; Mom never slept that late. Abby trotted up the stairs and, as she'd suspected, the bed was made and Mom was nowhere in sight.

Maybe she had just run out for a gallon of milk or something. But on Christmas morning? Abby peeked into the garage, finding the car still parked inside.

"Mom?" Abby called out.

No answer.

Abby went to check out the laundry room. Mom wasn't in there.

"Mom?" she said again. Again, Mom didn't answer.

Abby gazed at the Christmas tree, memories stirring of Christmases gone by when her family used to sit around the tree on Christmas Eve and behold it with wonder. That was then. Now it seemed ridiculous to think this lifeless thing could hold any kind of promise or magic. Underneath the tree a shattered burgundy ornament littered the gifts. Mom must have knocked it down while stuffing presents under the tree and not bothered to pick it up. Maybe she no longer saw the point in trying to hide what was broken.

Or maybe Mom had just given up. Abby's heart raced. Had

Mom lost it this time? Had she allowed Christmas without Dad to be the straw that broke her?

How could she?

"Mom!" Abby cried out in panic.

"I'm right here," came a tiny voice from behind the stairs. Abby turned as her mother poked her head out. She looked awful; her face was red and swollen. She'd been crying. Surprise, surprise.

"Why didn't you answer me?" Abby demanded.

"I didn't want you to see me like this," Mom said. "Not on Christmas."

"I thought something had happened to you." Abby was mad. She couldn't help it. "I thought you'd—"

"I'm just having a bad morning."

"What's new?" Abby realized she was being unfair, but so was Mom. Couldn't she try to hold it together, just for one day? For Abby? For Josh? For herself?

Mom's eyes met Abby's. She looked wounded, but only for a moment. "Well, excuse me for having feelings," Mom snapped.

"What—I don't have feelings?"

Mom shook her head and brushed past.

"I don't want to talk about this," she said.

"Talk about what?"

"Nothing!" Mom shouted. "Nothing's wrong. Right? Is

that how I'm supposed to feel? Well, fine. Merry Christmas. Go ahead and open your gifts."

Mom barged up the stairs and banged around in the kitchen while Abby rehashed the conversation in her head, trying to figure out what had gone wrong. Okay, so maybe she had been insensitive but, come on, she'd been tiptoeing around her mother for months, trying not to say or do anything that might set her off. It was no use. Mom was always so sad. She emanated sorrow; she carried the shadow.

Her sadness was infuriating.

I can't hurt anymore, Mom! Abby wanted to scream. *Don't you get it? If I don't get rid of this pain I'm going to go under, and you're not strong enough to pull me up!*

Abby took one look at the presents under the tree, realizing that she had no desire to open them. What was the point? There was no Santa Claus.

Instead, she slipped on her coat and boots and wandered out the back door. It was a gray, gloomy morning, warmer than it should be on Christmas, so that the snow was melting into slushy mud. She sloshed down the backyard hill and ambled precariously along the slippery, uneven lakeshore. Mom's rule of thumb was that if the ice shanties were up, the ice was strong enough to walk on, and though a couple of shanties stood out on the main lake, on a warm day like this Abby didn't trust the ice, especially on the bay.

Her head was throbbing and her jaw ached. She'd fallen into the habit of clenching her teeth while she slept, and she realized that she was still clenching them now. She couldn't help it; she was so angry with herself. Angry that she was angry. Mom was trying her best. Abby knew she was. But she wasn't trying hard enough.

She kept walking. She didn't know where she was going until she got there—the front porch of Spence's bungalow. In all the years they'd known each other, Abby could count on one hand how many times she'd been inside his house. She never knew why; it was just a given that he hung out on Abby's side of the bay. It dawned on Abby that there must have been a reason Spence didn't want her there. She turned and retreated down the steps. She should get back home, anyway, to apologize.

The door creaked open behind her.

"What are you doing?" Spence asked. Abby turned to face him. She couldn't decipher the look on his face. Was he mad or surprised to see her, or both?

"I'm sorry," she said, feeling herself blush. "I shouldn't have . . ." Abby started for the road. "I'll call you later."

Spence hurried down the porch steps and grabbed Abby by the arm. "No, wait. I just meant what are you doing here on Christmas morning instead of home with your family?"

Abby looked at the ground, ashamed. "My mom and I kind of had a fight."

"About what?"

"I really don't know." Abby's eyes wandered from her own wet boots to Spence's bare feet in the snow. "Why don't you have any shoes on?"

Spence glanced at his feet and grinned. "I saw you on the porch, and then you weren't on the porch and . . . why would you leave without even saying hi?"

She shrugged. "I didn't know if you wanted me here."

Spence laughed. "You know better than that."

Her eyes traveled from Spence's feet up to his face. He was wearing just a pair of shorts and a T-shirt. His cheeks were ruddy from the cold.

"Aren't you freezing?"

"I'm a hockey player. I live on the ice, remember? It's actually, like, tropical out here." Spence grabbed Abby by the hand and tugged her toward the house. "But let's go in."

Abby stopped, pulling Spence back with her. "Are you sure it's okay with your mom?"

Spence nodded. "It's fine. Come on."

The living room looked exactly the same as it had the last time Abby had seen it—tired old blue-and-white-striped couch, saggy blue recliner, scarred Sauder coffee table, and a couple of metal tables set up to hold lamps and ashtrays. The carpet, which might have been white once upon a time, was stained beyond repair. Everything smelled like stale tobacco. The only difference was the short, squat tree in the corner of the room. It was dressed in multicolored lights and some stringy garlands, accessorized with a dozen or so mismatched ornaments. A few wrapped gifts hid underneath.

"Like the tree?" Spence asked, shutting the door behind her. "I got it half price at Broadview. Decorated it myself."

"It's nice," Abby said. "Really nice."

He dropped onto the couch and patted the cushion beside him. "Let's gaze in awe."

Abby stepped on one boot to pull her foot out and then did the same for the other. She hung her coat over the back of the chair.

"Where's your mom?"

Spence didn't falter. "I don't know. She didn't come home last night."

"What do you mean? Where is she?"

"Probably at Tim's," Spence said, nodding his head toward the gifts. "He's the latest. And the greatest. Look, see? He left me a present."

Abby sat down on the couch, burying her hands underneath an afghan to warm them. "Are you going to open it?"

Spence shrugged. "Probably, later. They have to come back sometime. My mom didn't take her makeup bag."

"You're not worried at all," Abby said.

"No. She does this sometimes."

Abby settled back into the couch. It was so worn that the wood frame poked her spine. She sat straight up again.

"I can't believe she left you here alone on Christmas."

Spence's smile disappeared. "Like I said. She'll come back later."

Abby tucked one leg underneath her and pushed a wisp of hair out of her eye. She studied Spence's tree, fixed up with so much loving detail that it tried its hardest to pull its belly in, abs tight, to stop slouching. It was the most beautiful tree Abby had ever seen.

"So?" Spence said. "Did Santa bring you everything you wanted?"

No. He couldn't.

"We didn't open presents yet. You know . . . Josh wasn't even up."

Spence nodded, and then snapped his fingers. "Let's open something!"

"I thought you wanted to wait for your mom. . . ."

"It's not from my mom." Spence got up and dug under the tree until he found a sloppily wrapped present. He carried the box to the couch and showed her the tag.

Abby gasped. "Your dad sent you something?"

"Yep." Spence fingered the foil bow. "It came in the mail a couple of days ago, but I wanted to save it."

Spence hadn't seen his dad in years. Mr. Harrison was a drifter. Last Spence knew he was living in Vegas, working as a casino valet. He called sporadically; Spence had memorized every word his father had ever said to him.

"So what are you waiting for?" Abby said, nudging his shoulder. "Open it!"

Spence grinned as he carefully peeled back the tape, as if the wrapping paper were made of gold. He lifted back a flap and let out a loud guffaw.

"What?" Abby said, moving in to get a closer look.

Spence ripped the rest of the paper off in one yank. He held up the Star Wars Lego kit to show Abby.

"He still thinks you're four years old," Abby said, shaking her head.

"Hey," he said, still laughing. "This Star Wars stuff costs a fortune."

Spence, the only person Abby knew who could step into a puddle and thank it for cleaning his shoes.

"And what exactly are you going to do with that?"

"Are you kidding? It's Christmas morning! We're going to play with it!"

Spence tore open the box and dumped the contents onto

the floor. As he constructed the Death Star, Abby popped the heads onto the blocky action figures.

"I'm Princess Leia," she said, humoring him. "You can be Luke."

"Naw," Spence said. "I'm gonna be Darth Vader." He grabbed Darth and spun it around to face the Leia figure that still lay facedown on the carpet. He deepened his voice. "And now, Your Highness, we will discuss the location of your hidden rebel base."

Abby picked up Leia. "Shove it, Darth."

Spence sighed and shook his head. "Really now. Have you not seen the movie even once?"

She shrugged. "A long time ago."

Then Spence made the Darth Vader sound. *Suck-swoosh.* Pause. *Suck-swoosh.* Abby felt sick to her stomach. When Spence dropped Darth and turned around again to work on the Death Star, she shoved the figurine deep down between the couch cushions where he couldn't breathe.

And then she watched Spence playing with this little-boy toy, amazed at how little it took to make him happy.

"Doesn't it ever bother you?" she asked before she could stop herself.

"What? That you are completely unable to remember movie lines? Yes, it drives me nuts."

"No. Your dad. I mean, he thinks you're still a little kid

and that being a parent means remembering to send you a gift every few years. He has no idea how great you are."

Spence continued his construction project without batting an eye. "You know that old saying, 'You don't know what you've got until it's gone'? It's true. You also don't know what's missing until you've actually had it."

Abby wondered which scenario was worse. She was beginning to think Spence was the lucky one.

TWENTY

December to March

The new year was full of promise. Abby was ready to leave the old year behind.

Well, sort of. On the morning of New Year's Eve, the thought that tomorrow would be not only another day but another year—a year of new beginnings, not endings— should have made her feel optimistic. It didn't. This had been the Year of Dad. Dad had taken center stage; everything revolved around him. Leaving the year behind felt like leaving him behind.

Abby would no longer be able to say that her dad had died earlier that year. Now she would say he had died last year. And last year sounded like such a long time ago. Soon she would say that he had died two years ago, then three, then five, then ten. Before she knew it, she'd be telling people stories about what her dad did years ago, when she was a kid.

All she'd have to tell them would be the memories she already had, and even those would fade. Once she became an adult, Dad would be just someone she had known long ago.

On New Year's Eve Abby needed her pep squad; she wanted her friends.

Some kids, including Spence and Leise, were going to the all-night ski at Alpine Valley, across town near the high school, and had asked her to come with. New Year's Eve at Alpine was a big deal; a band played in the lodge and at midnight the ski patrol lined up for a downhill parade and fireworks were set off over Alpine's highest slope. The kids who had gone had boasted about how much fun it was, and Abby was dying to check it out for herself. Never mind that she'd never skied in her life; Abby didn't intend to start on New Year's, anyway. She could sit in the lodge and listen to music and drink hot cocoa and hang out with her friends.

She knew she wouldn't be able to go, though. Mom planned on staying home; she'd always said that going out on the roads on New Year's Eve was like playing Russian roulette. They used to have Billy Mohr's parents and the Beasleys over to ring in the New Year with cocktails, munchies, and euchre, but this year Mom said she wasn't feeling up to it. As Mom mopped the kitchen floor that afternoon, Abby sat at the kitchen table, trying to sway her to at least go out for dinner with friends so that maybe she'd let Abby go out, too.

"Why don't you give Charlotte a call?" she prompted. Charlotte was Mom's never-married friend from work, and the two of them went out to dinner now and then. "I'm sure she'd love your company."

"Charlotte has a date tonight, honey."

"What about Miriam or Judy?"

"They're married." Mom put her full weight into the mop, scrubbing like her life depended on eliminating a sticky spot on the floor. "They'll be spending the evening with their husbands."

"I'm sure they wouldn't mind if you tagged along."

"No, they probably wouldn't. In fact, Judy asked me to come to a party she's having this evening."

"So? Go!"

"I can't, Abby. I just can't. I'd feel like a third wheel."

"It's a party, Mom. There will be lots of people there."

"That's another thing," Mom sighed, taking a break from her mopping and wiping her forehead with her sleeve. "There will be plenty of couples there, along with some of the 'nice men' everyone has been trying to set me up with."

So maybe Mom was right. She shouldn't go.

"I've been put in the situation before. As much as they mean well, I don't think my friends realize how humiliating it is for me when they appoint themselves my personal matchmakers. We go out and these men show up and I swear

I can feel their eyes on me the whole night, scrutinizing what I look like and analyzing every word I say. Invariably they sit next to me the entire night, asking a million questions, personal questions, when all I wanted to do was get out and have a little fun. It's not fun. I assure you that any man past forty who is not married is single for a good reason."

"So can't you just tell these bozos to buzz off?"

Mom laughed. "I wish it was that easy. Besides, you know how I feel about driving on New Year's Eve. Every drunk in the country gets behind the wheel on New Year's."

Mom wrung out the wet mop and set it in the garage. She dumped the dirty water from the bucket into the sink, plunked a paper-wrapped pound of ground beef onto the counter, and searched through the spice cabinet for the fixings to make a meat loaf.

"Ask your friends to come over here, then," Abby suggested.

"Everyone has plans, Abby. Why are you keeping at me about this? Why is my staying home tonight such a big deal to you?"

Drumming her fingers on the table, Abby tried to think of something to say that sounded sincere and altruistic, but came up with nothing.

"Oh," Mom said with a smile. "I get it. You want to get me out of your hair so that you can go out, right?"

"Well . . . yeah."

"Forget it," Mom said quickly. "There's no reason for a fourteen-year-old to be out on New Year's Eve."

"But Mom, all the kids from school are going up to Alpine. It'll be safe—no one is driving and there are adults all over. Why can't I go?"

"Because you're fourteen, and—"

"Fourteen and a half!"

"Not quite. There will be plenty of time for late-night parties when you're older. You know, my curfew was nine o'clock until I went off to college. I wouldn't have dreamed of asking my parents to let me stay out past midnight, not even when I was eighteen."

Her *parents*. Didn't Mom know how much it stung to hear that word in plural?

"That was in the olden days, Mom."

Her mother laughed. "Yes, we had to make it home before dark so that the horses could still see the road to pull the buggy."

Then she went about her business, chucking the ground beef into a bowl with some bread crumbs and spices, kneading the mixture with her hands. Abby watched her mother, dressed in worn khakis and a faded blue Henley with the sleeves bunched up to her elbows, her short curls coiffed just so, her hands covered in a fatty mess of beef and bread crumbs and basil as she flattened the mixture into a loaf pan. Mom's life was so depressing. Abby flashed forward to a vision of herself in thirty years, trying to imagine her life being so pathetic. She couldn't picture it.

Mom didn't understand anything. She'd been the perfect kid, earning a 4.0 through high school and college, modeling for a department store to pay for what her University of Michigan art scholarship didn't. She'd abstained from anything that resembled fun. She was her own mother's dream. No wonder Abby was such a disappointment.

Abby would never be like that, no matter how hard Mom tried. Staying home, watching television with her, and listening to her cry herself to sleep, was undoubtedly the last way Abby wanted to spend New Year's Eve.

"So Josh is staying home tonight, too?"

"He's staying the night at Billy's."

"Wait, that's not fair—"

"I talked with Mr. Mohr and he'll be home all night. Josh will not be doing anything more exciting than you will."

"Yeah, right." Billy's parents were pushovers; there was no doubt in Abby's mind that Billy and Josh would be up at Alpine.

"Abby, I'm sorry, but you're staying home. End of story."

Abby's face flushed and her hands started to tremble. Slamming her fist on the table, she rose from her chair.

"You can't keep me in a bubble, you know." Abby's voice was loud and shaky. "I'm sorry that you're so depressed all the time, but I don't want to be as miserable as you are."

Mom looked at Abby, her jaw tight. "I want you to be happy, but I'm also going to keep you safe. You're trying to grow up too fast."

"You just can't face that I'm growing up!"

"Nonsense," Mom said, and went back to preparing dinner.

"Why don't you just get a life?" Abby screamed as she stomped up the stairs.

She went into her bedroom, intending to slam the door behind her to drive home her point, but instead she stood near the door, listening for her mother's sobs. She regretted her harsh words already. Sticks and stones could break bones, but words can kill.

But Mom didn't cry. She didn't even yell back. The silence was deafening.

She wasn't playing fair, laying on the guilt trip with her sneaky psychological tactics. Steam came out of Abby's ears as she sat on her bed and pounded out an email to Leise, detailing the woes of her confinement. When Mom stuck her head inside her bedroom door she growled at her to go away. Abby fell asleep at eight o'clock, leaving her bedroom light on to drive Mom crazy.

At eleven she woke to a knock on the front door.

"Josh?" Mom shouted.

Abby jumped out of bed and ran down the stairs to find Billy standing on the front porch with Josh, green in the face, hanging on to the wooden railing for dear life. Billy dragged Josh inside and deposited him on Dad's recliner.

"He's been drinking," Billy said quickly before bolting out the front door.

Josh slumped over in the chair, mumbling something incoherent and laughing to himself. Suddenly Abby didn't see Josh anymore. She saw Dad in that chair, fighting with morphine for control of his mind. She wanted to pummel her brother for bringing it all back. When she thought of Dad, she found she could hardly remember him healthy, so she'd stopped remembering. It was easier that way.

Mom didn't know what to do, so she called Mr. Beasley.

"Jim?" she said into the phone. "It's Josh, he's . . . can you please come over?"

Abby could have sworn that he walked through the front door before Mom had made it back to the living room. "Josh?" Mr. Beasley said loudly. "Look at me."

Josh raised his chin and tried to open his eyes, but his head rolled backward. Mom gasped.

Mr. Beasley pulled him to his feet, draped Josh's left arm over his broad shoulders, and hauled him up the stairs. Mom and Abby followed them into Josh's bedroom, watching as Mr. Beasley gently laid him on the bed.

Mr. Beasley snapped his fingers in front of Josh's face and Josh's eyes shot open.

"How much have you had to drink, son?"

"Ohhhh . . . two or three." Josh closed his eyes. "The room's spinning."

"Do you feel like you're going to get sick?" Mr. Beasley asked.

"Already did."

"What's wrong with him?" Mom asked anxiously.

Mr. Beasley turned to look at her and smiled.

"He's drunk, Helen."

"But he's so out of it. Do you think he has alcohol poisoning? Is there something I can give him?"

"Spaghetti pizza," Josh chimed in. "I need some of Aunt Fran's spaghetti pizza."

Mr. Beasley chuckled and shook his head.

"How's he gonna read?" Josh asked no one in particular. "It's too dark in there. He needs a flashlight."

Abby wanted to run out of the room, down the stairs, and out the front door. She wanted to sprint down the road and keep running until her legs gave out. But she didn't move.

"What's he talking about?" Mr. Beasley asked.

Mom shook her head.

"He's talking about Dad," Abby said quietly. "Josh left a book in the casket."

Mr. Beasley's eyes fogged, and he hugged Mom.

"He'll be okay," Mr. Beasley assured her. "He'll be just fine." Abby wasn't sure if he was talking about Josh or Dad. "Do you want me to stay?"

"No. I'm sorry to have bothered you. But you're sure there's nothing I can do for him?"

"I'll tell you what. Give him some water and check on him a couple of times overnight while he sleeps it off a bit. Wake him up bright and early tomorrow morning and make him shovel and salt the driveway. Then dust, vacuum, scrub toilets, whatever. By noon he'll never want to drink again."

Mom smiled and saw Mr. Beasley to the door. He hesitated. "You're sure I shouldn't stay?"

"No. I can handle it."

After he left, she looked almost serene as she walked upstairs to Josh's room. The calm before the storm. She stood over the bed with her hands on her hips and took a deep breath before erupting.

"I don't know how you expect me to handle all this!" Mom yelled. "I need some help here, you know. I didn't ask to be a single parent."

"I'm sorry, Mom," Josh said dully.

"You say that, but are you really?" She started for the

stairs but turned back again. "I've had it. Do you hear me? I've had it!" She slouched down in the middle of the hallway and covered her face with her hands. "I can't do this. I'm failing. I can't do this alone."

Abby approached her mother, but she pulled away. "You, too, Abby. I get it, you're angry that all this is happening. You need someone to take it out on and that lucky person is me. I don't want to be that person!"

"Mom—"

"You know what?" Mom said, standing and stomping toward the master bedroom. "I'm angry, too! Something has to change or I'm going to go stark-raving mad."

Mom arranged an appointment for the three of them to see a psychologist, Dr. Robert Robinson, a middle-aged guy with a lisp and an extremely distracting unibrow. He called himself "Dr. Robby." Honestly.

During the first visit Dr. Robby met with the three of them together, and Mom detailed the deterioration of her once-impeccable children into juvenile delinquents. She wanted to know what she was doing wrong and how she could help them. Dr. Robby informed Mom that it "wasn't uncommon for teenagers to act out grief in self-destructive ways" and that Mom had brought them to the right place.

The guy had turned Abby off at word one.

Dr. Robby scheduled individual appointments with Josh

and Abby, one after the other, for the following week. Abby knew she didn't need therapy, but she figured if she went along with it, maybe Mom would realize she wasn't as terrible as she thought and get off her back.

On her solo visit, Dr. Robby asked Abby about school, about her friends, about her relationship with her family; he even tried to get her to venture into the Land of Feelings. She gave him one-sentence or, more commonly, one-word answers and waited patiently for the next question. Dr. Robby wouldn't say anything for a while, pausing long enough for the silence to become so uncomfortable that she would want to spill her guts.

He didn't know how stubborn Abby was. He learned.

Then he blew it completely. "Your mom says you've been pretty angry," he said.

For bringing me here? Yes, angry doesn't even come close.

"Are you angry with your father for leaving you?"

Angry with Dad? Why would Abby be angry with Dad? Was Dad thrilled about having half his life stolen from him? He hadn't wanted to die. Dad was a victim; how could she possibly be angry with him?

"My dad died," Abby growled. Idiot. "He didn't leave me."

"Not on purpose. But do you feel like he abandoned you?"

Abby clenched her teeth to keep herself from telling the

guy to shove his theories right back up his butt where his head was, stood up, and stormed out. She grabbed her coat off the chair beside Mom in the waiting room, opened the door, and headed into the hallway.

"Where are you going?" Mom asked, wide-eyed.

"I'll wait in the car. This is a waste of time."

Abby strode out into the parking lot only to find the TrailBlazer locked. She kicked the car's tire out of frustration. Josh would be in with Dr. Know-It-All for the next hour, and it couldn't have been more than fifteen degrees outside. The office was in Birmingham, a suburb of Detroit Abby had only passed through once or twice in her life; she had no idea where to go to stay warm. She sure as hell wasn't going back in, so she sat on the hood of the car until her butt went numb, wishing she could pluck her heart out and freeze that, too, so she wouldn't feel anything anymore.

Mom cut back on her hours at work so that not only could she be at home with Josh and Abby before and after school, she could drive them to and from school. Abby supposed her mother suspected that they might play hooky or that during the half-hour bus ride they'd be ducking out of view of the driver and snorting ground-up Smarties or drinking Listerine or something. Maybe she thought that some of the other kids on the bus were bad influences. Or more likely, Mom feared that the bus might have a brake malfunction that would send it hurtling into the depths of White Lake, sinking fast with the remainder of her family inside.

Whatever the case, Josh and Abby were stuck being shuttled to school in Mom's SUV. It was humiliating. At least she had the decency not to drop them off in the student parking lot; she stopped in front of the main entrance, in the faculty lot. Still, they would hide their faces in shame as she drove in, and they'd leap from the car before it had stopped moving and make a mad dash to the school, hoping they hadn't been spotted. After school, they'd loiter near the main office until all the buses and most of the cars in the student parking lot were gone; then they'd meet her in the lot. The wait annoyed her, but she knew better than to come into the school to get them. That would have been a declaration of all-out war.

One icy day at the end of February, Josh and Abby slipped and slid toward Mom's car after school and climbed in to find Mom beaming. At Abby.

"Did you see what's posted out there?" She pointed at the marquee near the school's front entrance. "Softball tryouts are next week."

"Mm-hmm," Abby said offhandedly, using the heel of one of her shoes to scrape the slush off the other and letting it melt on Mom's floorboard. Abby had heard about the girls' softball tryouts, all right. How could she not? She could have sworn that every wall in the school was papered with flyers.

"So are you excited?" Mom asked. "Nervous?"

"About what?"

"About trying out for the softball team!"

Abby shrugged.

"You are going to try out, aren't you?"

Another shrug.

"Abby, you have to try out! You love softball, and you're so good at it!"

"I'm not good," Abby corrected. "I'm barely mediocre."

Mom dismissed her comment with a wave of her hand. "Oh, you are not. I've always thought that you played very well in summer ball!"

"You're my mother, and that was the Hi-White league. The high school team is more competitive."

"You did better than a lot of the Hi-White girls, and those are the same girls that will be trying out for the freshman team."

"There is no 'freshman team,' Mom, only JV and varsity."

"Well, so what?"

"So I'm not good enough. End of story."

"But you love softball," Mom insisted.

"*You* love softball."

"I don't know what's wrong with you."

"Nothing's wrong with me. If you're so obsessed with softball, why don't *you* play?"

"Abby, you can't just—"

"I'm tired of you trying—"

"—throw away an opportunity like this—"

"—to live vicariously—"

"—because you lack self-confidence!"

"—through me!"

Josh cleared his throat and said he was hungry and could they continue this conversation at home and not in the parking lot? Mom shifted the car into reverse and backed up slowly.

"This conversation's over," Abby grumbled.

"No, it's not," Mom insisted.

"Yes, it is."

"I don't think so."

"Whatever."

The following Monday, Abby stood with her back against the bleachers in the stinky gym, twirling her mitt on her index finger as she waited alongside her fellow JV softball team hopefuls to be assigned a tryout station by the coach and her assistants. Her mother had threatened to march Abby into the gym herself—and, even worse, make her go back to see Dr. Robby—if she didn't make the decision "on her own" to go to tryouts. So she went—but Mom couldn't force her to put any effort into it.

"This group," barked the coach—who couldn't be identified as male or female by voice or appearance—separating ten girls from the line, "go over to the north end of the gym with Sarah for catching-and-throwing skills review." A redhead wearing the team cap raised her hand.

"Group two"—another ten girls—"will go outside with Olivia to Field B for fielding review." Abby let out a sigh of relief. It was snowing outside, for Pete's sake. No way was she going to trudge through a foot of snow in her sneakers to stand shivering in the field so that she could prove to some chick that she could catch a fly ball. "Group three"— that included Abby—"go upstairs with Ashley to the batting cage."

The coach assigned another group to sprint in the hallway, and him- or herself escorted a cluster of girls who had expressed interest in pitching to the south end of the gym.

Along with nine other girls, Abby followed her leader— blonde, ponytailed Ashley—upstairs to where a batting cage had been set up. A couple of girls Abby knew from the Hi-White League, both of whom had been on the All-Star team, were the first to grab helmets and race for the cage. Katy Townsley, a house of a girl, shoved her way inside first and took a confident stance at one end of the netted cage.

Crack. Crack. Crack. Katy smacked every ball that came at her, sending them flying into the net. When her turn was up, she reloaded the machine and handed the bat to Tamika

Jakubic. Tamika nailed every pitch, too, smirking and swaggering out of the cage when she'd finished.

Abby was last in line, and as her turn at bat approached she decided that she had to pee and could not wait one more second. She took off for the locker room, and when she started back up the stairs afterward, her group was heading down.

"It's time for rotation," Ashley scolded. "You missed your turn. I can't evaluate you."

So of course there was no point in staying. As the rest of her group grabbed their mitts and coats to head outside for fielding evaluation, she slipped out into the hallway and away from the gym and fiddle-farted around until tryouts were over.

Mom was waiting in the parking lot just after seven.

"So, how'd it go?" Mom asked excitedly.

Abby slumped in her seat. "I was cut."

"What? On the first day?"

"Told you I wasn't good enough."

Mom looked at Abby sympathetically and patted her knee. "It's okay, honey. At least you gave it your best shot. Maybe next year."

Abby shrugged. Guess she showed her.

TWENTY-ONE

April

Josh turned sixteen in the first week of April, and Mom handed him the keys to the Impala. Occasionally. Josh had been on house arrest since New Year's Eve, and besides, he didn't have sole custody; Mom was the Key Master. She allowed him to drive to school, with the stipulation that he had to drive Abby as well—and then, only if the weather was perfect. If there was a slight dusting of snow on the ground, which there often was until mid-April, or if the Channel 4 weatherman forecast even a drizzle, Josh and Abby would be stuck riding with Mom.

On the days Josh drove, he'd usually stop at Billy Mohr's house and swing by to grab Spence as well. Abby was okay with the backseat; it was her comfort zone. Back when the Impala was Dad's, Josh and Abby always sat in the back while their parents sat in the front, Dad's hand sporadically leaving the ten-and-two position on the wheel to hold Mom's. Sitting in the front seat now would be just another reminder that everything was not as it should be.

The annoying part was that Josh insisted on leaving half an hour earlier than he needed to so he could get one of the first parking spaces in the student lot. And, wouldn't you know it, Josh invariably parked next to the brand-new silver Mustang convertible Logan Pierce's parents bought for his sixteenth birthday. Abby had to get up even earlier to be in top form each morning. Logan sometimes shot her a smile or an occasional hi, but Josh barred her from leaning against the cars and hanging out with him and his boys before school. Which was best, she guessed. Word had spread that Logan was going out with Paige Quinlan, the most ridiculously beautiful girl in the sophomore class. Abby couldn't stand even to hear about it, much less to be there when Paige strutted up to Logan's Mustang, smiling coyly, her dark hair spilling around her shoulders in a purposeful messiness that Abby could never achieve, her miniskirts showing enough of her perfectly toned legs, sleek and tan, to make any guy's tongue fall out of his mouth.

So Abby passed the time before first bell with Spence, sitting on the veranda looking over each other's homework or hanging their legs off the school's loading dock, eating granola bars and drinking SunnyD until the food-service truck showed up to unload.

"What's eating you?" Spence asked one morning, tearing open a bag of pretzels and sending a few over the side of the loading dock.

"Is that your breakfast?" Abby asked.

Spence shrugged. "I haven't had time to go grocery shopping. I found these in the back of the pantry."

Abby looked at Spence with pity and admiration. Though his mother simply tossed him whatever tiny scraps of love she had left over, Spence never once complained. He just kept on surviving. Maybe that's why he and Abby understood each other so well. They both knew what it was like to wish for something so long that you forgot what your wish was in the first place. Only Spence kept on dreaming, while Abby knew that unrealistic hope was, well, hopeless.

"So, really," Spence repeated with his mouth full, "what's bugging you this morning? You're awfully quiet."

"I am?" Abby hadn't noticed. Sometimes she and Spence could sit for hours and say next to nothing, but never once feel like something was missing. Each of them always knew what was up with the other.

"Maybe not just quiet," Spence clarified. "You seem kind of sad."

"I'm not sad," Abby said quickly.

Spence held up a hand. "Okay, wrong emotion. Perturbed?"

She looked across, into the student parking lot, where Logan Pierce still stood near his car, now with his arm draped around Paige Quinlan.

"Oh, *I* see." Spence crumpled his empty pretzel bag into a ball and squeezed it in his fist.

Abby snapped her head around. "What?"

"It's that Pierce guy. You still like him?"

She stared at her shoes, watching them appear and disappear as she swung them back and forth over the edge of the dock. She couldn't find the right answer to Spence's question. "How can you like him so much," he added, "when you don't even know the guy?"

Abby crossed her arms over her chest and made a face. "I know him. He's been to my house lots of times."

"To see Josh." Spence jumped off the dock to throw the destroyed pretzel bag in the nearby Dumpster. "I know Pierce better than you do."

Abby snorted. "How's that?"

Spence stretched his arms over his head. "Doesn't take much to know that the guy's a dolt."

Abby gritted her teeth and glared at him. "So you say."

"And I'm right. I mean, if I were going to ask anyone out, I'd ask you."

"Well, apparently Logan feels differently."

Spence shook his head and started to walk toward the school. "I wasn't talking about Logan."

Abby watched him go through the loading-dock doors and down the long hallway. She expected him to turn around and wave good-bye, but he didn't. She continued to stare down the hallway long after Spence had turned the corner and disappeared from view.

Abby had only one thought: *come back.*

The yearning filled her heart before she could lock it out.

Stay away from boys.

Especially Spence, that's what Dad had meant. Her father had seen this coming, and she had been too stupid to pay attention.

The parking lot was filling up, and kids were filing into the school, but Abby stayed put. It seemed that every time she stood on her own two feet the rug was pulled out from underneath her and—*whoosh*—everything changed.

TWENTY-TWO

June

Abby and Spence never talked about that morning again, but for the rest of the school year it flitted around them like fireflies whenever they were together. It was strange and uncomfortable, so Abby kept a safe distance. She had no idea how she could keep it up during summer vacation, which she couldn't imagine spending without him.

Abby's cousin Wendy saved her. Wendy's Minnesota wedding, just after school let out, was a three-day reprieve; by the time she got back, she hoped, things would be back to normal. They'd just pick up where they left off, Spence doing his summer chores and swimming and boating with Abby in between, and she would no longer have to wonder if either of them had said hello in a different tone of voice, or looked at the other too long, or looked away too quickly, leaving something unsaid lingering in the air.

Mom let Josh drive for about half the trip to Duluth. She sat so stiffly Abby could actually see her head over the headrest, and she kept her arm draped over the console between the driver and front passenger seat with her fingers splayed outward, ready to grab the wheel at any given second. Mom made Josh travel in the slow lane—wouldn't let him pass anyone, not even the semitrailers going fifty-five—and then just about hyperventilated every time another car had to merge. It was entirely too stressful, so Abby turned on her iPod. It was fun enough just watching Josh's ears and neck turn red as he tried to hold back his frustration.

After making it past the Michigan/Illinois border, they drove through Illinois farmland and around downtown Chicago and past signs listing the names of outlying suburbs, and Abby fell asleep before they'd even made it into Wisconsin. She didn't wake until they were near the Minnesota border, where Duluth lay just on the other side.

They checked into the Sheraton late Friday evening. While Mom and Grandpa Warner and Aunt Marlene and the others staying at the hotel congregated in the lounge, Josh and Abby took Katie and Krissy to the pool. They played the game that Dad had invented when they stayed at hotels with pools. He'd throw in change from his pockets, and they'd dive in. After coming up, Josh and Abby would count their change and see who had "earned" the most. Dad used to toss in quarters and, every now and then, silver dollars, but now they played with the pennies Mom had dug out of the bottom of her purse. They didn't even get through one round before the hotel manager came to holler at them about coins screwing up the pool filter. Just as the manager stormed off, shaking his head as if to say "where are the parents, anyway?" Aunt Marlene came to fetch Katie and Krissy, announcing that Mom wanted Josh and Abby to call it a night, too.

Back in the room, Mom, who had set the ironing board up and was pressing Josh's shirt and dress pants, gestured to the credenza behind them. The tantalizing smell of pepperoni and cheese filled the air. As they bowled each other over to get to the pizza first, Abby caught sight of a fantastic light-green dress that had been laid out on the bed with a pair of strappy, low-heeled shoes beside it.

"Is that the dress you're wearing?" Abby asked, stopping to watch Mom set the iron on end and rearrange Josh's shirt. The iron let out a puff of steam.

"No," Mom said. "It's yours." Abby beheld the dress with awe. "You like it?"

"It's okay, I guess."

"Good." Mom grinned, not fooled for a second. "I can't wait to see it on you."

Pizza could wait. Abby took the dress into the bathroom to try it on. She liked it even more on than off. It fit perfectly, as did the shoes. When she looked at herself in the mirror she could almost see a classy-looking young woman—if her hair wasn't wet and disheveled and her eyes red and psycho-looking from the chlorine.

Mom knocked. "Let me see."

Abby opened the door slowly. Mom sucked in her breath. "I knew the moment I saw it. That dress was made for you."

Abby glanced at herself sideways in the mirror.

"Yeah," she said. "I . . . it's nice . . . I'm glad you bought it."

"You're welcome." Mom chuckled as she headed over to grab a slice of pizza before Josh ate it all.

The next day Abby did the dress justice by curling her hair into soft waves and then sweeping it into a relaxed updo, like she'd practiced at Leise's. She put on some makeup, but lightly for Mom's sake, and hooked in a pair of silver dangly earrings. After she'd finished, she tried to picture herself strutting before Logan Pierce and watching his eyes pop out of his head, but found that what she really wished was that Spence could see her. Spence, who had seen Abby at her worst, would most appreciate her at her best.

The Norths arrived at the church at one thirty and greeted Abby's relatives, most of whom she'd last seen at the funeral.

"Abby?" her aunt Shirley said. "Is that you? My goodness, the last time I saw you, you were a little girl. You've become a beautiful young woman."

Abby smiled and blushed. She hoped that Mom was taking note. Abby was not a little girl anymore; she was a woman.

Then Deanna showed up with an engagement ring.

Everyone gathered around, oohing and aahing over the one-carat diamond. Brad stood next to Deanna, shaking hands with the men and accepting hugs from the women. Mom stood with her arm around Deanna's waist, smiling proudly. Abby couldn't remember her mother ever having looked at her that way.

Just before two o'clock, an usher escorted the Norths to their pew, a few rows back from Aunt Shirley and Uncle Dub. Soon a recording of Pachelbel's canon began to play and bridesmaids in pale pink taffeta shuffled down the aisle with groomsmen in gray tuxedos. There they went, one, two, three . . . seven couples approaching the altar and splitting off, standing in two separate lines at the front of the church.

Abby envisioned her own wedding—minus a groom for now, of course—and made a mental list of the girls she might ask to be bridesmaids: Leise, maybe Foley, she couldn't leave out Deanna . . .

The first few strains of the wedding march played and the crowd rose and turned toward the back of the church. Wendy, wearing a gown that made her look like Cinderella at the ball, appeared in the doorway on the arm of her dad, Abby's ex-uncle Cal. Father and daughter walked slowly down the aisle,

Wendy smiling from ear to ear and winking at a few people. Uncle Cal wiped a tear from his eye. When they reached the altar, Cal lifted Wendy's veil, planted a tender kiss on her cheek, and then hugged her tight, whispering something into her ear. Abby averted her eyes. When Mom touched her knee, she jerked away. All this pomp and circumstance was ridiculous, Abby told herself. She'd never want to be part of something so theatrical. Mom would never be able to afford it, anyway. And Dad wouldn't be there to give her away. No, a big wedding would not be in her future.

After the ceremony ended, Mom, Josh, and Abby piled into Mom's SUV and headed for a reception at the local VFW hall. They found their names on place cards at a table near the dance floor and sat down to rehash details about the wedding with Deanna and Brad and Aunt Marlene and Grandpa Warner. Uncle Cal arrived, still looking shaken up, and Wendy waltzed into the room with her new husband. Then the hundreds of guests went nuts, cheering and clinking glasses and snapping pictures and throwing confetti.

Dinner was served buffet style. Josh and Abby piled their plates with roast beef and garlic mashed potatoes and green beans almondine and sweet rolls. Josh dug into his immediately and went back for seconds, while Abby pushed the food around on her plate. The bride and groom were floating about, hugging and talking to people and posing for pictures. Krissy and Katie were whining about wanting cake, and Deanna was busy polishing her new ring, and Mom was talking about mutual funds and mortgage rates and other yawn-inducing subjects with Grandpa and Aunt Marlene. Abby sat silently taking it all in, incensed at her mother for putting her through this torture and wishing Spence were there to suffer alongside her. He would have made the whole experience somewhat endurable.

Just as Mom was finishing her dinner, a tall man with thinning grayish-brown hair walked up to the table.

"Helen?"

Mom turned to look at him, gasped, and jumped out of her chair.

"Denny!" she shrieked. He hugged her tight, smiling and swaying back and forth. Neither let go for what seemed like an eternity.

Mom pulled back and held both of "Denny's" hands in hers.

"It's been such a long time!" she exclaimed. "I'm so glad to see you! I knew you and Shirley still kept in touch, but I didn't realize that you'd be here!"

Denny smiled. "It's good to see you, too, Helen. I've been thinking a lot about you since I heard about Sam. I'm so sorry. Did you get my card?"

"I did. Thank you, and I apologize for not replying, but things have just been . . . you know . . . it's been a tough year."

"I understand completely." He paused. "I lost my wife five years ago. It's hard to go it alone."

Mom deftly changed the subject. "So how are you? I hear that you're living in Chicago now?"

"Sure am," Denny replied. "Both my kids live in the suburbs now—in Schaumburg—and I wanted to be near them. Businesswise, it doesn't much matter where I live; I travel pretty much nonstop anyway. I'm in engineering consulting and do quite a bit of work for the automotive companies, which takes me to Detroit a lot."

"Oh, so you still come out my way, huh?" Mom was acting in a way Abby had never seen before.

"All the time."

Abby cleared her throat, and Josh nudged Mom with his elbow.

"Oh," she said, looking at Abby. "I'm sorry. These are my kids, Abigail and Joshua." Mom pointed across the table at Deanna, who was gushing to Cousin Joslyn. "And that's my daughter Deanna over there."

"Good to meet you," Denny said, shaking Josh's hand, then Abby's. At the touch of Denny's hand, Abby felt herself wanting to cave in, a feeling she could only describe as homesickness.

"Hi," Abby muttered, turning to Mom. "Can I go make a phone call?"

"Sure," Mom answered, handing Abby her cell without looking her way. "Go ahead."

Abby hurried outside and stood near the parking lot, dialing Spence's number. He wasn't home, so she left a quick message.

Then she stared at the phone, willing it to ring. She was sure Spence would call her back as soon as he could. Why she was so sure she didn't really know, and she didn't know why she thought talking to Spence would somehow put everything right. But it would. At that moment she missed him so much her insides ached.

Abby detested the thought of going back inside. The reception was a drag. Wendy was spoiled and arrogant and fake and, besides, she looked fat in her wedding gown.

"Hey," Josh said as he lowered himself onto the curb beside her. She'd been so lost in her thoughts she hadn't heard him.

"Hey."

"Whatcha doin' out here?"

"Pondering ways to end world hunger. How about you?"

Josh shrugged. "Peace in the Middle East, I guess."

He fiddled with his tie. He hadn't even come close to getting it tied right—Dad had always helped him with that—and soon he took it off entirely and stuffed it into his pocket. "Let's do something."

"Like what?"

"I dunno. Play a game?"

"A game. Any suggestions?"

"Thought you might be able to think of something."

A wicked grin spread across Abby's face. "How about Truth or Dare?"

Josh snorted. "I don't care to know any more about you than I already do."

"Fine. We'll skip the truth part and stick with dares."

He raised one eyebrow. "Only if I get to dare you first."

"Deal."

Josh tapped his lip and squinted his eyes in deep concentration. Then he smirked and nodded. "I dare you," he said, "to go stand out by the road, wait until you see a car about to pass by, and pick your nose."

"No!"

"Chicken."

"This is so juvenile." Yet, determined to prove herself, she scuffled along the dirt driveway to the main road and stopped about ten feet away.

"Closer!" Josh shouted.

"You said out by the road," Abby hollered back. "You did not specify a particular distance from it, so bug off."

"Fine."

When an old VW bus rumbled toward her, Abby bent her finger to the second knuckle and placed it to her nostril. The middle-aged hippies inside honked as they passed, and Abby turned toward her brother victoriously.

"Ha!" Abby said. "Now it's my turn to dare you."

"You cheated. Your finger wasn't in your nose."

"Yes, it was!"

"It most certainly was not. If you're not going to play right, let's not play."

"Okay, okay. But it's still my turn."

"All right. Shoot."

Abby thought for a minute while surveying the parking lot. There were a few clusters of people in the lot, some smoking cigarettes, others chatting near their cars. Then it came to her.

"Stand right where you are and, as loud as you can, perform the song 'I'm a Little Teapot,' accompanied by all corresponding body movements."

Josh, looking completely nonplussed, began to sing.

"I'm a little teapot . . ."

"Louder!"

"I'M A LITTLE TEAPOT, SHORT AND STOUT . . ."

The people in the parking lot turned their heads to stare, and Abby took off and hid around the side of the building so Josh would have to go it alone, laughing so hard she could barely hear him finish. Then a deejay started blasting music inside, almost drowning out Josh's performance. When Abby was sure he was done, she came out of hiding and walked toward her brother, doubled over in laughter.

The game went on, and neither of them refused a dare until Abby offered her brother the ultimate challenge.

The music in the banquet hall was so loud that it sounded like they had a speaker right next to them, and right then that cheesy old song "Celebration" by Kool & the Gang was playing.

"Go inside and stand in the middle of the dance floor and dance to this entire song."

"No way," Josh said. Abby knew that dancing alone was the one thing he would refuse to do.

"Bawk-buh-bawk-bawk!" Abby teased, flapping her arms. "That's right."

"Okay. You know the rules. Five bucks." Abby held out her hand.

"I don't have five bucks on me."

"You can give it to me later, with interest. Ten bucks."

"You've got to be kidding me." Josh headed for the door. "I'll do it."

Shocked, Abby followed Josh inside and into the darkened hall. Josh positioned himself behind a group of frantically shimmying women and stood there bobbing up and down a little. He wasn't cheating; that was Josh's version of cutting a rug. Abby laughed so hard her gut ached.

When the song was over, Josh swaggered toward her triumphantly, and the deejay asked everyone to clear the floor. It was time for Wendy's father to dance with the bride. Abby darted for the door. On her way out she saw that Mom was still sitting at their table talking with Denny. He was leaning toward her slightly and it appeared as if their knees were touching.

Abby tried calling Spence once more. This time he answered.

"Save me," she said.

"I'll hop on my bike right now," Spence replied. "But I don't know how long biking seven hundred fifty-eight miles will take."

"Seven hundred fifty-eight miles?"

"I MapQuested it."

A rush of warmth spread through Abby's body, and she remembered why, whenever life sucked, Spence was her lifeline.

They talked a while, about nothing, really, until a beep on the cell phone warned Abby that Mom's battery was just about cooked.

"I've gotta go," she said.

"Okay." Spence sounded as disappointed as she felt.

"Hey, Spence?"

"What?"

"I . . . I miss you."

She was relieved when the phone suddenly went dead. This was uncharted territory. Abby didn't know what had come over her. Or maybe she did.

Inside the reception hall, Mom was still engrossed in conversation with Denny. Josh and Abby lined up for cake, and by the time they made it back to the table Mom and Denny were out on the dance floor. They weren't dancing cheek to cheek; their bodies barely touched and they faced each other, talking and laughing as they swayed from side to side. Mom would have danced with Grandpa the same way but, still, seeing her mother dance with a someone other than Dad made Abby feel strange. Was it anger? Jealousy? Fear? Whatever it was left a bruise on her heart.

They finally left at ten o'clock. Mom and Denny enjoyed a long hug good-bye, and Denny promised that he'd call the next time he was in Detroit. Mom said that she'd like that. On the way back to the hotel she turned on the radio and sang along and didn't stop smiling for most of the ride.

"So who is this Denny guy, anyway?" Abby asked Mom as she pulled into the parking lot.

"He's just an old friend," Mom said, finding a spot near the front entrance. "An old boyfriend, actually. My high school sweetheart."

Mom? With a boyfriend? Abby couldn't imagine it.

"So, do you think he still likes you?"

She laughed and yanked the gearshift into park. "Like I said, we're friends. We're much different people than we were back in high school. Things change."

Her smile faded. She pulled the key from the ignition and looked down at her hands, caressing the wedding ring she still wore on her finger.

"Things change."

TWENTY-THREE

June, Continued

Denny called the following Friday. Mom sat at the kitchen table after work, talking and giggling during their hour-long conversation. Though Abby pretended not to be listening, she managed to hear enough to reassure her that nothing was really going on. After a while she allowed Mom the privacy she deserved and ran down to the Point for a swim. Mom was still on the phone when she got back, and when she finally hung up she told Abby that Denny would be in town in a few days and that they had made dinner plans.

"You're going on a date?" Abby asked as she dried her hair.

"No, not really." Mom looked through the fridge for something to prepare for dinner. "We're just a couple of old friends going out to catch up with each other."

"I thought you did that at the wedding. You talked to him almost the whole night."

"That was a couple of hours, Abby." Mom pulled a half-eaten ham out of the fridge and started slicing it for sandwiches. "It's been almost thirty years since we last saw each other. A couple of hours is hardly enough time to fill each other in."

Abby had to give her the benefit of the doubt. Maybe at one time Mom had had romantic feelings for someone other than Dad, but that was before she realized that he was the love of her life. You don't get to have that twice. Mom wasn't stupid; she had to know that. Therefore Abby didn't raise a fuss when Mom went out with Denny the following Wednesday evening.

It was weird, watching her mother get ready. Mom came home early from work and took a shower, even though she'd showered in the morning. She took more time than usual with her makeup and hair, making sure every curl was in just the right place. Abby went into the bedroom as her mother decided what to wear. She laid several outfits on the bed and sighed.

"I need some new clothes."

"What's wrong with this?" Abby asked, picking up one of her work suits by its hanger.

"Too businessy."

"How 'bout this?" She pointed to the pale-peach dress Mom had worn to the wedding, fresh back from the dry cleaner.

"Too dressy. And besides, Denny saw me wear that the other night." She paused and added, "Oh my Lord, I sound like you."

Abby tried not to be offended.

Finally Mom settled on a silk blouse and gray skirt that she sometimes wore to work.

Denny came by at six thirty. He greeted Josh and Abby and gave Mom a peck on the cheek. Abby cringed. Mom handed Josh a twenty for pizza delivery, and made a show of forbidding them from leaving or having friends over while she was gone. Abby watched from the doorway as Denny opened the passenger door and helped Mom inside. He turned to Abby and nodded with a smile. He waited for a smile in return—but didn't get one—before climbing into his car and pulling out of the driveway.

When the pizza came, Josh inhaled six slices while playing Xbox, and Abby nibbled while she read an article in *Seventeen* about troublesome facial hair. Electrolysis, lasers, waxing, shaving, creams . . . if only getting rid of Denny would be so easy.

"What?" Josh said as he played.

"Did I say something?"

"Something about getting rid of Denny." Josh stood and turned off the Xbox. He plucked the pizza box off the floor and wandered into the kitchen. "What's the problem? He seems like a nice enough guy."

Josh unwrapped a bag of popcorn and stuck it into the microwave.

"Don't you find it a little weird?" She reached into the cupboard for the popcorn bowl, then remembered what Dad had used it for—of course her mother had tossed it. Instead, she pulled out the biggest Tupperware container she could find and set it on the counter.

"Do I find what weird?" Now Josh was shoving a handful of M&M's into his mouth. The way he ate, he should have been a pudge.

"Mom having dinner with Denny."

"Dinner? No. People do it all the time." Josh gave Abby a once-over. "Normal people."

"You know what I mean, Josh. Think about it—"

"No. Don't think about it."

They agreed to watch a movie and played Rock-Paper-Scissors to decide who got to pick the DVD. Josh won three out of four, so Abby was stuck watching a stupid shoot-'em-up action flick. An hour into the movie, Josh fell asleep on the couch, but Abby didn't turn it off, trying to keep her mind occupied and her eyes off the clock. She wanted to stop wondering when Mom would make it home, and what Dad would think if he knew where she was.

While the ending credits rolled, she phoned Spence. "Hey, you."

"Hey yourself. Is your mom home yet?"

Abby shook her head, as if he could see. "What about yours? She around?"

Spence laughed. "Silly question. Of course she's not. She's out with Andreas. . . . He's the spice of the night. The Maltese Falcon."

"Is he a nice guy?"

Spence chuckled. "He brought me a Snickers, so I have to like him."

Abby wandered into the kitchen. "Seriously," she said, pacing slowly, "doesn't it bother you when your mom brings one guy after another into your life?"

"Only when she brings them home."

Abby halted abruptly. "You mean when they sleep there?"

"They're not sleeping." Spence quickly turned the tables. "Abby, if you're worried about your mom and this guy—"

"I'm not, really. I'm just not used to my mom going out with strange men."

Spence sighed. "I know. But you said they're just old friends, right?"

Abby leaned her forehead against the fridge. "He used to be her boyfriend."

"Used to be. She didn't marry him, right?"

"Right."

"So don't worry about it. Hey, I used to be head over heels in love with Heather Freeman when we were in kindergarten, and I'm not anymore. But we're friends."

Abby stood up straight. "Heather Freeman? The one with all the piercings and snake tattoos?"

"Yep. I used to follow her around school, and my heart was broken when she moved away during first grade to live with her dad in Indianapolis. When she came back our freshman year I didn't even recognize her."

"She looks like Marilyn Manson."

"I know! Not exactly my type, but we had biology and art together last year, and you know what? She's pretty cool. Actually a fun person to hang around with."

"Point taken."

There was a flash of light against the kitchen wall. Abby checked and saw headlights in the driveway.

"She's back. I'll talk to you tomorrow," Abby said quickly, hanging up.

Spy time. Abby crawled to the couch and peeked over the back to see through the picture window. Denny's Lincoln idled in the driveway, but Mom didn't get out for a while.

Finally Denny did, and went over to the passenger side to help her out. As he walked her to the door, Abby slid along the wall to the corner of the room where they wouldn't see her. They talked for another few minutes, though too quietly for Abby to hear.

The headlights ran across the living room wall and slowly disappeared as Mom stumbled inside. She literally tripped, nearly falling into the piano, and giggled.

"Whooops!"

"Hi, Mom," Abby said, sliding onto the couch next to Josh.

"Oh, hi there." Her mother wore a goofy grin. "How was your night?"

"Fine. How was yours?"

Mom's eyes lit up. Then she sighed. "Oh, not bad." She started toward the kitchen, but managed to catch her foot on the piano bench. As she caught herself, she exploded in laughter. Josh awoke with a start.

"Mom?" he said groggily, rubbing his eyes. "Have you been drinking?"

She held her hand up, her thumb and index fingers just centimeters apart. "Maybe just a wee bit. Just one glass of wine."

"You're kind of fun when you're sloshed!"

She snapped her fingers and did a few mini-Rockette kicks while singing the theme song from *Sesame Street*. Josh and Abby roared.

Mom theatrically sang and danced her way up the stairs. "Good ni-ight," she called before swaggering down the hall into her bedroom.

Josh and Abby couldn't stop laughing. Seeing her so happy was wonderful—but Abby's stomach hurt, and it wasn't from laughing.

THE NEXT MORNING MOM DIDN'T COME OUT OF HER ROOM. At ten thirty, four hours after Mom usually got out of bed, Abby went upstairs and knocked on the bedroom door. "Mom? Are you in there?"

"Mm-hmm."

"Can I come in?"

"Mm-hmm." Abby opened the door to find her mother still in her pajamas, sitting on the edge of her bed and staring out the window.

"Mom? Are you okay?" Mom shook her head. "Did something happen last night?" If Denny had so much as said an unkind word, Abby would let him have it.

"No." Her voice was barely a whisper. "Last night was wonderful."

"Then what's wrong? Why do you look so sad?"

"Because last night was wonderful." Mom started to cry softly.

Abby took a deep breath and counted to three. The first

words that popped into her head weren't exactly pleasant. "It really was a date, wasn't it?"

Mom nodded, still looking out the window. "Yes, I guess you could say that—but I don't want you to think that I lied to you. I was only fooling myself. Denny was a great guy at eighteen—but he's an amazing man now."

Her mother had actually gone out on a real date. Abby couldn't believe it. It was too soon.

"You broke up with him once, though, right? You must have had a reason."

Mom shook her head slowly. "During our senior year of high school his family moved to Nebraska, and he wound up going to college there. We were too young to handle a long-distance relationship. It was just too hard to stay connected."

Did you love him as much as you loved Dad? Abby wanted to ask, but she was scared to hear the answer.

"So . . . are you going to go out with him again?"

"No."

Phew. What a relief.

"Part of me wants to see him again, but most of me doesn't."

"I don't get it."

"You wouldn't understand," Mom said, her voice rising

and falling like a bird struggling with a broken wing. "You couldn't possibly. I love your dad and won't ever stop loving him. I know he's gone, but he's still . . . around me all the time. When I wake up, I expect to hear him singing in the shower. When I'm at work, I find myself waiting for him to call me during his lunch hour, just to say hello. When I come home and see his car in the driveway I imagine that he'll greet me at the door with a smile and a kiss. He's everywhere in this house, yet he isn't. He is all around me but I can't be with him." She took a deep breath and looked at Abby. "You have to understand—it's killing me."

"This might surprise you," Abby said after a long silence, "but I guess I do understand, kind of."

"I thought that maybe spending an evening with Denny would make me feel human again," Mom went on, "and it did. Temporarily. Now I just feel like a monster. How could I have—? How. Could. I?"

Abby wished she could find the right words to make her mother feel better, but she was at a loss. She was shamefully glad Mom felt like she did. "I don't know what to say."

"There's nothing you can say. I have to figure this out for myself."

Denny called that evening, and the next day, and the next, but Mom wouldn't talk to him. She made Josh or Abby answer the phone, all the while shaking her head and mouthing, "I'm not home." When Abby made excuses for her mother, Denny sounded sad, and his voice grew sadder every time he called. Abby almost felt sorry for him.

Almost.

TWENTY-FOUR

June 28

June twenty-eighth was the first anniversary
of Dad's death. Just another day on the calendar, Abby told
herself.

But she was sick that morning. She couldn't get out of bed.
Her mind drifted in and out, and she probably would have
slept all day if her stomach hadn't hurt so much. Last semes-
ter they'd studied internal organs in anatomy and physiology
class, and now she tried to remember where her appendix
was. She was sure that something had ruptured.

Mom was at work, and Josh was over at Billy's. Abby
couldn't drag herself out of bed to get to the phone, and she
was positive that without immediate medical attention she
would lie there, helpless and alone, and die.

At noon there was a knock on her bedroom door. She
hoped it was her mother, rushing home from work because

she had sensed that something was very, very wrong. She'd call an ambulance and save Abby's life. Then June twenty-eighth wouldn't be tragic; instead, it would be the day that Abby North was snatched from the jaws of death. It would be a day of triumph.

"Are you becoming a vampire or something?" Spence called out cheerfully. "Rise and shine, Sleeping Beauty."

So it wasn't Mom. It was much, much worse. Miraculously Abby found the strength to cover her face with her hands. Spence hadn't seen her without makeup in eons.

"What's the matter?" he asked as he came in.

Abby rolled over to face the wall.

"Nothing. I'm just not feeling well. You'd better leave before you catch something." Forget impending death. What about her unmasked zits and bed head?

"No one feels good if they stay in bed all day." Spence shook her shoulder. "Come on, get up. I biked into town and picked up breakfast from Mickey D's."

Spence knew that a sure way to win Abby's heart was a sausage biscuit and a hash brown patty, but even that didn't sound appetizing.

"Thanks," Abby mumbled. "But I'm not hungry."

"You need to eat something. You're getting too skinny."

"I can't eat, Spence, really. I'll throw up."

"I brought you something else." Abby's heart skipped a

beat. She looked up at Spence, and he cocked his head, staring at her oddly.

"What?" Abby said, covering her face again. She'd been right. Spence would see the real Abby and flee.

"You look good without all that crap around your eyes. You're so pretty."

Abby smiled and let her hand drift away from her face. The wings of dozens of tiny butterflies tickled the pain in her stomach away.

"Now come on, woman!" Spence said, pulling Abby by the hand. "Get your butt out of bed and come see what I brought you."

Abby let him help her out of bed and lead her downstairs into the kitchen. Two vases filled with roses, a half dozen in each, sat on the kitchen table.

"For me?" Abby gasped.

Spence grinned and nodded.

"But why two?" Abby asked, letting her fingers brush the soft rose petals.

"One is for your mom. I know it won't help much, but I thought that you could both use some flowers today."

Abby wrapped her arms around him and took a deep breath, inhaling his scent, filling her entire being with Spence.

"Thank you," she whispered in his ear.

"You're welcome," he said. Their cheeks brushed as they pulled away from each other and they stopped, their faces inches apart. Spence was the first to look away.

"Do you, um, have plans today?"

"Not really, except going to the cemetery with my mom after she gets off work."

Spence ran his fingers through his hair. She'd never seen him look so nervous. "Do you . . . *want* to have plans today?"

Abby smiled. "I'd love to."

Spence finally let his eyes meet hers again. "Okay, then. Go grab your bathing suit and let's get out of here."

They took the paddleboat out to Youth Island. Spence had thought of everything. He brought along a Styrofoam cooler packed with his homemade trail mix (Bugles, pretzels, and peanut M&M's) and cans of Coke, arranging it all on a blanket on a grassy spot near the steps of what had once been a building.

Decades earlier, Youth Island had been a church camp with a lodge and several cabins. Legend had it that a bonfire had gone astray and caught the lodge on fire, and the fire had spread to all the cabins, burning them down with the campers still inside. For most of her life Abby had avoided being there after dark; she'd heard stories about people spotting the ghosts of children on the island, shrieking and running for safety that did not exist.

Youth Island didn't scare her anymore; she didn't believe in ghosts.

Though she still wasn't hungry, she tasted a bite or two of Spence's concoction and took tiny sips of Coke, which he'd poured into champagne flutes from his parents' wedding. He was trying so hard to brighten her day, but she still didn't feel right. The day was pleasant enough—sunny and warm, without a cloud in the sky—but somehow this made Abby feel as if God were mocking her. *You think this isn't just another day? Well, I'll show you!* If it were raining, or cloudy at least, she'd have known that God was sad, too.

Spence leaned back on the blanket, propped up on one elbow and picked just the M&M's out of the snack mix. He reached into the cooler and tossed a photograph in front of her. She picked it up and studied the picture of the faded bluish-greenish Chevy Cavalier.

"Whaddya think?" he asked. "Classy ride, huh?"

"You're getting this car for your birthday?" Abby asked excitedly. Mrs. Harrison had enrolled Spence in school late, so he was an entire year older than Abby. He'd turn sixteen in just a few days.

Spence spat out a laugh. "Are you kidding? I'll be lucky if my mom even remembers my birthday." He sat up straight and looked over Abby's shoulder at the photo of the car, beaming. "I'm buying it myself. All these years of being Handyboy weren't for my health. Not only have I been able to foot the bill for hockey, I've saved up enough to buy a car."

She took his hand and gave it a squeeze. "That's awesome, Spence. Really."

"So I'll be able to drive you to school in the fall, instead of Josh."

Abby snorted. "Right. Like my mom will allow that."

"Why wouldn't she? She trusts me, I think."

She didn't know how to explain her mother's fear of catastrophe. You'd think Mom would feel better having her kids in two different cars—that way if one were to get creamed in a crash, she'd still have one kid left. But then she'd still have someone left to live for, and maybe it was the living that scared her more than anything.

"I'm excited for you." *Excited* wasn't exactly the word. Spence's being able to drive was just another indication that life was changing way too fast.

She closed her eyes and let the sun warm her face, imagining she was a little girl again, napping on a blanket at the Point while Mom sat beside her, rubbing her back and reading a book, and Dad splashed in the water with Josh, trying to get him to take off his water wings. Her mom had once told her about a book she read that claimed that the entire universe is made up in our minds. Abby wondered whether if she concentrated hard enough she could go back in time.

"So how are you feeling today?" Spence asked, interrupting her meditation.

"Hot," Abby said, opening her eyes and fanning herself with her hands.

He smacked her arm. "You know what I mean."

"And hungry," she lied, sitting up to grab a handful of trail mix and shovel it into her mouth. She chewed it slowly, fighting the gag reflex when she swallowed. Today, no food was good food. She chased it with a large gulp of Coke and swore she could feel the carbonation attacking the starch in her stomach. She shoved the Tupperware container away and felt a gigantic burp working its way up her esophagus. There was a time when she would have just let a belch fly in front of Spence, but now she turned away from him and let the air out in a puff, deflating quietly.

"You can talk about it, you know," Spence said to her back.

"Talk about what?" Abby wanted no part of contributing to her own misery. When she turned back toward Spence he was on his feet, slipping his shirt over his head. "I don't feel like swimming," she said, shielding her eyes from the sun with her forearm.

"You will after you swing," Spence said, grinning.

"Uh-uh." She sat up and shook her head. "No way." She hadn't braved Youth Island's hilltop rope swing since she was about nine. Back then she'd thought nothing of entrusting her life to a thirty-foot length of rope and a tree branch that had withstood fire and years of abuse, letting the rope carry her over land and water and having blind faith that when she let go she'd fall safely into the waves. The first time she'd tried, she'd made the leap and held on all right, but had released the rope a little too early, landing on her knees in the still-too-shallow water and skinning them up something awful on the sand and rocks. It had been her first lesson in human fragility.

Spence shrugged. "Suit yourself."

He sprinted toward the north end of the island. She noticed that he even ran differently now, his stride longer and his arms swinging out to the sides to leave room for his expanding chest and thickening biceps. She found herself rising and hurrying after this intriguing stranger.

He was already halfway down the steep hill, grasping the knotted end of the thick rope that hung from the tallest, thickest tree in Highland. When he got back to the top of the hill, Abby ran her hand along the rope's rough surface.

"This has to be older than we are."

"Probably older than our parents, too," Spence concurred.

"And you think it's safe?"

Grinning madly, Spence walked backward, pulling the rope back as far as it would go.

"I guess we'll find out!" He grabbed the rope up high and

ran full tilt toward the steep part of the hill. And then he jumped, wrapping his legs around the rope and bellowing out a Tarzan yell as he swung out beyond the hill and over the water. When the rope had gone as far as it could, he let go and sailed downward, hitting the deep water with an enormous cannonball splash.

Abby got ready to catch the rope when it swung back, keeping her eyes trained on the water the whole time to make sure Spence came back up for air. He did, crowing like Peter Pan.

"You're crazy!" she yelled down at him.

"You're a wuss!"

"Girls can't be wusses!"

"Then you're just a 'fraidy cat!"

"What are you, six?"

"Just jump!"

Abby didn't think twice. She didn't even think once. Before she knew what she'd done, her feet had left the ground and she was hurtling forward through the air. She'd thought it would be hard to hold on to the rope, but actually she felt completely weightless, and her mind couldn't focus on anything but her own fear. She wondered if that's what it felt like to leave your body.

"Let go!" Spence hollered, and she did, free-falling until she was at once submerged in the cold water, deep enough that she didn't even touch bottom before bobbing back up to the surface. From underneath the water she could hear him cheering. When she finally came up, he pulled her a little closer to shore to where he could stand and slid one slippery arm underneath her legs and the other underneath her arms. He cradled her. Abby's fears had completely vanished.

"You did it!" Spence said, his face so close to Abby's that she could see her own drenched reflection in his blue eyes. Her entire body shook—maybe from the adrenaline rush. Or maybe because there was nothing left between her and Spence but a soaking wet tank top, shorts, and skin.

"You're freezing." He carried her until she could touch bottom, then took her by the hand and led her ashore.

"I forgot to take my clothes off," Abby said through chattering teeth, slipping out of her shorts and top and hanging them over a tree branch. Out of the corner of her eye she caught Spence eyeing her in her bathing suit.

"Yow!" some idiot yelled as he sped by in a red MasterCraft. They looked up to see four guys gaping at her as they passed. Spence started to flip them the bird, but Abby stayed his hand. She was less concerned with being treated like a piece of meat than she was with the pontoon boat that was anchored a few hundred feet ahead, in the path of the MasterCraft. She pointed wildly at the pontoon.

"Look, you morons!" she screamed. The guys waved. The

man and woman in the pontoon wrestled with the anchor, trying to pull it up before they got hammered.

"Look!" she yelled again. Maybe the driver thought she was calling him to come back and pick her up for a ride or something, for he turned the wheel so that the boat veered away from the pontoon. He must have noticed his close call at the last minute; he went back to the irate pontoon passengers, probably to apologize. Abby was the last thing on his mind.

In unison, Spence and Abby exhaled the breath they'd been holding.

She couldn't remember a ton from when she was a little kid, but one thing that stuck in her mind was the time Dad had taken Abby and Spence and Josh fishing and they'd almost been struck by a speedboat. Dad had stood in their rowboat and screamed wildly, waving an oar in the air to try to get the speedboat driver's attention as Abby and the boys were ready to jump out and swim to safety. The language spilling out of her father's mouth had been completely foreign. He was like a man possessed, scared out of his mind.

Spence turned to her. "Do you remember the time we went fishing with your dad—"

Abby stopped his sentence with her own mouth, pressed against his. For a moment, Spence froze, but then he melted into Abby. They grasped each other's hands and held them between their bodies, making a bridge between their hearts.

The whole rest of the world faded away.

Stay away from boys, she heard her father say from somewhere inside her head.

And she backed away from Spence and released his hands, feeling as if she had done something wrong. He looked stunned and bewildered. She wrapped her arms around his neck and held tight in apology.

Sometimes having a guardian angel isn't all it's cracked up to be.

"I'd better get home." Abby unwound herself from Spence, and turned to pull her clothes off the tree branch. "When my mom gets home from work she'll want to go to the cemetery. I need to go with her."

"I'll go, too," Spence said, following her up the hill.

"No." She quickened her pace.

He didn't let on whether it bothered him that Abby wouldn't let him into the part of her heart where she kept Dad. She couldn't. He wouldn't understand that when she tried to think about her father she still saw his body lying in a coffin, or that he was still alive, but barely. He would think her heartless for roaming aimlessly around the cemetery while Mom tearfully spoke to Dad's headstone. He'd think she was nuts for still making believe that an empty coffin was buried underneath the ground.

Wordlessly the two of them packed up their things, loaded them into the boat, and paddled toward home.

They docked the boat at the Stovers' and walked up Abby's backyard hill, to the door on the backside of the garage. She didn't invite him inside; her mother wouldn't want anyone around besides Josh and Abby. She didn't need to feel awkward about expressing her grief today; today, she was allowed.

Abby gave Spence a quick kiss on the cheek. Really quick, in case Josh was lurking. What would he think? Would he be mad at Spence for changing the rules of their longtime friendship, or would he wonder what the heck had taken him so long?

"Thanks for coming to my rescue today," she said, holding his hands in hers.

"No," Spence said. "Thank *you*." He shifted from one foot to the other, staring at the ground. "I wanted to be with you today because, you know, I thought you might need someone. And if you needed someone, I wanted you to need me. I guess that's kind of selfish."

"Spence, I'm the selfish one. You're always there for me, and I never give anything back."

Spence grinned. "Today you gave me all I've wanted."

Abby could feel herself blushing. "My mom should be home any minute."

"Okay, I'll go. See you tomorrow?"

Abby nodded. *And the next day, and the next, and the next.*

She watched him descend the hill, his wet towel flung over his shoulder, his cooler underneath one arm. He turned around and smiled, letting her know she was forgiven for sending him away.

But she had a hard time forgiving herself. Her mother had surely felt dismal and lonely all day—and Abby had let Spence take her away and cheer her up. She wasn't supposed to have had a day that was so normal.

It was more than normal. It had been amazing.

Mom was a mess. Her colleague Bob had driven her home and walked her to the front door with his arm around her shoulders. She came inside, blowing her nose into a soggy tissue. "Your mom was in no condition to drive," he explained to Abby. "I'm sure you're not having such a great day, either. I'm sorry."

She nodded but didn't reply. An awkward silence filled the room.

"Your mom's car is in the parking lot at work," Bob said, finally. "I'll pick her up in the morning and drive her in."

"Okay," Abby said, feeling as if she was giving him permission.

Bob turned to Mom. "Helen, seeing that Abby's here, I think I'll take off. Unless you need me to stay . . ."

"No," Mom said. "You go on home. I'll be all right. Thanks for being so good to me today." She gave him a hug, then wiped tears from her eyes. "I'm so embarrassed."

"Don't be so hard on yourself." He patted her gently on the shoulder. "I can't imagine going through what you are. I don't know what I'd do if I lost Sandy."

"You won't, not for a long, long time." She walked him to the door. "Say hello to her for me."

Bob nodded a good-bye to Abby as he left. She looked over at her mother. Though she didn't make a sound, her shoulders shook. She was crying again. Abby touched her shoulder and Mom flinched. Only slightly—but still, she'd flinched.

"Mom?" she said softly. "Do you want to take a walk or something?"

Her mother took a moment to reply. "No. I'm not up to it today."

"Are we going to the cemetery?"

"I went on my lunch hour." She started crying. When Abby tried to hug her, Mom hugged back weakly and pulled away.

She'd never done that before.

"Do you want to talk?" Abby asked.

"No, thank you. I saw Dr. Robby this morning, and I'm all talked out." Her mother went upstairs to her bedroom without saying another word. Abby sat down on the couch, bewildered.

Had she worked so hard at pushing her mother away that she'd actually succeeded?

"Where's Mom?" Josh asked as he came in. Abby pointed upstairs, and he went to check. He came back within minutes, shaking his head. So it wasn't just her. Mom didn't want Josh, either.

It felt strange not to visit her father at the cemetery that day, and Abby considered asking Josh to drive them there. But she couldn't leave Mom alone.

With MTV blaring in the background, Abby flipped through *People* magazine; Josh scanned *Sports Illustrated*. The remote control was MIA, so every now and then he'd get up and turn up the volume. Then he'd do it again. And again, until she was sure that one of the neighbors was likely to come over and tell them to knock it off. Mom never came downstairs, though.

Perhaps she was grateful that he'd filled the silence, too.

At eleven, Abby announced that she was going to bed. Josh wasn't ready to give in yet. She wondered if he'd stay up all night, upping the television volume to deafening levels for companionship.

Abby went upstairs and, finding light shining through the crack in Mom's doorway, peeked in to say good night. Mom was fast asleep with a book splayed open on the mattress beside her.

Life After Harry: My Adventures in Widowhood, by Virginia Graham.

Abby pictured Mom in black spandex, a bold capital W emblazoned upon her chest, flying through the air with her black cape streaming in the wind behind her, slaying the demons that haunted her day and night, ultimately defeating the Sorrow Monster.

Yeah, right.

Picking up the book and opening to the first page, Abby saw a message in Grandpa's unmistakable handwriting.

My dear Helen. Time to get on with it. All my love, Dad.

Abby put the book on the nightstand, but then thought better of it and tossed it underneath the bed. She figured Mom wouldn't finish it anyway, assuming it was about letting go of the past and forging on toward a new, bright future. She knew her mother could do neither. Denny was proof. He'd called several times now since their dinner, asking Mom to go out with him again, but she'd always made up a reason why she couldn't. She didn't need Grandpa Warner's help in "getting on with it." What she needed was time. It had only been a year.

A year. Abby still couldn't believe she hadn't seen her dad in a whole year. She'd changed so much since then. Would he still recognize her?

After she'd brushed her teeth and washed her face and put on her pj's, Abby crawled into bed and tried her darnedest to go to sleep. It didn't work; her stomach was hurting again, like someone had wedged a fist in her abdomen. Thinking of her kiss with Spence didn't help. It just made her feel more alone and, worse, like she'd done something wrong. Maybe Dad, wherever he was, knew that Spence was the only person who kept the shadow at bay. If he was around, maybe he'd tell Abby that her feelings were okay. But Dad wasn't around. Still. She had no way to ask his permission.

It wasn't a fist in her gut, but a hook, twisting and turning.

Warm milk. Mom had always given Abby warm milk to help her sleep when she was little. It worked back then to cure her nightmares; it might settle her stomach, too. Midway down the stairs, she heard a strange sound coming from the living room. Actually, it was almost an absence of sound— Josh had turned off the TV, but there was something else.

Tiptoeing the rest of the way down the stairs, she stood near the bottom step and peeked around the wall. Josh was still on the couch, hugging his knees to his chest and rocking back and forth, sobbing.

She backtracked up the stairs as quietly as she could. She didn't want Josh to know she'd been there. She'd never seen him cry before; Abby never even knew he cried. He'd been waiting for her to leave so that he could grieve in private.

Seeing Josh crack was frightening.

Why couldn't she cry? If she could, maybe her stomach pain would go away. The emotions bottled up inside her were eating her alive. Her inability to grieve was cancerous.

Back in bed, she forced her thoughts into forbidden territory. She visited the world of cancer, she toured death and the funeral home and the burial, she voyaged through the "year after" and "years to come," dwelling upon the things Dad had missed out on and the events he was yet to miss. Her journey took place in the shadow; the destination was intended to be grief and sadness and, ultimately, tears.

But she was too angry to cry.

Why did God continue to punish her family? They'd done their time in the shadow; they'd had more than their fair share. They were trying to be happy. Why did the shadow still hover over them? Why wouldn't God show them any mercy?

Was it because the Norths weren't regular churchgoers? Because they didn't say grace when they sat down for a meal? Because she didn't say her prayers before bed each night? Because the only thing she could recite with the word *God* in it was the Pledge of Allegiance?

It was obvious. She was a fair-weather friend. She'd only turned to God in times of confusion or trouble, and now He was showing her. But Abby believed in Him! Didn't that matter?

I'm sorry! Okay? Now please—please—*let the sadness go away. Allow us to forget. Let us go on and be happy. If you hear me, give me a sign. . . .*

Abby lay still, looking at the black sky through her bedroom window, waiting for a flash of lightning, a clap of thunder, a shooting star, a bird, a bat, a June bug slamming into the window screen . . . anything. She wasn't picky.

But she saw nothing but blackness.

What about you, Dad? Are you still out there? Can't you see what's happening to us? Would you mind giving me one small sign to show that you care about us, even just a little bit?

Again, nothing.

Rage burned her stomach, swelled into her chest, shot into her limbs and her face until she thought she might explode. Rolling over and burying her face in her pillow, she screamed with all her might. She yelled at God, telling Him what to do with whatever lesson it was He was trying to teach her.

Then Abby screamed at Dad. She knew he hadn't wanted to die, but he sure was a crappy angel. He was supposed to watch over her family and protect them, yet he continued to let Mom be heartbroken and had left Josh and Abby to deal with it alone.

Oh, wonderful. Seemed Dr. Robby was right.

Lifting her face from the pillow, Abby slammed her fist into it. It felt really, really good. So she did it again, and again, with one fist, then the other, then both at once. It felt wonderful. It felt liberating. After a while her stomach felt a little better. Soon she was exhausted, but calm.

Rising from her bed, Abby crossed the hallway into Mom's bedroom and lay down in the bed beside her, in Dad's spot. Abby knew she could sleep there.

At least she still had her mother.

TWENTY-FIVE

July

Deanna and Brad came home for the Fourth of July. Deanna's scowl as she walked through the door around four in the afternoon made it clear that the two of them were on the outs. Brad skulked in after her, muttering a greeting and stewing in front of the TV while Mom and Deanna pored over bridal magazines at the kitchen table.

Brad asked Josh and Abby to go for a swim. As she headed off to suit up, Abby wondered if, now that she was older, she'd be expected to stay behind and help Deanna and Mom grill burgers and boil corn and set up the patio chairs on the back porch and talk mother-daughter stuff. She hurried to the Point before they could ask.

Brad's spirits lifted the moment he hit the lake, and the three of them had a blast playing water tag. It was the first holiday they'd spent together as a family since before Dad died, and for once things seemed quasi-normal. They couldn't feel *normal* normal, but Abby had to settle for almost. Forty-five minutes later Deanna rambled down the hill and announced that dinner was ready.

Brad and Josh fixed two burgers each and piled their plates with corn on the cob, potato salad, and chips. They sat at the picnic table on the back porch and dug in as Abby, Mom, and Deanna made their own plates.

"Mom," Abby said, "you made enough food to feed the whole neighborhood."

Mom looked at Brad and Josh. "I doubt that. Those two will be on to seconds before we've even taken our first bites. Why don't you make a plate for Spence before it all disappears?"

Abby's entire body tingled. It had been six days since her kiss with Spence, and the anticipation about when it would happen again was almost unbearable. They'd seen each other every day since, but they hadn't been alone yet, and Abby wasn't ready to go public with her feelings, even though Mom seemed to know something was up. She smiled knowingly at them as they played Scrabble at the kitchen table, not across the board from each other, but side by side, their legs touching. She hung around the vicinity when Abby talked to Spence on the phone, having conversations that stretched on to almost an hour each night before she went to bed. She continuously made comments about what a great guy he was and how lucky a girl would be to have him for a boyfriend and how she'd always imagined Abby and Spence becoming a couple one day. Abby didn't take the bait, though. She didn't want to jinx anything.

"I'm not sure he's coming," she said, which was true. Spence was helping one of his mother's friends put new vinyl siding on his house. He'd promised to make it to the Point for fireworks, but wasn't sure about dinner.

She left a seat beside her at the table for him, though, just in case.

Everyone ate, except for Mom. She was just pretending. Ten minutes after sitting down on the woven lounge chair, her plate was still full. Finally she set it aside, stood and cleared her throat.

"There's something I want to talk to all of you about." After a long pause and a sigh, she dropped a bomb. "I'm thinking about selling the house."

Abby dropped her fork. Everyone was silent. Even Deanna.

"Why?" Josh asked.

Mom didn't answer right away. She buzzed around with a pitcher of lemonade, refilling everyone's cups, even if they were almost full to begin with. "A lot of reasons, but mainly because this house is just too much for me to keep up by myself."

"What do you mean?" Abby asked, offended. "Josh and I help you out. Josh mows the lawn, runs the sprinklers. . . .

I help out with the weeding and cleaning up inside."

"You do help," Mom said. "But it's more than just the day-to-day stuff, it's the general upkeep of this place. The house is almost thirty years old now, and in the past few years the furnace has had to be rebuilt, the well pump replaced, and the hot water heater fixed. Now the shingles on the roof need to be replaced and the driveway needs to be resurfaced and there's a leak in the basement and that septic tank isn't going to last forever. Do you have any idea how much it costs to put in a new septic field? This house is going to cost me a fortune and, frankly, it's becoming a headache."

"I can do the shingles," Josh said, "and resurface the driveway and fix leaks and stuff. I can learn how to do all that."

"And Brad and I can come home to help now and then," Deanna piped in.

"And me," Abby added, "and Spence."

Mom smiled and shook her head. "I know you're all willing to help, and thank you for offering. But in a couple of years Josh will go away to college, and then Abby, and here I'll be in this house by myself and what for? I don't need a house or a yard this size, and I won't get much use out of the lake. I'd be better off in a little house with a small yard, or in a condo or something."

"A condo?" Abby said too loud. Everyone stared at her as if to tell her to shut her trap.

And then Spence saved the day—as usual.

He came out into the back, all smiles, saying hello to everyone. He brandished his new driver's license and the pictures of the Cavalier—he'd be picking it up tomorrow.

Abby walked past him, through the garage, into the kitchen, and upstairs to change back into her clothes. Once dressed, she stood in the center of the room, staring at nothing in particular until Spence knocked on the door.

"Thanks for brushing me off out there," he said through the closed door.

"Sorry."

"Are you okay?"

She let him in. "Mom wants to sell the house."

Spence stopped dead. "And move where?"

She looked into his eyes and saw the same fear that she felt. "I don't know."

Happy Fourth of July.

CONNIE MONROE ("THE REAL ESTATE PRO") SOON BECAME Mom's best pal and Abby's worst nightmare. She came highly recommended by Mom's friend Charlotte, who had bought and sold three homes with Connie's help in the previous ten years. Mom contacted Connie not to list their house, but to "check out the market."

Connie should have shortened her name to "Con." The

first time she came over, bringing stacks of real estate listings, Abby listened from the bedroom. Connie commis-
erated with Mrs. North about the anguish of losing a
spouse. She was a widow herself. *How convenient,* thought
Abby.

"It's an important step in grieving," said Connie. She went
on to say that while "ambiguous feelings about selling the
home she'd shared with her husband" were normal, it was
imperative that she "make this step to accept her loss and go
forward with her life."

Rolling her eyes, Abby put in her earbuds, turning the volume up on her iPod loud enough that they could have heard
the music downstairs. Abby would have bet all the money in
her savings account that if they drove by Connie Monroe's
house on any given weekend they'd see her "dearly departed"
husband mowing the lawn.

That evening Mom sat at the kitchen table poring over the
listings, separating them into three piles: *Nice, Possible,* and
Ghastly. Before she went to bed, she paper-clipped each pile
and shoved them into a manila envelope. Abby took a look
when she was sure her mother was asleep.

The "Nice" listings were all houses—no condos—and
all of them were in her current school district. On one page
Connie had written down "three bedrooms, at least one and
a half baths, basement, no more than half an acre." Nowhere

did it say that Mom wanted a house on a lake or even one with a pool.

Abby stuffed the listings back into the envelope, figuring that her mother would look at some of these characterless places and realize what a Shangri-la she lived in. How could she not?

But Connie called day and night, wanting to know if Mom had looked over the listings and if she wanted to tour any of the homes, and was she ready to put their house up for sale yet? Mom agreed to look at some of the houses, and asked if Josh and Abby would go with her. Josh said that he would; Abby informed her mother that she had pressing plans to shave her legs and clip her toenails that would keep her much too busy. So off they went—only to get Connie to back off, Abby was sure.

But when they returned, Mom didn't kneel down to kiss the matted carpet or run her hands in awe over the faded kitchen cabinets. She showed no signs of remorse but instead immediately called Connie to further discuss some of the properties.

"So where did you go?" Abby asked Josh, walking uninvited into his bedroom.

"We looked at a few different places, some over near Commerce and a few in Orchard Acres."

"Did Mom see anything she liked?"

"Yeah."

"And?"

"If you're so interested, why didn't you come with us?"

Abby shrugged and left, so Josh wouldn't think she really was interested.

Two days later a red van pulled up in front of the house. Its middle-aged driver erected a FOR SALE sign in the yard with Connie Monroe's name and phone number on it in big, red, capital letters. Abby burst out of the front door as if he was committing murder right before her eyes, and he gave her a curious look.

After he left, Abby dialed Mom's work number with trembling hands. "Mom, can you tell me why there's a 'For Sale' sign in our front yard?"

Mom sighed, but didn't answer.

"Mom," Abby repeated, her voice shaking. "Since when did you decide to sell the house?"

"Honey, I told you on the Fourth—"

"You said you were *thinking* about selling the house! Did you forget to tell me that you'd made up your mind?"

"Abby, you've barely said a word to me since I told you I wanted to move."

"What am I supposed to say, Mom? That you should go ahead and do whatever makes you feel better? What about me? What about Josh? Aren't we supposed to have feelings about this? Don't we have a say in what happens in our own lives?"

"Don't I?" her mother snapped. "For the past year my life has revolved around you, and all you've done is try to push me away. I've spent my entire adult life putting my needs aside for everyone else. Isn't it time I started caring about me?"

"Give me a break. You can care about yourself without turning my life upside down. I'm going out there right now to take that stupid sign down."

"Don't, Abby. If you do, I'll just put it up again."

"And I'll take it down."

Abby slammed the receiver onto its cradle and stormed outside. She grabbed the sign and kicked and tugged on it, grunting and straining until she thought that one of her eyes might pop out of its socket. It was no use. The guy must have planted it in concrete.

When Mrs. Stover came outside to ask what she was doing, a sweating, panting Abby ran inside and into her room, where she paced the floor and slammed her fists against her thighs.

Calm down, Abby. Think rationally. She took a deep breath. A sign in the yard meant nothing. Mom hadn't bought another house, and theirs hadn't sold. There was still plenty of time for Mom to come to her senses. If Abby played her cards right, showing Mom that she was still her ally, she wouldn't feel so hard-pressed to focus on trying to handle things alone. Let Mom have her silly little sign in the yard. When it came time to sign on any dotted lines, Mom would crumble.

Abby had to be sure of that.

TWENTY-SIX

August

By late summer, plenty of prospective buyers had toured the house, but none of them had made an offer. For the time being, fate was on Abby's side, and she hoped that eventually Mom would tire of keeping the house spotless and take it off the market. She just had to be patient.

Abby turned fifteen on the sixth of August. Her last birthday had been just over a month after the funeral, and she'd awoken to find Mom sitting on the bed staring at a photo of her and Dad in the hospital on the day Abby was born. She'd cried when she gave Abby a present Dad had asked her to buy—the Scrabble Deluxe Edition—and when they ate dinner at Emperor's Palace, Abby and Dad's favorite restaurant, and when Abby blew out the candles on her cake and made a wish Mom knew wouldn't come true. That was the day Abby stopped caring about her birthday, and this year she wanted to just forget it.

Mom wouldn't let her. She'd been asking her for a wish list, but Abby hadn't given her one. What she wanted most couldn't be bought. Still, there were three presents on the kitchen table when Abby came downstairs. She didn't immediately dive into them, the way she once would have. Instead she leaned back against the kitchen counter, watching Mom whip up pancakes.

"Happy birthday," Mom said with a smile.

"Thanks." Abby glanced down at the notepad beside the phone. Spence had called. Already. "So where are we going tonight? Emperor's Palace?"

Mom poured the batter onto the griddle, three dollops that ran together so that the first pancake would look like Mickey Mouse. Dad's old trick.

"Where would you like to go?"

Abby shrugged. "Doesn't matter. Can Spence come?"

Smiling, Mom rifled through the utensil drawer until she found the spatula. "You and Spence have been quite inseparable these days."

Abby felt a blush creep up her neck and burn her cheeks. "No different from how we've always been."

Mom smirked. "Right." She carefully flipped Mickey

over and then looked at Abby thoughtfully. "Would you and Spence like to go out alone tonight?"

Pigs were flying outside, and below Abby's feet, hell was freezing over.

"Alone? By ourselves?"

"That's what alone means." Mom chuckled.

"You mean in Spence's car?"

"I guess. As long as he drives carefully and gets you home by curfew."

Before Mom could change her mind, Abby called Spence. He was as excited as Abby was, and told her that he'd pick her up at five and take her out to a nice restaurant. Abby didn't care if he took her to the bowling alley concession stand. What was important was that Mom was putting some slack in Abby's leash.

Abby hung up the phone and watched as her mother piled the pancakes high on a plate, wanting to kiss her for allowing her to go out with Spence, yet puzzled. Why didn't she want to take Abby out for her birthday? Had she made other plans to go out already? Surely there had to be a catch.

"Mom, are you going out on a date tonight or something?"

"No! Why would you ask that?"

"I don't know. I just—you never let me go out with Spence before, and . . . who are you?"

Mom laughed. "Look, it's not like from now on I'm going

to let you and Spence go off together every night, but this is your birthday and you deserve to spend it the way you want to. I trust you, and I trust Spence. I want you two to have fun tonight."

"You trust me?"

"Yes, I do."

When did that happen?

"But . . . don't you want to be with me on my birthday?"

"Of course I do. We'll spend the whole day together. Let's go shopping!"

Where was the thermometer? Abby needed to take her mother's temperature. Mom hated shopping. Her clothes had always been several seasons out of date, and she splurged on new shoes only when the old ones were falling apart. Clothing was simply a physical necessity, and she couldn't comprehend why it mattered that the popular girls at school never wore the same outfit more than once a month. Mom expected Abby to be as frugal as she was.

But not today. Not only did she buy Abby several new outfits, she also picked up a few things for herself. The tops, sweaters, and pants were casual but classy; not anything Abby would have chosen for herself, but still pretty fun. Who would have expected Helen North to be hip?

When they got home, Abby opened gifts. Mom gave her an alarm clock with an iPod connection, a ceramic straightening iron, and a cosmetic case stocked with makeup. Aunt Fran had dropped by earlier in the day and left a gift with Josh—a pink terry robe that might have fit when she was six. Aunt Shirley and Aunt Marlene and Grandpa Warner had all played it safe and sent gift cards. Thoughtful Josh gave her an Xbox game and sweetly tested it out for her while she went upstairs to get ready for dinner.

She wanted to blow Spence away, so she chose the white minidress that Mom had just bought her and paired it with the shoes she had worn to Wendy's wedding. She took her time in front of the mirror, applying her new makeup and using the straightening iron and, ta-da, she was done.

But not quite. She had a few pairs of earrings, but she needed something more to complete her outfit. Mom was downstairs talking on the phone with Grandpa, so Abby went to examine the contents of her mother's jewelry box. She'd look first, and if there was anything she liked, she'd ask permission to borrow something later. It was her birthday, after all; Abby was sure Mom wouldn't mind.

The jewelry box was on top of the bureau, next to a stack of cards from Denny that Mom had left unopened. There were a jumble of necklaces in the bottom drawer, some gold, some pearl, most much too formal. Then she spotted one that looked like tiny Petoskey stones, and decided it would be perfect, if only there was a bracelet to match. After untangling the necklace from its nest, Abby laid it out on a piece of paper next to the jewelry box. She found the matching bracelet in the middle drawer and struggled to put it on. She'd have to ask her mother to help her out.

As she picked up the necklace, her eyes were drawn to the boldfaced heading of the piece of paper it had rested upon:

PURCHASE AGREEMENT

Abby went numb.

When the feeling came back into her body in an explosion of nerves and nausea, she read on.

> The undersigned hereby offers and agrees to purchase, subject to easement and restrictive covenants of record, the following property in the township of Highland, county of Oakland, Michigan, commonly known as 709 Summit Drive together with all . . .

Several pages were paper-clipped to the first. She flipped to the last page and found her mother's signature on the seller line, together with the names of Walt and Jean Corcoran as the buyers, signed August fifth. Yesterday.

She had really done it.

The stairs creaked a warning, and Abby chucked the purchase agreement back on the bureau, turning to find Mom standing in the bedroom doorway.

"What are you doing in here?" Abby was too shaken to answer. "Did you—"

"When were you planning to tell me that you sold our house?" The words were almost a shout, and her mother took a step backward. *"On moving day?"*

Her mother avoided her eyes. "You've been taking the idea of moving so hard, and I didn't want to upset you on your birthday. I thought we'd talk tomorrow."

"Gee, thanks for thinking of me. Hope you didn't hurt yourself. So that's what the big shopping day was all about, huh? You thought that by buttering me up today, tomorrow I'd say, 'Oh, sure Mom, go ahead and do whatever makes you happy'?"

"Abby—"

"So is there anything else you want to tell me? Did you go ahead and buy a house, too?"

"No. Not yet." *Okay, all was not lost. She could back out of a purchase agreement. People did it all the time.* "But," she continued, "I'm going to put an offer on a place in Orchard Acres. You'll like it, Abby; I know you will. It's got bigger bedrooms and walk-in closets and two and a half baths—we won't all have to fight over the shower in the mornings—

and lots of kids from your school live in the neighborhood. You and Josh can just walk down the street to visit with friends."

"We don't need to walk. Josh has his driver's license, remember? And I'll have mine next summer. Don't tell me you're doing this for my benefit."

"Well," Mom said, unconsciously straightening the bedspread and fluffing the pillows, "I do think a change would be good for you. You've been so volatile, so angry—"

"Haven't I been better lately?"

Mom nodded slowly. "You've been acting better, yes. But I want you to *feel* better. I think you're having a hard time coming to terms with—"

"Don't analyze me!" Abby screamed. "*You're* the one who has to go see some half-witted shrink to figure out what to do with your life. If that works for you and Josh, fine. I don't need any help. But have you ever thought that maybe I'd be able to 'come to terms' with things if my world wasn't constantly being turned inside out? This is about you, not me. At least admit *that!*"

The doorbell was barely audible over the screeching white noise in her head. She tore down the stairs. She had to get away from Mom, fast. As Spence stepped inside, Abby grabbed her shoes and darted past him, running barefoot into the driveway and settling into the ripped cloth of the

Cavalier's passenger seat before he'd even turned around.

Spence stood on the front porch, visibly perplexed. Mom stood beside him, sporting a deer-in-the-headlights expression—and a camera. She couldn't be serious.

Abby was not about to pose for her; Mom had betrayed her. And Josh. And Dad. She'd betrayed all of them.

"Let's go!" Abby called. Poor Spence was stuck, disregarded in the heat of battle. He chatted with her mother—probably apologizing for Abby's behavior—before getting into the Cavalier's driver's seat.

"Great," he grumbled as he slammed the car door. "The first night your mom lets us go out together and we leave her in tears."

"Big whoop," Abby said, looking out the windshield at her mother. She stood on the front porch, her mouth in a straight line, wiping her cheek with the back of her hand. Abby turned away, considering herself off the hook; she would never, ever pity her mother again.

"Can we just go now? Please?"

Spence started the engine and backed out of the driveway.

"What happened?" he asked as the Cavalier jiggled and squeaked down the gravel road.

"Nothing." Abby didn't want to talk about it; she didn't want to think about it.

"Abby, you can tell me—"

"I said, nothing!"

The muscles in Spence's jaw tightened as he sped down Duck Lake Road toward M-59, taking out his frustration on the stick shift, jerking it into gear.

"Spence, slow down!" He did.

"Your wish is my command," he said stiffly.

"Why are you being like that?" she asked.

"Being like what?"

"Whatever. Forget it."

Abby crossed her arms and stewed. When they stopped at the main intersection in town, the car beside them honked its horn. She glanced over to see Leise in the driver's seat of her dad's van, waving madly. She'd just gotten her learner's permit, and her dad looked almost as excited as she did.

Abby's dad's face popped into her head as she recalled his fuzzy disappointment at not being able to drive with Josh. For a moment Abby imagined Dad taking her out for her first driving experience, but she pushed the thought from her mind. She waved back at Leise, hoping her smile didn't look too bitter.

With the windows up, Abby couldn't hear what Leise was saying, but she could read her lips. "Happy birthday."

Hunh. If she only knew. Abby would call her tomorrow. Or, on second thought, maybe she wouldn't. Leise would fail to see any downside to moving. She'd home in on the positives—more bathrooms, bigger closets—that's the stuff that would matter to Leise.

Mr. Spangler tapped Leise on the shoulder and pointed at the green light ahead. She hit the gas, and the car lurched forward. As they drove away, Abby could see him shaking his head. Abby so envied Leise that at that moment she despised her.

Spence was driving toward Waterford at turtle speed. She began to tap her foot. "It's six o'clock. If we don't get to a restaurant soon we'll have to wait for hours."

"We'll be fine."

Abby bit her tongue. She was angry at Spence, but had no idea why. She was mad at Mom, she was mad at Dad, she was mad at everyone and everything. It was a nameless, blameless fury, and it terrified her. She knew she should ask Spence to leave her alone for a while, so she could sort things through in her head, but where would she go? Home? Home wasn't home anymore.

They drove in silence to Andre's, a semi-classy restaurant in Waterford, just two doors down from the funeral home. She could see it when they pulled in: the double doors through which the pallbearers carried the coffin, the parking lot where she had lost her mind. It seemed like such a long time ago; it seemed like yesterday. So much had happened since then, and Dad had missed all of it. He'd miss everything from now on—he wouldn't know where his family lived.

She couldn't tear her eyes away, but Spence didn't notice. After killing the engine he reached into his pocket and tossed a tiny black velvet box onto Abby's lap.

"Here's your birthday present," he said dully.

Abby stopped breathing and she stared at the box in her lap—a jewelry box. With unsteady hands she flipped open the box and found a gold heart locket. She lifted it out and opened it.

Spence had placed a tiny photo of Dad inside. Abby knew that photo. Mom had taken it at Cedar Point when Abby was eight, right after Dad had taken her on her first roller-coaster ride. His hair was standing on end, and he looked deliriously happy.

"You went with us on that trip," she said. "Why weren't you in the picture?"

"Because Josh and I were already back in the line."

Abby nodded and tried to smile.

"Thanks," she said, closing the locket and placing it back in the box.

"I'm sorry I didn't buy you something better," Spence said, staring at his lap. "I just thought . . ."

"No," Abby said lifelessly. "It's not that. I love it." She took the locket out and fastened the chain around her neck.

There was a silence. Then he sighed. "Look, do you want me to take you home?"

Abby's heart froze and a lump formed in her throat.

Oh, God, I did it. I pushed him away, too.

"No," she croaked. "Please."

Spence spun in his seat so that he faced her. "Then tell me what's wrong. You've been all over my case and I don't know why. You won't tell me what's going on at home and I just . . . I thought things between us were, you know . . . forget it."

This was all wrong. This was supposed to be a wonderful night. She wanted to apologize, but the lump in her throat made talking impossible. A single tear rolled down her cheek. It was such a foreign sensation that she had to touch the tear to be sure it was real.

"Abby?" Spence said, laying a hand on her forearm. She closed her eyes, ashamed at her tears. Why hadn't she been able to cry when she'd wanted to? When she was supposed to? "Oh, Abby, I'm sorry. Why won't you talk to me?"

"It's not you," she managed. And then she broke down.

Through hiccupping tears, she told him about Mom selling the house. Saying it out loud made her bawl even harder; it was still inconceivable to her that someone else would be living in her home, Dad's home. Mom was trying to get rid of all their memories. Hadn't he been the love of her life? How could she do this to him?

Spence leaned over to put his arms around her. She lay her head on his shoulder and held the locket, keeping Dad in the palm of her hand.

"Where will you be moving?" he asked.

"Orchard Acres."

She felt him relax. "That's just across town. You won't have to change schools; we'll still be able to see each other—"

"But she sold my house!"

Abby broke down completely then. She pulled away and buried her face in her hands, sobbing. He tried his best to console her, but no matter what he said—moving into a new house wouldn't be so bad; her mother wasn't doing it to hurt her; the more they saved on the house, the more Abby would have for college—nothing worked.

And no matter what she told herself—her father was watching over them; he was a guardian angel; he didn't deserve to lose his home—the truth kept coming through.

Dad was dead. Dead people don't have homes. If he were a ghost, he could float through walls and transcend time and place. He wasn't, so he couldn't. Dad was dead. Dead people don't feel happiness, or sadness. Dead people don't feel anything. Mom could do whatever she wanted; Dad—Samuel Lee North, Sam North, Mr. North, husband of Helen, father of Joshua and Abigail—was never, ever coming back.

Abby swallowed an anguished scream, and sobbed without sound. Spence had run out of words. Suddenly everything seemed too quiet. She heard the *shh . . . shh* of cars whirring by on M-59, which became the *shh-bmp* of the scratchy 45, and then the *suck-swoosh* of Darth, deep inside her head.

Through the windshield she could see the darkened funeral home. How many corpses lay inside those walls, alone in the dark, dressed and made up to be gawked at by a parade of mourners? How many of them were mothers and fathers? How many little girls were fooling themselves into believing that they had guardian angels that watched over them? Had any of them had asked for a sign of the afterlife and actually received one?

Spence reached over to wipe a tear off Abby's face.

"Tell me what you need," he said, his voice straining with desperation. "What can I do?"

Abby couldn't answer him. There was nothing he *could* do. He could never give her what she needed most: her dad there to tell her he was fine, just fine, and that everything would be okay. Resting her head on the window, she closed her burning eyes and hugged herself. And then she let out the grief that had been building for over a year, and all of the tears she hadn't cried.

SPENCE AND ABBY NEVER MADE IT INTO THE RESTAURANT. Abby's tears wouldn't stop. Instead, he bought them a pizza from Little Caesars and drove back to Highland.

"I don't want to go home," Abby begged.

"Okay," Spence said. He parked at the end of Summit, got a beach towel from the back of his car, and led her by the hand down to the Point. Thankfully, it was deserted.

He spread the towel over the grass and guided Abby down with him so that they sat facing each other with the pizza box in between. He opened it and offered her a slice. When she declined, he tossed it back in and closed the box again.

"I'm not really hungry, either." He pushed the box off the towel and onto the grass. Then he pulled Abby close and kissed the top of her forehead. She looked out at far-off Youth Island, once a place alive with laughing children and camp-fire songs, now dark and lifeless, abandoned. Haunted. No one had rebuilt the camp. No one lived there. They'd left it to the ghosts.

Dad would have to live with the Corcorans.

Spence held her tight and she nestled into him, soothed by his warmth, his strong embrace, the rise and fall of his chest, the sound of his breathing, steady and calm. He pointed at a grassy area near the Fischers' backyard.

"Remember the tree house in that big sycamore tree that used to be over there?"

Abby nodded into his shoulder. "Yeah, Mr. Fischer built it for his kids when they were little. That was the best tree, and the best tree house."

"Until lightning hit it."

Abby remembered the morning after the storm. Spence had come to fetch Josh and Abby early in the morning to show them the tree, split down the middle.

"You cried for, like, weeks," she said.

Spence sighed. "Yeah, I did. That was my spot. There were times when I was a kid that my mom used to get so mad, I just—I knew she didn't want me around. So I'd go . . . sometimes to Griffin's house, or yours, but mostly to the tree house. Even slept there a couple of times."

Abby gasped and looked up into his face. "You did? Why?"

"My mom had a friend over. And I hated it."

"But why didn't you come to my house? My mom and dad would have let you stay."

He shrugged. "I know they would, but I just felt like, y'know, you were a family, and I was this extra kid, and I didn't want to be a fifth wheel. I didn't want anyone feeling sorry for me."

Abby could relate. "But you were always part of my family. Never an extra kid."

"I know. But that wasn't all of it. I was kind of afraid back then that if people knew I was out running around all night, someone would come and take me away. Away from my mom. Away from my home. Away from you, and Josh, and everyone and everything I'd ever known."

Abby entwined her fingers with his. "My parents would have let you come live with us."

He looked down at her and chuckled. "And room with Josh? I wouldn't have gotten any sleep, knowing you were right there in the next room."

"Spence, we were, like, nine years old."

Spence stared into her eyes. "And I think I knew, even then, that"—he hesitated, but only for a moment—"that I loved you."

Abby bit her lip, wishing she could say those words back, but she knew that saying "I love you" is ominous. She tilted her chin so that her lips met Spence's. She started to cry again. Her tears rolled over their lips, salty and sweet. Abby ran her fingers through Spence's hair while she kissed him, wanting to hold this moment for a lifetime. When they stopped, their faces remained so close that she could feel his hot breath.

"So how did you live without it?" she whispered.

"What?"

"The tree house."

Spence traced her hairline and tucked a lock of hair, damp from tears, behind her ear. "I guess I just decided that I didn't need a place to hide." His fingers mapped her jawline and tickled her chin. "I figured out that my mom wasn't really mad at me. She was mad at—I don't know—life, I guess. And when she's dating someone, when she really likes a guy, she's happier.

"I stopped trying to make her into the mom I thought she

should be and let her live her life, even if sometimes that made me unhappy. I knew I had a lot of people who cared about me, and it was the people in my life that were important, not where I lived, and not some stupid tree."

Abby knew what he was trying to say to her, but the thing was, her childhood home wasn't a stupid tree. Spence's tree had disappeared. Abby's house would stay put. She was the one who had to leave.

She pulled back suddenly. That was it.

"You're right," she said. "It doesn't matter where we are, as long as we're together."

Spence smiled. "Right."

"So let's go somewhere!" Abby said, unable to contain her excitement. "Just us."

He stared at her, puzzled. "Where?"

Abby bolted upright. "I don't know. Anywhere! Anywhere but here. Let's just get in your car and drive. And keep driving."

"Abby—that's not what I meant—"

"Please," she begged, clutching Spence's arm. "I just want to stay with you."

"You will," Spence said, taking her hands in his. "I'll never leave you."

"Then let's go," she said almost frantically. She stood and tried to pull him up with her. He wouldn't budge. "Let's get away from here, away from everything."

"Abby," he said slowly, "think about what you're saying. I know things are tough right now, but—"

"But what?"

"You know we can't just run away. That's crazy."

Her stomach turned. She let go of him and backed away. "You think I'm crazy."

"No! I didn't say that—"

Abby turned and started up the hill.

"Abby," he pleaded, following her. "Wait." He grabbed her arm and tried to turn her around.

"No!" Abby said, pulling away and running up the hill as fast as she could. "Please, Spence, just leave me alone!"

She sprinted to the house and threw open the door without looking back, humiliated. She'd lashed out at him again— and again, he hadn't done anything to deserve it. She felt so out of control. Maybe she *was* going crazy. Spence was probably figuring that out pretty quickly, and it was only a matter of time before he couldn't deal with it anymore. She had to get rid of him before he broke her heart. She should have listened to Dad.

Mom was waiting in the living room, and rose from the couch in panic when she saw Abby stumble in and slam the door behind her.

"What happened?"

"Nothing." Abby shielded her eyes from the brightness of

the living room. Her head was throbbing. She trudged up the stairs, and as she crawled into bed she heard the Cavalier's engine start up and its wheels crunch on the gravel road. Alone in bed, she finally allowed her despair to charge at her full force and pummel her, stomping her into the ground. She didn't resist. She just lay there and took it.

Okay, shadow. You win. YOU WIN! Are you satisfied now?

Mom came upstairs shortly thereafter. Abby had been expecting her.

"Honey?" Abby tried to look at her mother, but the hallway light stung her eyes and seared into her brain. She turned away. "Honey, I'm sorry." Abby nodded and curled into the fetal position. "Talk to me, Abby."

"I want to go to sleep, Mom. Please? Just let me go to sleep."

Mom left, shutting the door behind her.

Abby closed her eyes. Was this was it was like for her father when he knew he was dying? To just close your eyes, surrender, and drift away? No more thoughts, no more worries, no more pain.

TWENTY-SEVEN

August and September

Spence called and kept calling. Every time, Abby told him she couldn't talk and hung up. And then she cried. Soon she stopped answering the phone altogether. Hearing his voice was much too painful. She didn't want to care about him anymore. She didn't want to care about anyone anymore.

Mom wouldn't answer the phone, either, afraid it might be Denny. He still hadn't given up. Josh had to play receptionist, screening calls and taking messages and telling lies until he stopped answering the phone, too.

And the Summit Drive house was sold. Mrs. North bought the house in Orchard Acres. Josh had already seen it. Abby stonewalled; she didn't want to give her mother the slightest idea that she was okay with the move, but her mother tricked her.

On the way back from Abby's annual dental checkup, they drove by the house. Out of the corner of her eye she saw the bland, pre-fab box on its barren quarter-acre lot. There was no flower garden, the shrubs had faded, and the yard was a flat stretch of brown grass lacking even a shade tree. In the back, there was a rickety old shed and a small patch of woods so scant that you could see the houses beyond, houses that looked exactly the same as this one, aside from slight differences in color.

Mom went on and on about all the changes she wanted to make: she'd plant a flower garden here, a tree there, hang ferns over the porch, trim the shrubs, paint the shutters and the garage door, and so on and so on. Now her excuse for selling the Summit Drive house because it was too much work didn't fly. Josh and Abby would give Mom grandchildren before she'd even finished up the outside of this house, and who knew what the inside looked like. Mom wasn't selling the Summit house because it needed too many repairs; she was getting rid of the Summit house because she couldn't deal with the memories.

On the way back, Abby shook inside. She couldn't imagine ever living in that hole. It was nothing like their real house; it would never feel like home.

Mom kept packing, divvying out Dad's stuff between Josh and Abby and holding a garage sale to get rid of much of the rest. As if this wasn't bad enough, she had the audacity to invite strangers *into their home* to sell off pieces of furniture during the garage sale.

The first item to go was the rust-orange couch, which she said wouldn't fit in the new living room. As much as Abby had poked fun at that couch over the years, watching two guys load it onto a trailer made her feel like part of her heart was being ripped out. Mom had bought that couch when Dad was healthy, and he had had a ball razzing her about it. Abby had sat on that couch when Dad announced that he was going to die, and Mom had slept on it every night until he did. After Dad was gone, Mom and Josh and Abby had taken turns sleeping on it when they were restless in their own beds. That couch had given them comfort, and Mom was sending it away.

Just like Abby was doing to Spence.

Abby marched upstairs and wrote KEEP OUT! on a sheet of paper in permanent marker and taped it to her bedroom door. She wouldn't put it past her mother to try to get rid of some of her things, too, trying to help Abby shuck the past and move on.

To keep herself occupied, Abby arranged the things of Dad's that she'd found in a couple of boxes labeled SAM on the floor of her mother's closet—his wristwatch, his eyeglasses, his college diploma, his teaching awards—on the shelves of the bookcase in her bedroom. Interspersed with the memorabilia were the framed photos she'd pulled out of one of the boxes: Dad as a baby, as a child, as a young man in his navy uniform. Then she put together a photo album that contained all the pictures she could find with Dad in them: Dad holding a newborn Abby, Dad helping miniature versions of Josh and Abby open Christmas presents, Dad kissing Mom in the kitchen, Dad leading the graduation ceremony at the high school where he worked.

Abby found herself staring at the photos, concentrating hard on every feature, every line, every visible mole or imperfection on her father's face. Sometimes, nowadays, she couldn't totally remember what he looked like. He had been dead only a little more than a year; she couldn't let him fade from her memory already. By the time she was grown, there would be nothing left. She vowed to memorize him.

On Saturday evening, after the garage sale, Mom came in and saw the Dad Shrine, but made no comment.

"You'd better start packing some of your things," she said instead. "School starts on Tuesday and we'll be moving on Friday. You won't have much time during the week."

"I'll get to it," Abby snapped.

"Spence is here. He wants to see you."

"Tell him I'm sleeping."

Mom sighed and ran her fingers through her hair. "You

need to talk to him, Abby. I don't know what happened between you two, but you can't just run away and hide like this."

Abby snorted. "Why don't you tell Denny that?"

Her mother shook her head and walked out. Abby plugged her ears so she wouldn't have to hear Spence's voice downstairs, and she didn't come out until Mom called upstairs that dinner was ready. If she weren't starving she'd have stayed in her room, and when she walked downstairs into a disaster area, she wished she had. The house was a shambles—boxes and newspaper and rolls of packing tape were scattered about everywhere.

And they now had no kitchen table. Mom had sold it.

"Where are we supposed to eat?" she asked, taking a scoop of homemade macaroni and cheese.

"Outside on the picnic table," Mom replied.

"No thanks." She dumped the contents of her plate back into the casserole dish, too nauseated to eat. Abby knew she needed to see a doctor about her stomach problem, but she didn't want to tell Mom about it. Let her find out when it was too late. Boy, would Mom be sorry then.

TUESDAY WAS THE START OF SOPHOMORE YEAR. JOSH drove her to school, but as soon as they got there, they split off and acted as if they didn't know each other.

At Lakeside High, the first day of school was never educational. Instead, it was reserved for finding classrooms and lockers and getting textbooks and, most important, hanging out with friends Abby hadn't seen all summer. They were lax about tardiness during the first week, so she spent a good chunk of the day in the hallways. She ran into Spence only once, in the hall before algebra, and she ducked into the classroom to avoid him. Mr. Petty, the teacher, gave her a smile, marking something in his attendance book. At least dodging Spence had given her the opportunity to brownnose.

After school Mom was waiting in the student parking lot. Mortified, Abby rushed to the car, hoping to get out of sight as quickly as possible.

"What are you doing here?" she said in a loud whisper.

"I came to pick you up so that we could go shopping for new bedding for your room."

"I don't want new bedding."

"Come on, it'll be fun. Oh! There's Josh. Let me go grab him before he takes off."

"No!" she blurted, horrified by a vision of her mother running across the parking lot. "I'll get him."

Josh glared as she approached. How dare she speak to him in the presence of his friends? He deigned to follow her to the car—and as soon as he learned he was getting some new things for his room, too, he was happy enough to leave the

Impala in the lot and come along. Abby had her own agenda; she was determined not to let Mom buy her anything. She wanted her new room to look like her old room.

At the mall, Josh found what he wanted right away—navy-blue-and-forest-green sheets, pillowcases, and a comforter that he could take to college down the road. Abby amused herself by watching a twentysomething couple debate the pros and cons of satin versus cotton sheets.

"Your turn!" Mom said cheerily. When Abby didn't move, her mother brought over plastic-wrapped comforters and sheets to show her. Everything was much too bright and girly.

"I don't like those. How about this?" She gestured to a bed made up with a black comforter and black-and-white-zebra-striped sheets. "This is perfect!"

"Black? Oh, honey, I don't like black. Not for your bedroom."

"It's my room, isn't it?"

"What about this one?" She picked up a floral-patterned quilt with a red background. "It has a little bit of black in it."

"Flowers, Mom? Please."

The more alternatives her mother offered, the more Abby said no. "Fine," Mom said through clenched teeth. "I won't buy you anything."

"Fine," Abby replied.

"Fine."

Abby trailed behind on the way out. Josh lugged his big bag of bedding and prattled on about how he was going to fix up his new room. Just like a girl. Like a traitor.

Friday morning, moving day, arrived too soon. She had stayed up all night, unable to sleep. She couldn't believe it was the last night in her childhood home. It didn't seem possible. It didn't seem right. It didn't seem fair.

Eventually she had to get ready for school. All of her clothes were packed except for a pair of sweatpants and a T-shirt. Terrific.

Mom had threatened to throw away anything she left under the bed, but aside from her Magic 8 Ball it was all just junk. Even her old yearbook. Abby reached under her bed and pulled out the 8 Ball, closed her eyes, and concentrated.

Abby: This is a done deal, isn't it?

God: YES

Abby: So there's nothing I can do to stop it?

God: MY REPLY IS NO

Maybe the stupid thing had been sitting underneath the bed for too long. Or maybe Abby just wasn't asking her questions right.

Abby: But you're God. Can't you make miracles happen?

God: CONCENTRATE AND ASK AGAIN

Abby: Can you make the Corcorans back out?

God: CANNOT PREDICT NOW

Abby: You have to predict now! There's no more time! Will you give me a miracle? I promise I'll never ask for anything again!

Abby shook the Magic 8 Ball furiously, turning it upright and waiting for a count of three to look at the answer.

God: VERY DOUBTFUL

Josh hollered for Abby to hurry. She walked down the stairs for the last time. And she chucked the Magic 8 Ball into the garbage on her way out.

TWENTY-EIGHT

September, Continued

A moving van was in the driveway when they got home from school, and a trio of men was loading the last of their belongings into it. Abby sat on a folding chair in the driveway, watching the movers haul her life away. It didn't take long, and when they were finished the Norths followed the van to the Orchard Acres house.

When they got there, she took her chair out of the trunk and sat in the new driveway, in a stupor.

She sat there for hours, well after the movers had gone. She didn't come inside for the pizza her mother had ordered. When the sky darkened, Josh coaxed her inside and she walked into the new house for the first time.

The interior was infinitely more colorful than the outside, because it hadn't been updated since the seventies. The kitchen appliances and countertops were avocado green, the wallpaper dotted with orange and yellow flowers. Every room had a different color carpet: beige in the living room; brown in the family room; and green in the dining room, to match the kitchen. The bedroom carpeting was downright blinding: royal blue in the master bedroom, red in one smaller room, and orange in the other. The orange room—hers, as it turned out—was so bright it would probably glow in the dark.

Mom danced around the house, talking about her redecorating plans. By midweek there would be new carpet in all of the public areas, a color she called "sand," and she would strip the kitchen wallpaper and paint as soon as she could. New appliances and new countertops were on order. She'd found living room furniture that she liked, too, but wouldn't buy it until the carpeting was in. She'd taken the next two weeks off work to scrub and paint and organize and wait for this contractor and that, and she was eager to get started. She wanted to show Abby the basement, but Abby declined, instead retreating to the orange room, terrified. All her stuff was in there, but she knew there was no way she would get to sleep. As if her stomach didn't hurt badly enough in her old room at her real home.

Mom came upstairs several times to check in. Each time she did, Abby just shook her head. She didn't know what to say to her mother; Abby didn't even know who she was.

Boxes were stacked in every corner, but she couldn't bring

herself to unpack. Eventually she did fall asleep, sitting on the bed with her back against the wall.

But her slumber was anything but peaceful. She woke suddenly, startled and scared, not knowing where she was. Bushes crowded up against an unfamiliar window, trying to get in. Abby couldn't tell what time it was, since she hadn't yet plugged in her alarm clock. With trembling hands, she reached for a bedside lamp that wasn't there. Pressing her knuckles against her eyes, she tried to forget a nightmare that had seemed all too real.

Mom and Josh and Abby had been watching the fireworks at the Point, while Dad slept at home. In the middle of the display there was a misfire, and the Point was suddenly ablaze. The three of them ran up the hill toward home with the fire at their heels. The neighbors' houses had burned almost to the ground, and as they approached their own they discovered that it was on fire, too.

With Dad in it.

Mom hollered for the two of them to stay put while she ran inside the house to save him. The flames grew higher and she still hadn't come out; Abby was worried that both her parents would be burned alive. As she tried to find a safe way inside, Mom leaped from her bedroom window, landing catlike on the front lawn. She approached Josh and Abby, looking forlorn.

"Where's Dad?" Abby asked.

"He wasn't in there," her mother replied, shaking her head.

"Yes, he was!" Abby cried. "He was sleeping, remember?"

"He wasn't in there," Mom repeated. "I couldn't see him."

"Just because you couldn't see him doesn't mean he wasn't in there!"

Mom cocked her head and studied Abby, puzzled.

The house burned to the ground within seconds. Though Abby hadn't heard him scream for help, she knew Dad had been inside. He was gone.

"He was in there!" Abby sobbed.

THE NEXT MORNING, JOSH AND ABBY WALKED INTO THE kitchen to find Mom trying to act chipper as she toasted bagels and poured orange juice and attempted to find a clean place where they could eat. She detailed her plan for the day—clean out the kitchen cupboards, spread contact paper inside of them, put away kitchen goods, run to the hardware store for wallpaper-stripping supplies—and though she put as much enthusiasm into her words as she could, Mom's mouth was that straight line. Perhaps she was having second thoughts, after all.

The Norths huddled over the kitchen island with bagels slathered with cream cheese on paper plates in front of them.

But, again, Abby couldn't eat. After Josh had finished, she begged him to take her for a ride. He glanced at Mom, who nodded her permission, and the two of them took off in the Impala.

"Where do you want to go?" Josh asked.

"Home," Abby said.

"Abby," Josh said cautiously, "Mom sold the house."

"I want to go home!" Abby insisted.

"Somebody bought the house!" Josh said louder.

"I don't care! I want to go home!" Abby knew she was being irrational, but she couldn't help it.

Josh shook his head but drove toward the tri-level on Summit Drive. When they got to the dirt road, there was a moving van in what had been her driveway just the day before. She bit her lip when she saw a curly-haired little blonde girl running around in the front yard with a roly-poly beagle chasing behind her. How she hated that little girl.

"Let me out of the car. I feel sick."

Josh drove past their—the—house and parked in front of the Fischers' place at the end of the road. Abby ran down to the Point. Fred, the Fischers' old basset hound, lay at the base of his tree. He lifted his head and gave a wag of his tail. She crouched beside him with her head between her knees, inhaling deeply to fight off a wave of nausea.

Josh rambled down the hill and stood beside her while she

tried to catch her breath. Grabbing a handful of rocks, he started tossing them one by one into the lake. The ripples mesmerized her. Funny how such a small thing could create such disorder, causing waves that grew larger and larger until they silently ceased to exist.

"Why can't everything just go back to normal?" Abby said in a small voice.

Josh's hand stopped in midair.

"There's no such thing."

TWENTY-NINE

September, Continued

Starting school was the only thing that kept Abby from going over the edge completely. During "Welcome Week," the halls were strewn with crepe paper and hand-painted banners reading WELCOME BACK TO LHS! There was the usual pep rally on Wednesday, and this year the PTO sponsored a new fund-raiser—Friday Flowers. A station had been set up outside the cafeteria during the first couple of days of school at which kids could purchase a carnation for another student and write a personal message, and on Friday the previous year's student council reps would deliver them during homeroom.

Abby didn't buy any carnations and hoped she wouldn't receive any, but she was afraid she'd get one from Spence. So far she'd successfully dodged him at school and ignored his phone calls; if he persisted in hounding her she was bound to break down and talk to him, which would lead to talking about what had happened on her birthday, a day she'd like to erase from existence.

She was a mess, and sooner or later Spence's well of understanding would dry up. She'd had enough heartbreak to last a lifetime, thank you very much. She'd decided it was better to be the leaver than the one who is left.

Abby pondered ways to play sick on Friday. Making herself throw up wouldn't be all that hard, but that was disgusting. She could probably pull off a fever—she had done it a few times by putting her face up close to the lightbulb on her bedside lamp until just before Mom came in to feel her forehead. She could tell her mother the truth about her stomach pains, but then she'd take her to the doctor, who would tell Abby what she already knew: if you cram too much into a suitcase it might rip open, and if you stuff all the bad thoughts and feelings into your stomach, eventually you'll bust at the seams.

But Mom was still off work. She'd be home on Friday. Abby would rather brave it out at school.

On Friday, two girls waltzed into Abby's homeroom carrying armloads of carnations, and the room fell silent as they passed them out. Squeals and giggles followed when the lucky recipients read their private messages. Abby waited and watched the stack of flowers the girls held become smaller, until one of the girls had empty arms and the other had only two carnations left. Abby's racing heart slowed. She was almost in the clear.

But not quite. The girl with the last two flowers searched the room and walked toward Abby. She handed her both carnations, one red and one pink. Two? Abby was admittedly intrigued. She read the message on the pink carnation first: BFFAE! (Best Friends Forever and Ever), from Leise. Abby wished she'd have thought to send Leise one, too.

On to the red. She braced herself for the message, hoping Spence hadn't written anything too mushy, or she'd have to cry in front of her entire homeroom class.

But the carnation wasn't from Spence.

The message read, *The alphabet is all wrong, because U and I should be together.* Signed by Logan Pierce.

Abby stared at the little piece of paper, shocked.

Erica Nichols, sitting next to her, peeked over Abby's shoulder at Logan's note and drew in a sharp breath. Soon half the girls in homeroom were reading the message for themselves. Before the end of third period, she'd be one of the most envied girls at Lakeside—a tenth-grader who had caught the eye of the most popular boy in the junior class. By lunchtime, gossip would have Logan and Abby going to the homecoming dance, and by the end of the day they'd be boyfriend and girlfriend.

"Have you been seeing Logan?" Erica asked, jumping up and down.

"Why didn't you tell us?" Dakota punched Abby in the arm.

Abby just shook her head, too stunned to speak. She'd seen Logan a couple of times over the summer as he came and went with Josh, and she'd had her usual heart palpitations when she saw him, but, she just now realized, she hadn't thought about him at all in between.

She reminded herself that she'd dreamed about this day for years. She wanted to be as excited as her friends were for her. But she was apprehensive. This was it; she'd reached her goal. She'd crossed the finish line and could move on to the next race. Spence would surely hear about this, and now he'd stop bugging her. That's what she wanted, wasn't it? She tried to tell herself that was so, but she couldn't shake a panicky feeling. Spence hadn't sent her a flower. Had he gotten over her already?

When the bell rang, everyone walked out of the room in a pack, but when Dakota spotted Logan near the gym, she nudged Abby and the group scattered.

Logan was eyeing Abby like she was a piece of candy. She wanted to run back into homeroom, to pull herself together, to remember the dozens of dreams she'd had about Logan, about this very moment, to remind herself how she was supposed to be feeling.

The smile on Logan's face wasn't the same as the cocky grin in her middle school yearbook. This Logan was not faded black and white, frozen in time, with the captions "Most Popular" and "Best All-Around" underneath his picture.

That Logan was a fantasy. This Logan was taller and huskier. He had large hands and thick forearms and a fuzzy upper lip. He was no longer the page sixty-seven Logan Pierce. This Logan Pierce was almost a man, an undeniably gorgeous man, but nonetheless a man who could no longer fit into the old T-shirt Abby had lost in the move, and she didn't know him at all. She never had. Not like she knew Spence.

Why hadn't Spence sent her a flower?

"Hey," Logan said as he sauntered toward Abby where she'd stopped cold in the middle of the hallway.

"Hey," Abby replied, jostled by impatient upperclassmen on every side. Logan took her by the hand and led her to a cluster of windows opposite the gym.

"Thanks for the carnation," she said shyly.

"What?" Logan yelled—the hallway was at rock concert–decibel level.

"I said thanks for the flower!" she shouted.

"No problem." Logan gave a sly grin. "Now you know I've got my eye on you. I gotta run—catch you later?"

Abby nodded and Logan squeezed her hand. Then he

rushed back to the gym, giving her a wink before disappearing inside.

Her homeroom friends appeared out of nowhere to get the lowdown.

"So did he ask you to the homecoming dance?" someone asked. She shook her head.

"He will." Dakota patted her back to give her the encouragement she thought Abby needed. "Don't worry."

Abby wasn't worried. Not about that, at least.

Why hadn't Spence sent her a flower?

ABBY HADN'T GONE TO THE HOMECOMING DANCE LAST year, and neither had Josh. Back then they were still trying to claw out of the rubble. Going out and having fun had felt like a betrayal, and their mother was too fragile to be left home alone for long. So they'd skipped the dance, opting instead to stay home playing Scrabble with Mom. Spence had joined them.

This year was different. Spence was out of the picture. She'd heard through the grapevine that Josh had asked Nikki Richardson to the dance. Mom was giddily busy with her home-improvement projects. They were moving on, and Abby thought she should, too. She hadn't seen Logan for the rest of the day, giving her several hours to come to the conclusion that if he asked her to the dance like everyone said he would, she would say yes. Maybe Spence wouldn't mind as much as she'd thought he would. Maybe he wouldn't care at all.

Leise convinced her to get into the homecoming swing, so they stayed after school for a sophomore float meeting. This year's theme was breakfast cereal characters. They came up with as many characters as they could think of: Tony the Tiger; the Honey Smacks frog; that annoying bird that exclaims, "I'm cuckoo for Cocoa Puffs!"; Cap'n Crunch . . . After what felt like hours, they finally chose Toucan Sam. They'd get their idea to the homecoming committee before the seniors could steal it and begin work next week.

Afterward Leise and Abby sat on the steps near the parking lot waiting for Mrs. Spangler to pick them up.

"Did you talk to Logan this afternoon?" Leise asked.

"No, I didn't see him."

"Do you think he's going to ask you to the dance?"

Abby shrugged.

"If he does, will you say yes?"

"I guess."

"Do you like him?"

"I've liked him for four years, Leise!"

"Yeah, I know, but . . . why?"

Abby raised her eyebrows. "Are you kidding me? Have you *seen* Logan Pierce?"

"Okay, so he's cute. I'll give you that. But I heard Paige Quinlan talking to Amaya Kish the other day in the bathroom, and Paige was telling her what a jerk he was when they were going out."

"Well, of course she'd say that," Abby said. "He broke up with her."

Leise set her lips into a smile. "Whatever. They're history. So you still like him. But what about Spence?"

A uniformed football player fresh from practice came jogging off the football field toward the school. His head looked extra-small poking out over his extra-large shoulder pads. Leise knew it was Logan before Abby did.

"Speak of the devil." Leise got up and walked over to the veranda, where a group of girls stood gossiping. Leise deserted her.

Abby rose to her feet and tried to smile at Logan. It took more effort than it should have.

"Water break," he said, as if Abby had asked. He wiped sweat from his face and tucked his helmet under his arm.

She nodded, not sure what to say.

And there was something else. Though he stood a few feet away, his BO was strong enough to knock her to the ground.

"I only have a minute—gotta get back before the coach reams me out—but there's something I wanted to ask you."

"Yeah?" Abby was blushing, and she hated herself for it. So much for playing it cool.

"Do you have a date for the homecoming dance yet?" She shook her head. "We should go together."

Abby had rehearsed this scene all day. She opened her mouth to say yes, but a whistle from the football field drowned her out.

"I have to go," Logan said, tossing his helmet into the air and catching it. "So are we on?"

Abby nodded and smiled faintly. "On."

Logan smirked and ambled toward Abby, kissing her on the lips. Luckily it was just a peck.

His breath was deadly. This had not been part of her dream.

As he ran off, Abby turned and looked up at the veranda, expecting to see Leise beaming and giving her a thumbs-up.

Instead, Spence stared at her, slack-jawed. She wanted to run to him, to wrap her arms around him, to explain everything—but he averted his eyes and walked away. Now Abby would be rid of him for good, just like she'd wanted.

Hadn't she?

THIRTY

September and October

The music vibrated through the barn louder than Abby thought the decrepit structure could endure. Erica's parents had renovated a century-old farmhouse on what was now acres and acres of grassy fields, and they had offered up the ramshackle old barn for building the sophomore homecoming float.

Convinced it might crumble down on them, Abby and Leise and a few other kids sat outside in the bed of the truck that belonged to Mr. Buchanan, their class sponsor, making tissue-paper flowers, while those inside constructed the float's frame out of chicken wire and papier-mâché. The dance was just two weeks away, and Toucan Sam still looked more like a misshapen potato than a bird.

Abby sat in the center of the group while they worked, fielding questions.

"Who are you and Logan doubling with for the dance?"

"What does your dress look like?"

"How are you going to do your hair?"

"Do you know who nominated you for homecoming court?"

"Are you guys like a couple now?"

She answered, rapid fire: One: I don't know. Two: Don't have one yet. Three: No idea. Four: Don't know that, either. Five: Not exactly. The girls thought she was playing it cool, but really Abby wasn't as into this homecoming thing as much as they were, and she honestly had no idea where she stood with Logan.

She supposed that maybe they were somewhat of a couple. Mom wouldn't allow her to go on any real dates with him, but was okay with them hanging out after school. "Hanging out" meant that she watched him practice with the football team or lift weights in the gym. She probably wouldn't have minded doing either, if he'd paid her any attention.

During football practice, she sat on the bleachers with the other players' girlfriends, mostly juniors and seniors; most of whom didn't give her the time of day. When Logan was lifting weights, Abby kept track as he grunted and perspired, all the while watching himself in the wall-to-wall mirror. After he finished, he always came over and gave her a distracted kiss—more to show possession than affection—before going off to shower.

Then he'd drive her home. All the way there, she listened

to him gloat about his skill and agility in football and the exaggerated amount of weight he could lift.

He never stayed long after dropping her off, either. Sometimes he played a few games of Xbox with Josh, totally ignoring her. And Josh wouldn't say more than a couple of words to him. Logan had broken an unspoken rule between guys: date whomever you want, but your friends' sisters are off-limits.

Funny, though, that Josh hadn't minded when the guy was Spence.

After a couple of weeks of this, she wondered if Logan knew anything about her at all. He sure hadn't been interested enough to ask. And she didn't offer. Why waste her breath? *He's under a lot of pressure*, Abby told herself. *Maybe after football season ends, he won't be so wrapped up in himself.* The thing was, she wasn't so sure she'd make it to the dance, much less the end of the season, without strangling him. It was too late to change plans for the dance now, though, so she'd stay positive and hope for the best.

Headlights approached and a car stopped about twenty feet away from the truck.

"Abby!"

She couldn't recall ever being so happy to hear her mother's voice. She finished her last flower and tossed it into a bulging plastic bag.

"See you later," she said, hopping off the truck.

"'Bye! Call me later!" This came from several girls. She supposed she should be elated about her newfound popularity, but to be honest it was a little disconcerting that people liked her more now that a particular guy had deemed her worthwhile.

She climbed into the car, which smelled like paint thinner. Abby cracked a window.

"Hi, honey. Did you have fun?"

"Uh-huh." Abby looked over and stifled a laugh. Mom's brown hair was spotted white.

"You look like a calico cat," she said, forgetting that she was still officially not talking to her mother.

Mom put a hand to her hair and giggled. "Just finished painting the hallway. Haven't showered yet."

Mom yakked all the way home, asking Abby if she would help her move the furniture in her room away from the walls so she could get started with painting in there, telling her about the great deal she had found on new carpet for the bedrooms upstairs and the fantastic contractor who would come at the end of the month to install it.

Abby just listened. Turning the house upside down was her mother's new method of distraction, and though Abby wouldn't have said so under torture, it was actually starting to look pretty good. The kitchen was now a sunny yellow that went well with the newly installed brown-speckled granite countertops and maple cupboards and floors. The living room was painted cream to match the new red-and-cream-upholstered furniture. Soon everything would be fresh and new. Her father's corduroy recliner was the black sheep of the living room—but it looked just right with Mom's pencil sketch of Dad hanging over it. She had constructed a shrine of her own.

The dining room walls were now peach, although there wasn't any furniture yet. Instead Mom had set up an easel and desk so that she could start painting watercolors again. She hadn't painted a thing since before Dad got sick.

So the interior of the house was decked out in happy, and most days her mother seemed happy, too. Traitor.

Abby spent most of her time at home locked up in her orange hell, but she had to leave the bedroom now and then or she'd die of starvation or an exploded bladder. As the weeks passed, she'd learned her way around the new house, no longer bumping into walls in the middle of the night trying to figure out where the bathroom was or opening every kitchen cabinet to locate the drinking glasses. She even halfway admitted (to herself) that it was kind of nice that she could walk to her friends' houses.

Mom continued to have one-sided conversations with Abby, and had started to bring up Dad more often, but not always with regret or sadness. She talked about the good times they'd had, and his funny idiosyncrasies. Abby some-times found herself laughing along. Thinking about him didn't always sting so much now, but it did bring pangs of guilt. Was Abby getting over losing him already? She was supposed to feel only sadness when she reminisced. How cold was she?

That was when she always reminded herself that she was at war with her mother. Mom had no right talking about Dad at all. She had betrayed him; she had betrayed Abby and Josh. Anger was a much less confusing emotion to deal with.

THE NEXT MORNING LEISE AND HER MOTHER STOPPED BY unannounced. While Abby's mother gave Mrs. Spangler the grand tour, Leise ushered Abby into her bedroom and tossed a little black, strapless dress onto the bed.

"Try it on!" she said, clapping.

Abby picked it up by its hanger. "Whose is it?"

"My cousin Shelby's. She wore it to homecoming last year and gave it to me. I love it, but it doesn't quite fit right over my hips. She's built more like you."

"Like a twelve-year-old boy, you mean."

Leise playfully slapped her on the arm. "She's slender. Like you. Please put it on . . . I'm dying to see it on you."

Abby took the dress into the walk-in closet. It was silky and soft and—Leise was right—fit like a glove. An impatient

Leise came into the closet and helped her zip up. When Abby turned around, Leise gasped.

"Kind of skimpy, huh?" Abby said, wincing.

Leise shook her head, took her by the elbow, and pulled her out of the closet. She led Abby into the bathroom across the hall where she could see herself in the full-length mirror. A smile spread across her face. She'd planned to ask her mom to take her to the mall, but now there was no need. This dress, made of black stretch taffeta, was sophisticated and simple, and looked like it had been designed just for her.

The bathroom door was open. Mrs. Spangler stood in the doorway, grinning, and Mom stopped in the hallway behind her, an odd look on her face.

"What?" Abby said, self-consciously crossing her arms over her chest. "You don't like it? It's not too tight or anything, and the hem is at my knees and—why don't you like it?"

"I do like it," her mother said slowly. "It just makes you look . . . older."

"Older?"

"Mature."

Abby loved the dress even more.

ABBY DIDN'T SEE MUCH OF LOGAN DURING THE WEEK before homecoming—he and his teammates were busy gearing up for the biggest game of the season against their rival, Milford High. They met up between a few classes, but Logan didn't have more than a few words to say that didn't have to do with football. Not until Friday, that was. Ironically, game day.

Friday was the day they announced the winners of homecoming court over the PA during homeroom. For Abby, just being nominated was more than she'd ever hoped for. She hadn't expected to win, and, really, hadn't wanted to. At halftime, the girls elected to court would be escorted to the middle of the football fields by their fathers. Abby didn't have one of those.

Turned out she had nothing to worry about. Leise was elected to court, and Abby was thrilled for her.

Logan didn't win, either, and he was completely bent out of shape about it. He found her in the hallway right after homeroom.

"Can you believe Chris Andrews won Junior Prince? Every nerd in the school must have voted for him."

"He seems like a pretty nice guy."

"He's a tool. I should demand a recount."

"Are you serious?"

"Why not?"

She gave up.

On the eve of the dance, Leise and Abby got ready together

at Abby's house. Leise smiled as she watched Abby do her hair, makeup, and nails with precision, like the star pupil she was. Mom took a few pictures of the girls together while Josh fiddled with his tie in the bathroom and sprayed on so much cologne that the house was going to smell like the fragrance department at Macy's for a month.

Billy Mohr, Leise's date, showed up at a quarter till five and was uncharacteristically tongue-tied and awkward when he saw Leise, stunning in her flowing silver dress. Mom's eyes nearly popped out of her head when Josh's date, Nikki, teetered through the door in five-inch pumps, wearing a little hot-pink number that didn't leave a whole lot to the imagination.

All the parents had come along to take pictures. After Abby and Josh suffered through a few obligitory family photos with Mom, Abby sat at the kitchen table watching the photo shoot—the boys placing corsages on the girls' wrists, the girls pinning boutonnieres on the boys' jackets, posing in front of the fireplace, two by two, and then all four of them together— until Josh finally announced that enough was enough. They were driving out to Novi for dinner, and didn't want to be late.

"I wish you were going with us," Leise said as they headed for the door.

"Me too," Abby said, but she'd let Logan make the plans.

Besides, there was no way Josh could have stomached being with Abby and Logan all night, and Abby felt likewise about Josh and Nikki. "I'll see you at the dance."

Abby stood in the doorway, waving, while the parents took more pictures in the driveway. They didn't stop until the Impala was out of sight.

By the time the Spanglers left, Logan still hadn't arrived. Mom came inside and Abby retreated to the bathroom to check her hair and makeup again. After applying a fresh coat of lip gloss, she came out to find Mom staring at the clock.

"He'll be here soon." Abby nodded, but she was starting to wonder. Maybe this was all a big joke. *Ha-ha, Logan Pierce asked Abby North to the homecoming dance and then stood her up. Good one! She really fell for it, didn't she?*

But before she could launch into an all-out panic, she heard a car pull into the driveway and she looked out the front window to see Logan strolling up the walkway, his cell phone stuck to his ear. Abby checked the clock on the wall. 6:20. Their dinner reservation at the Highland House, the only decent restaurant in town, was in ten minutes. They were meeting other couples there, though, so Abby didn't sweat it. She did, however, think that his tardiness was rude.

But she didn't make a fuss when Logan walked through the door, looking more handsome than ever in his charcoal suit.

"You look nice," she commented once he got off the phone.

"Thanks," Logan said. "You, too. We'd better go or we'll be late."

"I'd like to take a couple of pictures," Mom said, and Logan sighed loudly. They posed arm in arm in front of the fireplace, and after taking two pictures, she got Logan's boutonniere out of the fridge and snapped a photo of Abby pinning it to his lapel.

"Your corsage is in the car," Logan said while tapping out a text.

"Do you want to go get it?" Mom prompted.

He hit SEND and flipped his phone shut. "We really have to go."

Mom made a face, but didn't press any further. She followed them out into the driveway and hugged Abby. "Be careful."

Abby turned to find Logan standing beside the Mustang's open passenger door, looking irritable. Mom took one last photo of Abby sliding into the car carefully, to avoid rumpling her dress, and waved as Logan shut her door, nearly amputating the heel of her shoe. Logan handed her the boxed corsage—he didn't even pin it on her—and Abby caught sight of her mother, mouth open in shock.

On the way to the Highland House, Logan continued to complain about not being elected to homecoming court, but thankfully he stopped when they met their friends. Met Logan's friends, that was—some strangers from the team and their perfect, conceited dates. The girls were all a year older than Abby, and during dinner they ignored her completely.

They sat boy-girl-boy-girl around the table, and while the guys shouted over each other about plays from last night's winning game, the girls gossiped about mutual friends, lowering their voices while discussing juicy details and scowling at Abby as if she were intruding. So she quietly polished her silverware until her Greek salad came and then ate in silence. When the girls took off for the bathroom to refresh their lipstick, they didn't invite her.

When the witches returned, Logan put an arm around Abby and said the first words he'd spoken to her since they'd arrived: "Come on outside. I've got a surprise for you."

A limousine waited in the parking lot. A chauffeur held the door open and Logan's friends started to pile in.

"Is this ours?"

"Yep," Logan said, kissing Abby on the cheek. The garlic didn't help his breath one iota. "Ever been in a limo before?"

"Yeah. Once."

"Well, what are we waiting for?" He got in first. She could hardly wait to get to the dance and see some friendly faces.

Once they were seated, Logan placed a hand on Abby's knee and kept it there for the duration of the limousine ride, and he held her hand as he escorted her into the school. They stopped at the photography station to have their picture taken, and then Logan met up with a few of his teammates in the hallway. As they relived last night's game—again—Abby tried to come up with something worthwhile to contribute to the conversation, but finally resigned herself to being the smiling arm charm.

When she spotted Josh and Nikki and Billy and Leise coming through the door, she excused herself—though Logan didn't acknowledge that he'd heard her—and slipped away to join the crowd clustered around Leise to congratulate her.

Leise accepted the accolades like the princess she was, before turning to Abby.

"Having fun?"

Abby gave a sidewise smile and a shrug. Leise took her by the hand and squeezed.

Music started playing in the gym.

It was packed and hot. Leise leaned toward Abby and said something, but the music was so ridiculously loud Abby had no idea what it was. She followed Leise's gaze to the dance floor and was instantly clued in.

Logan was going berserk, swiveling his hips and jerking and shaking like he was having some sort of seizure. He spun around and clapped his hands together and jerked some more, pulling the nearest hot girl close to join him in what he must have thought was dancing. The girls surrounding him, mostly freshmen, moved in closer, each hoping to be the next one to catch his attention.

Abby couldn't help but laugh—not just at Logan's "dance moves," but also at the Logan-worshipping girls. That had been her. It now seemed so ridiculous to have spent so many years obsessing over a complete stranger. She could have held deeper conversations with a stack of pancakes than with Logan Pierce.

Spence and Leise had tried to warn her, but she'd refused to listen. Liking Logan had been a habit she couldn't kick. It was kind of like when she used to suck her thumb. Her mom said that she'd had to fight tooth and nail to get her to stop before starting kindergarten. Later, it seemed repulsive, and Abby couldn't fathom why she'd done it in the first place.

With raised eyebrows, Abby's eyes went from Leise to Logan and back to Leise. She shook her hips and did a little jerk. The two of them nearly doubled over with laughter.

Billy bowed before Leise and asked her to dance. She took his hand and let him lead her out onto the floor, keeping a watchful eye on Abby as they swayed back and forth. Abby didn't fully understand until she saw Spence walking arm in arm with Kristen Barker.

Though Kristen wasn't the prettiest girl in school, there were things about her—her never-ending smile, her warmth and enthusiasm—that made her glow. She was one of those girls who became popular by personality alone. She was a nice girl. She was the female Spence.

Spence and Kristen danced, but not get-a-room-type dancing like Logan was now doing with some cute little blonde freshman. Instead, the two of them were slightly apart, looking in each other's eyes and talking and laughing, just like Mom and Denny at Wendy's wedding. They looked so happy.

When Abby couldn't stand watching anymore, she walked out into the hallway. Still, she felt as if the walls were closing in. Sprinting to one of the outside doors, she stepped out onto the veranda. Leise was outside within seconds, easing down onto a bench beside Abby, both of them shivering in the crisp October night.

"Forget Logan. Come on inside and dance with us girls!"

"I don't feel like it, Leise." Abby puffed out a breath and watched its white mist dissipate into the darkness. "I'd rather sit out here a while."

"It's freezing!" Leise said, hugging herself.

Abby shrugged. "It was too hot in there, anyway."

Leise sighed and folded her manicured hands in her lap. "Are you upset that Spence brought Kristen to the dance?"

"Are you kidding me? No! I dumped him—that's ancient history."

"And that doesn't bother you—"

"Of course not! Spence can go out with whomever he wants to. Why would you even ask me—I have no right to—" She jumped up and took a few steps away from Leise. "It's over."

After a long silence, Leise stood and crossed her arms across her chest. "We're friends, right?" The yellow light of the overhead lamp made a halo around her crown.

"Of course we are."

"So if I say something you don't like, you won't write me off forever?"

"No, I guess not. Why?"

"Because that's what you do, Abby."

"I don't know what you're talking about," Abby mumbled, scratching the polish off one thumbnail with the other.

"Look," Leise said, leaning in so that Abby had to look at her, "I know you've been through a lot over the past couple of years, and I can't say that I know how you feel because I don't. Both my parents are still alive. It just seems like you're hell-bent on making sure you'll never be happy again."

"What do you mean? All I've done for the past two years is try to be happy, to try to be normal like everyone else. My God, I'm dating Logan Pierce, aren't I? Well, maybe we're not . . . *whatever*, but I've had a crush on him since the sixth grade and now here we are!"

"Yeah." Leise laughed. "Here we are, you and me, out here while Logan is in there making a fool of himself."

"Is that supposed to make me feel better?"

Leise waved a hand in the air. "This isn't news, Abby. Logan is a self-absorbed jerk and you know it. He doesn't have the capacity to care about anyone the way Spence cares about you. And yet you treated Spence like garbage so you could be with someone who treats you like garbage. You'll have to explain that to me, 'cause I just don't get it."

Abby stopped pacing. "Spence *did* care about me, Leise. Past tense."

"How is he supposed to feel? You chased him away!"

"And? That's what I do, right?"

"You don't have to."

Abby walked slowly toward the concrete half-wall that surrounded the veranda. The fluorescent lighting illuminated the wall and created a dark shadow beyond, making it appear as though if she hurdled the wall she'd fall into infinite blackness.

"It doesn't matter," she muttered. "Spence is here with Kristen. He's moved on."

"Abby, Spence and Kristen are just friends. He's had one eye on you since the moment he saw you."

Abby's heart skipped a beat. "Really?"

"Really. Why don't you go in there and talk to him. Tell him you're sorry about everything and ask him to give you another chance."

"I can't," Abby said, shaking her head. "Not here. It wouldn't be right."

"Then do it tomorrow."

"I don't think I can do that, either."

Leise let out an exasperated sigh.

"Look," Abby said. "We're going to graduate in a couple of years, and Spence will go one way and I'll go the other. Nothing lasts forever, so why bother continuing a relationship that's going to end anyway? It's easier to let go now, rather than later."

Leise raised her eyebrows and nodded. "Oh, I get it. You're so afraid of losing people you love that you're never going to love anyone again?"

"Thanks for the pop psychology." Abby rolled her eyes. "How much do I owe you for this session, doctor?"

"Okay, push me away, too." Leise turned on her heel and walked toward the door. "I'm going inside. I'm leaving you." She stopped and looked at Abby over her shoulder. "But not for good."

A surge of techno escaped through the door as Leise opened it. Abby wrapped her arms around herself for warmth. Goose bumps prickled up and down her bare arms and legs, her teeth were chattering, and she swore her breath could see its breath, yet she wasn't ready to go back inside. She tried not to think about the things Leise had said, fully aware that her doing so made Leise right. But Leise didn't understand what it was like to be Abby. No one could understand. Well, maybe someone could . . .

Abby went back inside. Leise was chatting with Billy near the gym doors. She motioned for Abby to join them, and Abby held up a finger to tell her to hang on a sec. Josh and Nikki were loitering just down the hallway near the photographer's station, and when he saw her alone, he looked concerned.

"You okay?" he mouthed, and she nodded. She *was* okay, but she needed someone to talk to. It wasn't Leise or any of the other girls, though. The person Abby needed most wasn't there.

When Josh looked the other way, she pulled the cell phone out of her clutch and dialed.

"Mom? Can you come and pick me up? I want to come home."

THIRTY-ONE

October, Continued

Abby told Leise and Josh she was going, but didn't bother finding Logan. By the time she got home and threw on sweatpants and Dad's Stuckey's T-shirt he still hadn't called, so she didn't know if he was mad or glad or hadn't noticed yet that she was gone. Whatever the case, she didn't care. Mom started a fire in the fireplace and just as the two of them had curled up on the couch together with a cup of hot chocolate, Abby's cell phone rang. In no mood for a confrontation with Logan, she considered letting it go to voice mail.

"Answer it," her mother said, pulling an afghan off the back of the couch and spreading it over her lap. "You at least owe him an explanation."

Abby nodded, set her cup of hot chocolate on the coffee table, and went into the kitchen for her phone. When she checked the caller ID she almost dropped it.

It wasn't Logan calling. It was Spence. Abby walked trancelike back to the couch and sat down.

"Hello?" she said timidly.

"Abby?" He was shouting to be heard over the noisy crowd. "What happened? Josh told me you went home. Are you okay?"

"Yeah, I'm okay. Just sitting here with my mom."

"Oh. Is *she* all right?"

Abby smiled. "Everything's fine." He sighed, but didn't say anything. Tears welled in her eyes.

"Don't worry about us, okay? I want you to have a good time tonight." It was hard to get the words out, but she wasn't lying.

"And I want the same for you."

Abby looked at her mother. Her eyes were wide with curiosity. "I will."

"Okay, then . . ." Spence hesitated. "All right. Bye."

"Spence—"

The line disconnected. Abby crawled underneath the afghan and rested her head on her mother's shoulder. Mom stroked her hair while Abby's fought back tears and lost.

"Will you tell me what happened?"

"It was a disaster," Abby said, sniffling. "Logan was a complete jerk."

Mom sighed. "I never knew what you saw in that boy."

There was a long silence. Abby got the sense that her mother was about to say something important, but needed to be careful with her words. It was the first real conversation they'd had in a long time. "What about Spence?" she said at last. "Why did you stop talking to him?"

Abby shook her head. "I don't know. I miss him."

"I miss him, too. Why don't you call him tomorrow? Ask him to come over for dinner."

"He brought another girl to the dance."

Mom paused. "But that didn't stop him from calling to check on you tonight, did it? He'll always be your friend."

Abby sat up and grabbed a tissue from the box on the end table.

"Problem is," she said, blowing her nose, "I don't know if we can go back to being just friends . . . and I don't think I want to."

"Well, then, what do you think you should do?"

She grabbed another tissue and wiped her eyes. She knew her eye makeup must be smeared everywhere, but it didn't matter anymore. "I don't think I need any guys in my life. Dad was right."

"Is that what this is all about?" Mom chuckled without humor, sliding an arm around Abby's shoulders. "He told me about that day, you know," she said softly. "The day he yelled at you and Spence when he thought you two were getting a little too close. He felt awful about it. He knew he was wrong, that he'd just been unprepared to watch you grow up. It was scary for him." Her voice caught. "He just loved you so much, Abby."

Abby buried her face in her hands. She was unprepared for this—it felt like she had brought him into the room with them, like Dad was talking to her himself.

"But you know what?" Mom said, hugging her a little tighter. "He loved Spence, too. He knew what a great support he was for you—for all of us—when he was sick, and I know that if Dad was here, he'd give you his blessing to date Spence. I know that for sure."

Abby thought about the times Spence had shared with her family while they were growing up and how Dad really did treat him like his own son. And she realized that while these memories ran through her head she wasn't seeing the gaunt, pale, sick Dad or the body lying in a coffin in a gray suit; somewhere along the line, the real Dad had found a place in her mind.

Abby picked up her cup of hot chocolate and sipped slowly. And then she smiled.

"Remember when we were little kids and Spence came over all bummed out because every boy in his Cub Scout troop was bringing a parent along for their camping trip? Spence said he wasn't going to go, but Dad insisted, and went with him. Dad came home after those two nights dirty and cold, but so happy."

"Which was saying a lot," Mom said, laughing. "He hated camping. Remember when we got our new computer, and your father, for the life of him, couldn't figure out how to hook it up? Spence came over and had it running in about ten minutes flat. He never let him live that down."

Soon they weren't talking about Spence anymore. Just Dad.

"Remember when Dad ripped the seat of his pants at your third-grade field trip to Kensington Metropark? He spent the rest of the day with your teacher's sweater wrapped around his waist, determined not to ruin your day by going home."

"Remember the time Dad got us lost in Macon trying to find Civil War battlefields? We spent three hours in that car with no air-conditioning driving around on Georgia back roads because he was too proud to ask for directions."

"Sometimes Josh acts just like your father. I swear when he's got a book with him in the bathroom I'm afraid I'll never see his face again. Remember how long Dad would take, even with the rest of us banging on the bathroom door, about to wet ourselves?"

Abby remembered, Abby remembered, Abby remembered. And when Josh came home just after midnight, he nestled onto the couch with them and, together, they remembered even more. When they finally retired to their own rooms in the wee hours of the morning, Abby crawled into bed exhausted but peaceful, feeling like she'd finally get a good night's sleep.

For the first time since the move, she felt like she was home.

THE NEXT MORNING ABBY STAYED IN BED LONG AFTER SHE was awake, staring up at the framed pictures on her bookshelf. Then she looked through the photo album she'd put together. It was in chronological order, beginning with Dad as an infant in his mother's arms, both of his parents gazing at him adoringly, their faces filled with love and hopes and dreams. He grew up with the turn of each page, the photos changing from sharp black and white to fuzzy faded colors. Once Abby entered some of the pictures, she changed in the flash of a bulb as well.

Finally she set the book down. And when she did, she saw the ugly brown-and-cream quilt and winced.

She'd snagged the fall Pottery Barn catalog out of the mail a few days ago, and had found a few things that she really liked. She flipped back and forth between the violet-and-green-striped duvet and coordinating sheets, dust ruffle, and curtains, and the set in a blue-and-yellow floral. Either would work in her new room. She hadn't yet asked Mom if the offer to redecorate still stood, but she was pretty sure it did.

The phone rang and Abby closed her eyes, willing it to be Spence. If he called, she wouldn't have to work up the guts to call him. Leise was right; Abby needed to apologize, whether or not that meant things could ever go back to the way they were.

"Abby?" Mom called. "Deanna's on the phone. She wants to talk to you."

Deanna? Her sister Deanna? Deanna never called Abby, ever. Intrigued, she hopped out of bed, slipped into her robe, and made her way to the kitchen. "Hello?"

"Hey, little sister. Up and at 'em."

"Like you didn't just roll your sorry butt out of bed five minutes ago."

"I didn't!"

"Did too."

"Did not!"

"Whatever. So what's up?"

"Brad and I set a wedding date."

"Oh, yeah? For when?"

"February. Valentine's Day. Won't that be the coolest anniversary?"

"Uh-huh." She wouldn't believe they were really married until she witnessed the ceremony with her own eyes. Knowing them, they'd have some huge fight the day before and Deanna would call it off, or Brad would get cold feet.

"So I have a request."

"Shoot."

"Will you be my maid of honor?"

Abby was too shocked to answer. She had assumed that Deanna's girlfriends would be the bridal attendants—and one would be the maid of honor.

"Abby?"

"Yeah?

"Don't you want to be in my wedding?"

She paused. "Well, sure, but I'm surprised you asked me."

"Why? You're my sister!"

"Yeah, but . . ." She glanced at her mother. Mom was grinning madly; she'd known what was up. Abby smiled back. "Just don't call me your maid."

Deanna and Abby chatted about wedding plans: the church, the reception, the dresses, the flowers. Brad was going to ask Josh to be a groomsman. She told Abby not to tell him; Brad wanted to ask himself.

After she hung up, she wandered into the living room. Josh was sprawled on the couch, absorbed in a magazine. "Deanna and Brad set a wedding date, Valentine's Day."

"Right." He snickered. "I'll believe they're getting married when I see them do the Chicken Dance at their reception."

"How 'bout 'I'm a Little Teapot'?"

Josh laughed. "That's so last year." He brought the magazine closer to his face, squinting in concentration.

"What're you reading?" He showed her the cover. It was a course catalog for Michigan State. "Aren't you getting a little ahead of yourself?"

"It's Billy's. I'm just curious."

"Are you gonna go to MSU?"

Josh shrugged and kept reading. There were more college catalogs on the floor next to him, and she went through them. University of Michigan, Grand Valley State, Northwood, Central Michigan, and a few out-of-state schools: Ohio State, Auburn, Texas A&M, University of Hawaii.

"Hawaii?"

"Dream big, sister."

The U of M catalog was filled with photos of dorms and the football stadium and adult-looking students enjoying a joke with a professor. She tried to put Josh in some of the pictures, but couldn't. It seemed inconceivable that in less than two years he'd leave Highland for good. And then Abby would, too.

What would happen to their mother?

"Where's Mom?" Abby asked.

"I dunno," Josh replied without looking up. "Maybe she's outside."

As Abby stood, she caught sight of their mail carrier's

white Jeep driving away. She slipped halfway into her sneakers and hurried out to get the mail, hoping no one would see her in her robe.

Bill, bill, sweepstakes entry form, doctor appointment reminder postcard, bill, card addressed to Mom from Denny. He hadn't called in weeks; Abby had thought he'd given up. Maybe this was his final farewell.

At the very bottom of the pile was a plain white envelope with "Abby" written on it. She recognized Leise's writing. There was no address and no stamp; she must have put it in their mailbox herself. As soon as she got inside, she tore it open and unfolded the piece of notebook paper inside.

> *God give us grace to accept with serenity the things that cannot be changed, courage to change the things which should be changed, and the wisdom to distinguish the one from the other.*
> —Reinhold Niebuhr

Leise had given her the Serenity Prayer, and on the bottom she'd jotted down a phone number Abby knew by heart. Spence's.

Abby started to stuff it back into the envelope. Then she changed her mind, went into the kitchen, and tacked it to the fridge with a magnet. And then she read it again. And again. And again.

Looking for Mom, Abby wandered into the dining-room-turned-studio. A freshly painted watercolor was propped against the wall. It was in her mother's unmistakable messy-but-cool style—a chubby, golden-haired toddler girl holding a bouquet of daisies. Though the little girl's eyes were closed and the daisies half covered her face, Abby could tell it was meant to be her.

There was another painting in progress on the easel. It showed a field of daisies that seemed to stretch on forever, the most distant flowers so small that they appeared to melt into one another and join the sky. The plastic wastepaper basket nearby was filled with wadded-up tissues.

Through the window, she saw Mom in the backyard. She watched as her mother heaved the lawn mower into the aluminum shed out back and then returned to the garage, hauling out watering cans, garden hoses, lawn sprinklers, and hedge trimmers. She turned back to the paintings and the wastepaper basket full of sorrows, and it dawned on her: Mom hadn't gotten over losing Dad; she was just trying to get through life without him. And she was doing it. Alone.

Mail still in hand, Abby opened the door to the garage. "Hi. Whatcha doin'?"

Mom set some gas cans on the porch and wiped sweat

from her forehead. "Just moving the summer stuff into the shed so that Josh can park in the garage over the winter."

"Do you need some help?"

Mom gave her an odd look, surely wondering what favor she wanted. "No . . . but thanks for asking. I think I've got it under control." She lifted a glass of iced tea off the porch railing and took a sip. "Maybe you can help me clean up inside, though. Aunt Fran's coming for dinner. I called her this morning."

"*What?*"

Mom gave a sideways smile. "You heard me."

"Interesting." She paused. "This came in the mail." She held out the card from Denny. Mom removed her work gloves. She opened the card, smiled wistfully as she read, and slid it back inside the envelope. She stared at it with an expression Abby could not read.

"You should call him," Abby said.

"Who?"

"Denny." Her mother gave her a look. "You've blown him off for this long and he still hasn't given up on you? He must really care about you. You should call him."

"Really?"

"Really."

"So you're going to call Spence then, too?"

"I will if you call Denny," she said with a grin.

"I'll think about it," she said, handing the envelope back. "Will you take this inside for me?"

"Sure," Abby said, but she didn't move. "Feel like taking a break?"

Mom sighed. "I've got a lot to do yet, hon, but . . . what do you need? Want me to drive you somewhere?"

"No. I haven't even showered yet. I was just wondering if you wanted to go out back and throw a ball around."

Mom's jaw dropped. "A softball?"

"No, a bowling ball—yeah, a softball. I've been kicking around the idea of trying out for the team in the spring, and my arm's pretty rusty."

"But you didn't even play summer ball!"

"I know. So I'll need all the practice I can get before March. Could you help me? Please?"

Her mother beamed. "Of course I will. You go on in and get dressed. I'll finish up out here, and then we'll play."

"Deal," Abby said, heading for the door and grasping the handle. Then she turned back.

"Hey, Mom?"

"What, honey?"

"I love you."

Mom's eyes brimmed with tears, but she was smiling. "I love you, too."

Inside, Abby chucked the mail onto the kitchen table and

went to get dressed. On her way through the living room she passed Josh and glanced at the pencil drawing of Dad that hung over the recliner. She was suddenly reminded of something she'd heard a wise man, the wisest man she'd ever known, say: *The Earth never stops spinning, Abby, no matter how fast you run in the opposite direction.*

"Dad," Abby whispered, touching the glass that held Dad, "I get it now."

She walked into the kitchen and picked up the phone, hoping Spence would answer.

THIRTY-TWO

October, Continued

Later, Spence joined the Norths for a surprisingly pleasant dinner with Aunt Fran. He and Josh and Mom chatted away like he'd never been gone, and Aunt Fran went over and above, complimenting Mom about how fantastic the new house was. Abby was quiet for most of the meal, wishing it was just her and Spence, alone, so they could talk, though if they were alone she wouldn't know where to begin. She snuck quick glances at Spence throughout the meal, hoping he wouldn't catch her. But he was looking right back.

"That was delicious, Helen," Aunt Fran said after they'd finished.

"Thank you," Mom said, sitting back in her chair and patting her stomach. "But you know what we need to top it off? Ice cream. Spence, would you mind running into town to pick some up?"

"I'll go," Josh offered.

"You've got homework," Mom said quickly. Josh jumped. Mom must have kicked him under the table.

"Sure," Spence said, pushing his chair back.

"Abby, why don't you go with him?"

Abby stood and smiled. "Okay. What should we get? Moose Tracks?"

"Whatever you kids want is fine. Take your time—we're not going anywhere."

She followed Spence outside and climbed into the passenger seat of his Cavalier, the scene of her breakdown. He turned on the radio, maybe to distract her from remembering.

"Where should we go?"

"I dunno. Rite Aid?"

"Works for me." He drove out of the subdivision toward town. Neither said much at first, but their unspoken words buzzed around them loud and clear: *What happened? What now?*

"The new house is looking good," he said, breaking the ice.

"Yeah." When he'd first gotten there, her mother had whisked him around the house, pointing out all the improvements she'd made. Spence had seemed sad that he hadn't been called on to help. "It's not so bad."

"And so do you," he added. "You look good, I mean."

"Um, thanks. You too." Awkward. She wanted to kick

herself. Was this how it was now? Neither of them knowing what to say to the other? She turned up the radio a notch to fill the silence, while she struggled to find a comfortable subject.

"So hockey starts soon," she finally said.

"It already started. Our first game is right before Thanksgiving."

Abby was mortified. Had their friendship always been so one-sided, with Spence paying attention to what she cared about while she took for granted that she knew enough about him? She began to panic. What if this evening proved to Spence that he was better off without her in his life?

She picked at her cuticles, racking her brain for something to say that would redeem her.

Spence laid a hand on hers. "Bad habit," he scolded, tightening his grip. "And you're shaking."

Abby laughed nervously and stared out the window. She felt her eyes prickling. She couldn't cry, not now. That would only make Spence think of what happened the last time—

"I'm glad you called," he said quietly.

"I hope Kristen's not mad," she said.

Spence laughed. "Kristen's got a boyfriend in Ohio. He couldn't make it up for the dance, so she asked me if I'd take her." He turned his head slightly to glance at

Abby. "You know who I would have wanted to take to the dance, if she wasn't already going with a knuckle-dragging blockhead."

Abby gave a laugh-sob. "I can't believe you're even talking to me."

Spence nudged her. "After all these years . . . don't you know that no matter what happens, I'll always be your friend?"

Abby wished she still believed in the word *always*.

Then she took a deep breath, and braced herself. "My friend?" she said carefully. "Or my boyfriend?"

He smiled, and she could tell he was blushing. "Well, now . . . I guess that's up to you." His hand tightened over hers, and she squeezed back.

As they pulled into Rite Aid, she noticed the marquee at the plaza entrance—the place where people in Highland announced weddings and births and anniversaries, knowing that you couldn't pass through town without seeing the sign.

Posted in big black letters, was the message:

HAPPY BIRTHDAY, HOPE!

Abby laughed.

"What's so funny?" Spence asked.

"A sign," she said with a grin.

"Huh?"

"Nothing," Spence wouldn't get the joke. It was between Abby and Dad.

Amy Ackley inherited her passion for reading and writing from her father—a writer, creative writing teacher, and literature addict. She earned BS and MSA degrees in business and wore a variety of career hats (court clerk, flight attendant, and labor relations specialist, to name a few) while spending late nights with her childhood love, writing fiction. *Sign Language*, her first novel, was drawn from the loss of her father to kidney cancer when she was a young teenager, and was the winner of the first Amazon Breakthrough Novel Award for Young Adult Fiction.

Ackley lives in southeast Michigan with her husband and an assortment of high-maintenance animals, including three daughters.